HOPE
UNBURIED

A HOPE UNBURIED

KIMBERLEY WOODHOUSE

BETHANYHOUSE
a division of Baker Publishing Group
Minneapolis, Minnesota

Published by Bethany House Publishers
Minneapolis, Minnesota
BethanyHouse.com

Bethany House Publishers is a division of
Baker Publishing Group, Grand Rapids, Michigan

Printed in the United States of America

Library of Congress Cataloging-in-Publication Data
Names: Woodhouse, Kimberley, author.
Title: A hope unburied / Kimberley Woodhouse.
Description: Minneapolis, Minnesota : Bethany House, a division of Baker
    Publishing Group, 2024. | Series: Treasures of the Earth ; 3
Identifiers: LCCN 2024002303 | ISBN 9780764241703 (paperback) | ISBN
    9780764244087 (casebound) | ISBN 9781493448180 (e-book)
Subjects: LCSH: Women paleontologists—Fiction. | Missing persons—Fiction. |
    Fraud in science—Fiction. | Deception—Fiction. | LCGFT: Christian fiction. |
    Thrillers (Fiction) | Novels.
Classification: LCC PS3623.O665 H67 2024 | DDC 813/.6—dc23/eng/20240129
LC record available at https://lccn.loc.gov/2024002303

Scripture quotations are from the King James Version of the Bible.

Scripture quotations are from the King James Version of the Bible.

Cover design by Peter Gloege, LOOK Design Studio
Cover image of woman by Ildiko Neer, Arcangel

Baker Publishing Group publications use paper produced from sustainable forestry
practices and postconsumer waste whenever possible.

24 25 26 27 28 29 30   7 6 5 4 3 2 1

This book is lovingly dedicated to my friend

Renette Steele.

Thank you for traveling back to your old stomping grounds to help me research my dino series. You are a wealth of information, a huge help, and so much fun to spend time with.

I hope and pray that one day all those beautiful stories you have inside will blossom and bless the world around you.

Keep on keepin' on.

DEAR READER

Thank you so much for joining me for the conclusion of the TREASURES OF THE EARTH series. I have loved writing these books and highlighting women in paleontology, the Bone Wars, and what it took to work on a dig during the Great Dinosaur Rush.

In this story, we'll get to see Earl Douglass—the man whose quotes you've been seeing at the top of each chapter in the series—in his work at the Carnegie Quarry.

Even though I've studied his journals and writings and have spent time speaking with his granddaughter, please understand that what I don't know firsthand has been created in my mind. It's called artistic license in the fiction world. I don't wish to take away from the man that he was or the fantastic work that he did. He was—above all—a man staunch about honesty and truth.

In that same vein, I allowed myself to get creative with what went on at Dinosaur National Monument in those early years. We know there were a lot of visitors. We know there was a lot of digging at the quarry. Those are both facts. A good deal of the rest is from my imagination.

A Hope Unburied tackles several issues.

A big one—and one that I hope doesn't offend—is the fact that judgmental and legalistic attitudes have always been present within the body of believers (and in non-believers too). Now don't go getting mad at me, I'm sure we can all admit that at one point or another we've been judgmental. This just shows us that we are all human. We're sinners. And we've been struggling with the same issues since the beginning of time. There's nothing new under the sun, right?

Another issue is from the perspective of science without faith. I wanted to show how you can feel stuck between a rock and a hard place because you can't please anyone. No matter what you do.

During the era when this book takes place, after the main years of the Bone Wars, it was still very difficult for paleontologists. There were a number of reasons for this. First, it was a cutthroat field (there was still stealing and sabotage going on). Second, the field didn't have the greatest reputation because of Cope and Marsh. Third, women struggled to find their footing in paleontology—just like most women of that day in any kind of work outside the home. And fourth, there was still a huge divide between science and the church.

Ever since the publication of Darwin's book, there had been a split. Before his book, most of the prestigious scientists claimed to be believers. (Gregor Mendel, the father of genetics; Georges Cuvier, the father of paleontology; Isaac Newton; Galileo Galilei; Johannes Kepler; Louis Pasteur; Carl Linnaeus; James Clerk Maxwell; and Nicolaus Copernicus, to name but a few.) But after the book came out and the theory of evolution spread, a chasm opened up. Many in the church believed you couldn't have anything to do with science because you would be negating the Creator. Those in science believed you couldn't have anything to do with religion because believers were ignorant. And if you were a woman in science, well, many tried to make you give up. As soon as possible.

So you can imagine how difficult it was for a woman of faith trying to find her way in this scientific field.

It is a wonderful thing to be able to glimpse back into history and see the struggles of mankind. As we learn and grow, we find there is so much to gain in knowledge if we simply look to the past.

As Winston Churchill said, "Those that fail to learn from history are doomed to repeat it."

Enjoy the journey,
Kimberley

"Go forth into nature and see what she has to show thee. Enter the silent wood and lose thyself in thoughts un-thought before. Let fancy construct worlds unknown—fairy worlds of the mind. All this is wonderful, but the wonder is of thyself the mystery of the mind and that matter can arrange itself, know to perceive, to perceive other forms, other arrangements of matter and then to think beyond, to construct a new world of its own yet of fragments of the old."

~Earl Douglass—Saturday, January 28, 1888

PROLOGUE

"I was full of courage and the highest hopes."

~Earl Douglass

Life would be so much easier if there weren't so many rules.

Eliza Mills trudged through the tall grass. At fifteen, she was almost grown up. And the past couple years had been filled with not only her studies but with Grandmama insisting on more and more rules.

"It's not polite for you to insert yourself into adult conversations, dear."

"Ladies do not wear pants out in public, no matter the job to be done."

"Must you insist on digging in the dirt right before a society party?"

She mimicked her grandmother under her breath, made faces, and took even longer strides—yes, in her pants—to the surprise that awaited.

"Where are you taking me *this* time?" Devin Schmitt—her best friend, confidante, and classmate—dragged the heavy bag

11

of tools, foodstuffs, and assorted paraphernalia along the dirt path as he followed her.

Devin's grumbling broke through her own negative thoughts, and a chuckle escaped her lips. His presence made everything better. Grandmama couldn't insist upon more rules out here. They were out in the glorious, not-a-cloud-in-the-blue-sky weather to enjoy the day. *And* her surprise. She lifted her face to the warm sunshine. "You'll see." Her voice floated on the breeze as she tossed the words over her shoulder. Oh, how she loved to tease him.

For six years, he'd traipsed along with her and helped her with whatever grand idea she had. Once his dad said they were old enough to venture out on their own, of course. As her private tutor, Mr. Schmitt was in charge. Grandmama and Grandfather paid him a handsome sum to not only educate Eliza but to ensure she was kept out from underfoot.

When she and Devin were younger, that meant exploring the world together through books and studies, tucked away in the east wing of Mills Manor. Mr. Schmitt often took them outside for their lessons as they studied bugs, birds, trees, and vegetation.

But as they grew older, dear Mr. Schmitt understood they needed to stretch their legs and enjoy the fresh air on their own, especially since he'd hurt his knee and couldn't keep up with them.

It was her only escape from all the ridiculous lady training her grandmother insisted upon these days.

"You do love to torture me, Eliza." Devin's voice carried to her on the breeze.

She turned and glanced back at him, wiggling her eyebrows then venturing forward once again.

His groan floated up to her along with the birds chirping and the swishing of the grass against his summer coat. "How much farther?"

She stopped in her tracks and swung her long, red braid over her shoulder as she swirled to face him. Narrowing her eyes, she placed her hands on her hips. "You should know better than to ask that question."

"As the one toting all your stuff, *again*, I think it's perfectly within my rights to ask just such a question." He set the bag down and mimicked her posture. "That bag gets heavier every time we go anywhere. I'm beginning to think you do it on purpose."

"A gentleman always carries a lady's things." Her chin lifted with the taunt.

"Which I have done and will continue to do, but what did you put in there? An anvil?"

Her lips parted ever-so-slightly as she did her best to suppress her grin. His annoyance wasn't real. "I have no need for an anvil, Devin Schmitt, so why would I do such a thing?" She clasped her hands in front of her and put on her most innocent look.

His eyebrows raised and he stared her down. The challenge in his eyes was as plain as the grassy knoll underneath her feet.

"Fine." She broke eye contact, lifted her hands upward, and let out an unladylike grunt. Good thing Grandmama wasn't present to hear that. "You just have to spoil the surprise, don't you? We're almost there." With that, she turned on her heel, knowing full well that he would pick up the bag and follow.

He always did.

Their path took an incline up a rocky hill, and she focused on her steps so she wouldn't trip and fall back into Devin. Making him take a tumble backward with her bag of goodies wouldn't be a nice thing to do, and he might refuse to come with her next time.

Huffing and puffing at the top of the hill, she waited for him to join her and then grabbed his hand. "You're going to love this. Just wait." Thrills zipped up and down her spine as she imagined his face when they accomplished their task. This was what made her feel alive. Even if she was about to have them knee-deep in muck.

As she dragged him toward her surprise, she swallowed back the sorrow that threatened to overwhelm her every time her thoughts went to the future. He'd be off to university before too long, and these days of dashing off together to explore would come to an end.

She blinked several times and forced the reminder to the back of her mind. "Look!" She pointed toward the drying creek bed.

He squinted. Leaning forward, his eyes narrowed even more. It was almost comical how hard he tried.

She watched and bit her lip. Over the years he'd gotten better at seeing what she saw, but most of the time, his guesses were incorrect.

"Is it . . . a fossil?"

"Look who has gotten so smart." She let the sarcastic words drip from her mouth and then smacked his arm with a playful swat. "Of course it's a fossil, silly. Don't you see the shape?"

He studied it for a moment longer. "You're the expert when it comes to this, I'm afraid I don't see anything specific jumping out at me."

"It's *clearly* a baby alligator, Devin. Come on." She raced toward the small fossil peeking out of its hiding place.

"An alligator. *Clearly*. In *Pennsylvania*. Where we have alligators around every corner."

She just laughed and led him down to the trench.

The afternoon passed with them digging through all the mud and dirt that surrounded the rock and fossilized layer. The time was filled with their shared excitement for subjects his father had promised to cover this term, laughter over how much mud covered them both, and the discovery that her "fossil" was exactly what she thought. It wasn't the full skeleton, but the skull was enough to keep her smiling. She'd have several months of contentment working on retrieving the fossilized bones.

"An alligator in Pennsylvania. Who knew?" Devin sat down on the dry grass above the trench, wiping his hands on a towel.

"Deposited here by a great flood, no doubt." She plopped down in the grass next to him, wiping her hands on another towel. Tossing it aside, she pulled her knees up to her chest and wrapped her arms around them. The pants she wore were filthy, but she would cover them with a skirt before she returned home. The real reason she'd brought him out here today wasn't just another of their explorations, or Devin following her and helping her dig up fossils. Eliza hadn't been certain when the right time would present itself, but at this moment, she couldn't contain the request any longer. "Will you promise me something?"

"It won't get me in trouble, will it?" He elbowed her side and sent her the lopsided grin she loved so much.

"I'm serious, Devin." She stared into his blue eyes, hoping he'd take the hint.

"I'm sorry. I won't tease." He gazed back at her, and his face softened from mischievous to earnest attention.

As she held his gaze, the blue of his eyes intensified. Deepened. Maybe it was simply her imagination, but no matter. She adored his eyes and the way he looked at her. "Promise me we'll always be best friends. That we won't ever let anything come between us." She drew her bottom lip in between her teeth as tears pooled in her eyes. Blinking as fast as she dared, she still couldn't keep them from forming. This wasn't how it was supposed to go. She hadn't wanted to get all emotional and talk about him leaving.

For several seconds he studied her. He didn't tease her or get annoyed that she was tearing up, but he also wasn't saying anything. At all. Finally, he broke their connection and looked out toward the horizon. "You're my best friend. Never doubt that. But promising forever? I don't think your future husband would appreciate you being best friends with a man. Especially not the son of your childhood tutor."

He always knew how to rile her up and steer the attention off himself. How she hated it when he brought up class! "Oh, posh. I can't lose you, Devin. I can't. You're the only person in the whole wide world who has ever understood me. You'll be leaving for university after only three more terms. Three! My future husband—whoever it is, *if* I even marry—will just have to deal with the fact that I won't be *me* without . . . you." The begging in her voice made her cringe, but he had to know how important his friendship was to her.

Holding her breath, she watched him. But he wouldn't even look at her.

"Why aren't you saying anything?"

The moments that passed felt like an eternity. But then he turned and met her gaze once again.

A single tear slipped down her cheek.

Reaching his hand forward, he wiped the tear off her face and then pulled his hand back. "I promise"—his voice cracked, and his Adam's apple bobbed as he swallowed—"I will always be your best friend."

She surged toward him and wrapped her arms around his neck. She could handle whatever life dealt her as long as he was by her side.

Eliza pulled back, kissed his cheek, and then sat in the grass again. "I promise I will always be *your* best friend. *Nothing* will come between us."

Back at the manor, Devin waved good-bye and shoved his hands into his pockets. As he walked home along the familiar lane, his eyes slid closed for a moment, and he relished the memory of Eliza's warmth as she'd thrown her arms around him. The feel of her so close made his skin tingle.

Her thick, red hair crowned her like a halo. Every time he saw her—which was every day—she grew prettier and prettier. Why did she have to tug and yank at his heart like this? It was difficult enough to keep his feelings to himself.

When he'd wiped the tear off her cheek, his heart had flipped. It was the most intimate gesture he'd ever allowed, and all it did was make him want more.

His feet tripped over something, and he snapped his eyes open.

What had he just done? He'd made a promise to her that he doubted he could honorably keep. A man's word was his bond. What would she think of him when he let her down?

Their lives would surely take them down different paths. He wanted to be a teacher like his father. She wanted to travel the world and dig up bones.

Still, her words had reached deep inside him and woven their way into his heart. He'd carry that moment with him for the rest of his life.

At sixteen years old, Devin's heart was already completely and utterly committed to Eliza Mills. Not that she would ever guess that her chum from all these years wanted more from their relationship. And not that he would ever say that aloud to anyone.

Even still, he would follow her to the moon. Of course he'd made the promise! He was a fool to even question it.

"Master Schmitt, if I might have a word." The booming voice brought him back down to earth, and his feet stuttered to a stop.

Devin glanced around. Mr. Mills—Eliza's grandfather—was in one of his many horseless carriages. Good heavens. The man had driven up without Devin even noticing! Heat flooded his face. This was what happened when he thought of her.

He cleared his throat. "Good afternoon, sir." With a stiff turn, he placed his hands behind his back and bowed toward the man. At least he still had some manners while his mind had been off lallygagging.

The man didn't exit his vehicle, just stared at him. Then he spoke to his driver. "Meet me at the gate. I wish to have a private conversation with the young man."

The door whooshed open, and Mr. Mills's imposing figure soon stood before him.

Devin straightened and gulped back his nervousness. Mr. Mills had never taken the time to speak to him privately. *Never.*

The driver drove the noisy machine down the lane. Silence surrounded them like a heavy cloak.

Devin swallowed, tugged at his collar, which felt all too tight, and blinked. What was the correct protocol? Speak only when spoken to? Talk of the weather? Ask after his family?

"Let's walk, shall we?" Mr. Mills didn't wait for a response, just took long strides. The cane in his hand was clearly for decoration. The man was spry and quick.

Realizing he still hadn't moved, Devin croaked out a response. "Yes, sir." He forced one foot in front of the other and focused on breathing.

"I wish to speak to you about my granddaughter."

More heat rushed up Devin's neck. A million different thoughts and questions sparked for attention.

"Let me speak plain and simple." The man stopped his steps, gripped Devin's shoulder, and speared him with an intense gaze. "My granddaughter spends a great deal of time with you and speaks of you with great admiration." He narrowed his eyes.

"Yes, sir." It seemed the only response. The hand on his shoulder was almost as heavy as the bags Eliza made him carry on their adventures.

The grip tightened. "Your father has informed me that you

will be off to university soon. Well done, young man. I will see to it that you have the very best education."

Devin narrowed his gaze a bit. What was the man offering? To put in a good word for him? Regardless, it was something that deserved his gratitude. "Thank you, sir."

"Mrs. Mills and I have enjoyed seeing you grow into an honorable young man. You have indeed been a loyal friend to Eliza." The man released his hold and took up his walk toward the gate again.

Devin joined him, feeling one hundred pounds lighter. If that's what they thought of him—

"But there comes a time when every man needs to understand his place. Eliza is from a family of great wealth. Generations of my family built this empire. It's in our blood. You, son, are not from old money. You're not even from new money. You are from no money at all. Your father is a simple tutor. You, frankly, are a different class."

All sense of lightness evaporated. Devin's stomach threatened to tie itself into knots. Mr. Mills wasn't saying anything he didn't already know. But *why* was he saying it?

"I need your word, son, that you will never pursue my granddaughter for courtship or marriage. It's clear she cares for you as a friend, but that friendship can *never* be encouraged to grow beyond what it is now. Am I clear on this point?"

He swallowed against the large lump in his throat. "Yes, sir."

"And I have your word on that account?" Mr. Mills's green eyes were the same color as Eliza's, but the ice within them threatened to stab Devin.

He swallowed again and lifted his chin, doing his best to convince his legs to hold him upright. How could he go against her grandfather? No matter how he felt toward Eliza. He couldn't. And being her friend was better than nothing. "Yes, sir. You have my word."

Mr. Mills held out his hand. "Gentlemen always shake on such an important bond."

Devin reached forward and shook the man's hand. The iron grip made his hand ache.

"You have a bright future ahead of you, Master Schmitt. I'm thankful to be a part of that." And with a brief nod, Mr. Mills surged forward and took long, fast strides toward his waiting vehicle.

Devin could only stare after the man. His legs felt weak and wobbly.

For the second time that afternoon, he'd made a promise.

And for the second time . . . his heart couldn't take it.

What had he done?

one

"They went out into Nature
With firm and joyous tread
To read in Truth's great volume
Whatever there was said."

~Earl Douglass, from his poem
Nature's Noblemen

Eliza rushed to the director's office, her long, slim skirt keeping her from going as fast as she wished. What was so important that he'd interrupted her latest tour and put someone else in charge?

A million different thoughts rushed through her mind. What if they fired her? Was that possible?

She was responsible for bringing in scads of donors and new exhibits. Which brought in customers. They wouldn't get rid of her . . . would they?

On top of that, her grandfather and Mr. Carnegie had been friends for many years. Not that she had gotten this job because of that. She didn't need the job. Didn't need the money.

21

She wanted it.

She'd *earned* her way here.

Stopping outside the door, she put a hand to her stomach, inhaled slow and deep through her nose, and straightened her long, embroidered jacket that matched her skirt.

She rapped on the door.

Mr. Childers opened the door and dipped his chin at her. "Miss Mills." He stepped aside and held out an arm. "Please. Join us."

Us? She swallowed the lump down and entered the room. Her eyes widened. "Mr. Carnegie!" Stepping toward him, she smiled and then hugged the man she'd known since she was a child. Who cared about society's rules when they were in private?

"My dear, you are looking lovelier with each passing year." He released her and offered her a seat.

"Thank you." Smoothing her skirt, she took the proffered chair. If Mr. Carnegie himself was here, what on earth could this meeting be about? She sucked her bottom lip in between her teeth and then resisted the urge to chew on it. What was it with her and all this nervous energy?

"I've asked you here because Mr. Carnegie has a proposition for you." The director sat behind his desk.

"Oh?" She gazed back at her grandfather's longtime friend.

Carnegie took the seat beside her. "You remember Mr. Douglass who works for me and found the first bones out in Utah?"

Butterflies took over her insides. She put a hand to her throat. "My goodness, yes, I've long wanted to meet the man behind Dinosaur National Monument. When it opened up last year, I wanted to be on a train west immediately. I've been so eager to see it with my own eyes."

The grin beneath his white beard and mustache made his eyes sparkle. "Well, if you are amenable, I'd like to have you go out to Dinosaur National Monument for the summer as a representative of the Hall of Dinosaurs here at Carnegie Institute. Since—at this time—the monument is nothing more than our quarry with nothing official for visitors, I believe your help making it more accessible for the guests is just the thing."

Her throat squeaked as she gasped, and it was useless to try to contain her giddiness. Her lips lifted, and she tapped her foot as if a lively tune was playing on the Victrola.

Mr. Carnegie's amusement was clear as his grin widened. "I've always admired your enthusiasm, Miss Mills. At first, your expertise would be required to help the sightseers understand what it is we are doing out there. It's taking valuable time away from the dig for the workers there to have to stop and explain their process. And if Mr. Douglass needs your assistance in the actual quarry, I told him you would be up to the task."

She gasped. "Truly?"

"Yes." He leaned back in the chair, appearing content with himself. The smile that lifted his rounded cheeks always made her think of St. Nicholas and Christmas. This wasn't his reserved smile for his colleagues or business associates. No. This was the giant smile that she'd loved seeing as a child. The one that showed the man was utterly happy.

"That is a huge honor, sir. I would be thrilled to go. And even more ecstatic to dig with Mr. Douglass!" Keeping her seat was more difficult than she imagined, but she forced herself to think of calm and sedate things. And pressed her palms to her knees to keep them from bouncing along with her tapping boot. After all, Mr. Childers was also in the room. She had to appear professional.

Mr. Carnegie rubbed his beard. "I'd even be willing to lend your expertise to the monument permanently, if you so desire. At least, as long as we are digging in the Carnegie Quarry for my Hall of Dinosaurs. You would still be an employee of the institute, and we could offer your services there. I'm inclined to agree with Earl's vision that the future generations need to see the bones and fossils in their resting places after we have produced an adequate amount of displays for the museum. Many have been excavated from the quarries, which is tremendous, but allowing people to see the great beasts' resting places—essentially trapped in time in the stone walls—will be a marvelous advancement for science and knowledge."

Her expertise. That's what he said. This amazing man didn't offer compliments up to make people feel better about themselves. If *he* believed in her and saw her experience and knowledge, there was hope that one day . . . the rest of the world would as well. To be recognized in the field of paleontology like this was more than a thrill. "That is very generous of you for the national monument, and I appreciate your confidence in me, Mr. Carnegie. More than you know."

"My dear, I know how long you've loved the field. And you've proven yourself through not only your studies and degree, but your passion and vision for the future of paleontology."

She put a hand to her chest. "That is high praise indeed, sir. Thank you."

"As much as I believe in Mr. Douglass, I believe in you. To inspire future generations, especially young people, to explore and learn. There is great potential out there in Utah." He stood. "If you are agreeable, I really must be on my way. But I wanted to ask for your assistance myself. I do believe this will be wonderful not only for the future of paleontology, but for the Hall of Dinosaurs, and for your own future as well."

She came to her feet and nodded to him. "I'm more than honored that you would think of me for this position."

"You're the *only* one I thought of."

She couldn't contain her smile. "While my first inclination is to agree immediately to your offer, I would appreciate a day or two to speak to my grandparents and to think and pray about it."

"Of course. That would be most wise." He placed his hat on his head and winked at her. "Just let Mr. Childers know your answer and we will make all the arrangements." And with that, the man whose name was on the building left the room.

Eliza blinked several times and took a steadying breath as she turned back to the museum's director. In all the time she'd worked here, he'd earned nothing but respect from her. He'd never questioned her ideas because she was a woman—and young at that—and he'd never treated her different from any other employee. Honest and steady. That's how she'd describe the man in front of her. "I'm a bit overwhelmed."

"It's a substantial offer, Miss Mills." His somber expression was difficult to decipher.

"It is."

"It will be a loss for the Hall of Dinosaurs if you leave, but rest assured, we will continue with the programs you have instituted." He nodded toward her.

"Thank you, sir."

He steepled his fingers together. His gray eyes were serious. "I must admit that I was resistant to the board hiring you at first."

His admission was no surprise. One, a woman as a paleontologist was not widely accepted. Two, she was young. Three, many people thought she got the job because of her family's relationship with Mr. Carnegie rather than her knowledge or experience. They just saw the little rich girl who knew nothing of dinosaurs.

For two years, she'd gone above and beyond to demonstrate her knowledge and worth.

The director continued, "You have proven yourself time and again, and I haven't once doubted you. You are an asset to the scientific community, Miss Mills."

Another compliment in the same realm as Mr. Carnegie's. Could this day get any better? "Thank you, sir." Making her way to the door, she allowed herself to revel in the excitement. "I had better get back to work, but I greatly appreciate your support and encouragement. It has been a privilege to learn from you."

He nodded again, a slight smile on his lips.

As she left the office and pulled the door closed behind her, she resisted the urge to squeal like a little girl. But once she was several paces away and was certain no one was watching, she twirled around, then released her joy in a long sigh.

Wait until she told Devin!

MONDAY, MAY 8, 1916 • PITTSBURGH

The newspaper crinkled as he shook it open. They'd done it. It had been official for eight months now. The sightseers were all visiting in droves. Not that they hadn't been fascinated ever since Earl Douglass found the bones there. Just thinking about it made his skin crawl.

The President had set aside eighty acres and called it a national monument.

He pushed his anger down.

He should have been the one to find the bones. It should be his name on everything. Carnegie should be singing *his* praises for his contributions to the world of paleontology, rather than relegating him to the insignificant work he did here.

Taking a swig of his coffee, he took a steadying breath. Plans changed. That was the way of life. And death. But his greatest strength was patience. He could be flexible. As long as the end result was the same, he could allow for some tweaks in his plans. He wasn't so arrogant to believe that everything would always go exactly as he wanted it.

The timing had to be perfect. Once he had Mr. Andrew Carnegie behind him, the world would see.

Whenever he mentioned paleontology, the upper class

would no longer share jokes behind their hands and newspapers as they recalled the lack of integrity shown by Cope and Marsh.

He would be the new face of paleontology. As he rose to the top, the accolades and respect would come pouring in. The field of science would have prestige once again.

When his men in Wyoming finished excavating his finest specimen yet, it would have the largest display next to Carnegie's beloved Dippy.

Yes, this could all be in his favor.

"Bring the crowds and hordes to view the dinosaur bones, Earl. Enjoy the ride while you can." He spat the words at the paper and set it aside. Shuffling through his correspondence, he tossed several letters aside, then spied the one he had been waiting for.

There was news from Wyoming. Ripping the letter open, he scanned its contents. With a frustrated growl, he balled the paper up and threw it across the room.

Nothing was going his way.

He took a deep breath and stood, crossing the plush carpet of his office, and snatched the crinkled letter off the floor. Settling back down at his desk, he smoothed the missive and read it again.

Not good news, boss. The skeleton that was promising in the beginning has yielded no more bones from the quarry. We need more funds to expand the digging area—maybe we just haven't looked far enough to the north yet. Awaiting your instructions. Please send telegram. —C

He plucked his glasses from the bridge of his nose and rubbed them with a cloth. Anger coursed through his veins. More money? He'd invested far too much already.

He glanced up at the clock. Ten minutes until he had to

meet with the junior paleontologists to begin a new display. Inhaling deeply, he worked to release his aggravation and then let out the air in his lungs with slow, pulsing breaths. Then he slid his glasses on, tucked the letter in his vest pocket, and stood. Work awaited. He grabbed his lab coat off the hook and slipped it on, making sure each lapel laid flat.

His ire had cooled. For now.

A few hours later, the late-spring wind tugged at his hat as he bounded down the steps of the Carnegie Institute toward home.

Finally, this wretched day was over. It would have been enough to learn about the impending disaster in Wyoming. But no. His junior paleontologists—the very men he had selected to help reach levels of brilliance under his tutelage— attempted to correct him about the placement of a spiked plate of the *Stegosaurus unglatus* just unboxed from the monument in Utah.

The nerve.

Still, his time with those two imbeciles hadn't been a complete waste. The skeleton Douglass sent would need a few plaster casts done for the back left leg. A common practice among museums when skeletons were almost completely intact. No one wanted to see a dinosaur with three legs or a missing tail—

His eyes widened.

That was it!

So what if they didn't have a *whole* skeleton. They could create what was missing out of plaster. And perhaps if they found a few other random bones where they were digging, they could be used to complete his new find. Maybe this was the best solution until he had more funds to expand the dig.

A voice shouted down to him. "Mr. Nelson!"

He cringed. Eliza Mills.

For months he'd had to endure the high-and-mighty lectures of that woman. Why on earth Mr. Carnegie allowed her to stay on was beyond any sensible man's comprehension.

He frowned, feigned he hadn't heard a thing, and turned the collar of his coat up, tucking his chin down between the tweed fabric. The delicate work that they did required precision. Intense study.

Just because her grandfather was Carnegie's friend should not have been enough to grant her a job. Much less keep it for this long. This was a man's field. And that was plain fact.

Paleontology's reputation needed to be restored, not ruined again. Adding a woman into the mix spelled disaster.

She called again, but it was cut off.

His foul mood today had started with her when he arrived and ended with her. Frankly, he was tired of putting on a nice face. He dared a glance back. She was heading back inside with the institute director.

Staring back at the museum, a new idea formed. It was a bit risky. He squinted in the chilly spring air. But in the long run, if he wanted her gone, it would be worth it.

~~~

MONDAY, MAY 8, 1916 • UNIVERSITY OF PITTSBURGH

Another school term was about to come to a close. Devin smiled out the window with the thought. It had been a good year at the university. His students had grown and, if their tests were any indication, learned a great deal.

But the summer break couldn't come soon enough. His mind and body were exhausted.

What had being a professor of English shown him?

It was draining, that's what.

It had been one thing to teach a class or two while he'd worked on his advanced degrees. Another thing entirely to take over the English department after the sudden departure of the head. A man who'd been there for years.

At least Devin had plenty of time to recover, rejuvenate, and plan for the next year. The Dean had promised him that.

He turned back to his desk and the stack of essays waiting for his red markings. Might as well tackle what he could for the next hour. It would be quiet here for a while and then he could head back home and check on Dad.

He pooled his energy, stretched, and rubbed his eyes before diving back into the grading.

Watching his father over the years and studying under him had only made Devin's love of learning and teaching grow. Before he could even read, the excitement of discovery and education had filled their small home.

It made him smile. There were many days he missed not ever really knowing his mother, but Dad had filled that void as much as he could. Devin really shouldn't complain. His upbringing had been wonderful. With plenty of opportunities thanks to the Mills family.

Thoughts of the family that had been his benefactor for so long kept him distracted from the essay he'd been trying to read—and brought Eliza to the forefront of his mind. Her grandfather had paid for every cent of Devin's education, not allowing a word of argument from him nor any from his father. And the man had been at every major event and graduation to shake Devin's hand and say how proud he was.

Mr. Mills never again mentioned the talk they'd had on that day in the lane, but Devin thought of it often—especially when his affection for Eliza would swell.

He shook his head and focused on the paper. Every day he had to push thoughts of her aside. And every day he struggled.

Knock, knock!

His head jerked up to see who it was.

The door opened a little, and an enormous green hat with some sort of feathers protruding out of the top preceded its wearer.

30

He'd know a hat like that anywhere. Eliza.

The object of his mind's wandering peeked around the door, eyed the room, and grinned. "Oh good, you're alone." She scurried to his desk and grabbed hold of his hand. "You simply won't believe it!" Tugging him from his seat, she began to spin around the room with him in tow.

It must be some pretty great news. "Whoa, give me a minute to put my pen away." Without letting go of her hand, he rushed back to his desk and laid it down, right as it dropped a fat blob of red ink. "See? We wouldn't have wanted that on your clothes."

"*Pshaw*." She grabbed hold of his other hand and around she twirled until she was breathless and almost lost her hat. Putting one hand up to balance the monstrosity, she giggled and released his other hand. "What is an ink spot when there is such exciting news to share? I had to tell you first."

"Tell me what?" Gone was his exhausted state. Seeing her made everything within him come alive.

She perched ever so daintily on the windowsill and covered her mouth with one hand. Her long green jacket and skirt matched her hat to perfection.

Eliza would never have it any other way.

Following her lead, he sat on the corner of his desk facing her and willed his heart to slow down. He crossed his arms over his chest. They were no longer children. Better prepare himself. Any day now, she'd tell him that she'd given her heart to someone. And his world would change.

Forever.

She released an almost imperceptible squeal and lifted her eyebrows. "Mr. Carnegie asked *me* to go to Dinosaur National Monument to the Carnegie Quarry as a representative of the institute and work there—lending my expertise, as he put it— for the whole summer! Permanently if I wish."

He hadn't seen such unadulterated joy on her face since

they were children. But his heart broke just the same. She was leaving?

Almost immediately, her smile drooped. "What is it? You're frowning."

"Not a thing." He forced an enthusiastic smile. "I'm ecstatic for you. Sounds like a wonderful opportunity."

"Don't try and fool me, Mr. Schmitt. What was that frown about?" Like a dog with a bone, she'd never let go if he didn't appease her with a legitimate answer.

"I'm sorry. It's been a long day, and it was probably from exhaustion."

"And?" She stood and stepped closer, analyzing him. One buttoned-up boot tapped the floor.

"The term is almost over. Lots to do. It's only my first year in this position—"

"*And?*"

Good grief, she loved to push. Fine. "I didn't like the thought of you leaving."

"Is that all?" She released a light laugh. "That's easily fixable. Since you're about to enter your summer break, why don't you come along? At least for a week or two?"

It was easy for her to say that. She always had an answer for everything. Eliza Mills had never let anything stand in her way. He, on the other hand, was not so fortunate. "I have a great deal to do this summer. It's not like I can just take off. There's planning and meetings and—"

"Oh, you'll have plenty of time to attend to all that. You have time owed to you. I know you do." Her green eyes flashed at him.

"While that is true, I have other responsibilities. Besides, didn't you tell me that Dinosaur National Monument isn't exactly close to any city? I don't think you will last very long out there." Maybe she would take the bait and get the focus off of him. He'd love nothing more than to spend his summer break with Eliza, but two nights ago—when he couldn't sleep for thoughts of her—he'd pledged to release her from his heart. This one-sided love affair wasn't doing him any good. Eventually she'd marry some rich fellow, and where would he be then?

Hands on her hips, she stepped even closer. "You don't think I will enjoy being away from the city?"

With a laugh, he dipped his chin at her. "I know you won't. You love digging and bone quarries and all that—but you *really* love the city. I give you three weeks tops."

She swatted at his arm. "I'll make it longer than that. Just you wait and see."

"Without Rufaloe's?"

The mention of her favorite bakery produced a twinkle in her eyes, and she licked her lips.

Yep. He knew her. "Or that milliner"—he pointed to the massive thing atop her head—"the one that makes these . . . gigantic creations you love to wear?"

A hand to the tip of it, she sent him a lopsided grin. "What? You don't like my hats?"

He gave her a little eye roll. "They're huge, and I'm always wondering when you will topple over."

"I think they're lovely. I will not be toppling over, thank you very much, and I happen to like how I look in them."

The slight defiant lift of her chin was adorable.

"Don't you?"

But he caught the hesitancy in her eyes. No matter what she said, she always sought his approval. "Eliza Mills, you will always be lovely, even when you're dressed in men's pants and covered in mud." It was as close as he could come to sharing his heart with her without breaking his promise to her grandfather.

"Spoken like a true friend." She removed her gloves, patted his hand, and leaned on the desk next to him. "Thank you.

And I'll have you know that I won't have any trouble out at Dinosaur National Monument. I might miss the city—yes, I'll give you that—but I'm excited to do what I love to do. It's an incredible opportunity. Especially for a woman."

"Yes, it is. And I'm thrilled for you." He bumped her with his shoulder. Sitting side by side was easier than looking her in the eye, but much more difficult because she was so near. He could smell her perfume—the soft scent of roses—and feel her warmth.

For once, he was thankful for the monstrous hats she wore because it gave them a buffer. Maybe her going out West would be good for him. To not see her every day and have the constant reminders of what could never be. Perhaps he could actually follow through with his pledge to release her. Once and for all.

"But what if I need you there?"

Her voice cut through.

"What?"

"You weren't listening, were you?" She released a little huff, stood up, and paced in front of him. "I *said*, you never answered my question about coming out to the quarry for a while. What if I need you there?"

"Why on earth would you need *me* there?" He tried to cover the question with sarcasm, but his heart still longed for her to say that she couldn't live without hi—

No. Stop it. This was exactly why he'd made the pledge.

Glancing around the room, she stepped closer. So close, her hat almost touched his forehead. "All those years I wrote the papers under a man's name . . . you promised you would stand in if I needed you."

This again? *Not* what he wanted to hear. "Ugh, Eliza. That was years ago. You've never once needed me to stand in, and you won't ever need me to. You're on your own two feet, you have a degree, and you are publishing all those scientific

34

papers under your own name now." He waved off the comment. "You've done digs with your own name. Besides, no one has ever come looking for the author of those papers. That charade is long past."

"But you promised."

If she started to pout, he'd throttle her. "Eliza, no. I will not be your stand-in. You don't need me to be. Aren't they pretty obscure anyway?"

Her cheeks tinged pink, and her eyes narrowed to slits. "Obscure?"

Now he'd done it. "That's not what I meant." He held up his hands. "I'm tired. I already told you that. What I meant . . . well, didn't you say that most of the scientific papers got buried after a while? I mean . . . since no one is talking about them right now, don't you think you're safe from having to answer for them?"

"You might have a point, Mr. Schmitt"—whenever she used his surname, he was in trouble—"but I think you're simply making excuses." Once again, she perched beside him. Close. "You don't want to go, do you?" She leaned to the side and eyed him straight on. "Or is it that you've had enough of me?"

He slumped his shoulders and shook his head. Was she really that clueless? "I've not had enough of you. But paleontology has always been *your* thing. If you'll remember, I teach English. I'm excited for you for the opportunity and to see you excel and spread your wings. Very few women have the chance to make a mark like you do."

With squinted eyes, she studied him. Apparently satisfied with his answer, she broke the connection and stared forward. "It still wouldn't hurt you to come visit."

There was no winning this argument. He crossed his arms over his chest again and nodded at his outstretched legs. "You are correct."

"So will you?" The words were softer this time. Not the Eliza who pushed to get her way. This was the voice of his friend. The one who sought his affirmation.

Her vulnerability in that moment was almost his undoing. "I'll think about it."

two

"I am having a grand time and am happy. Seem to be just in my element."

~Earl Douglass

Devin breathed in the scents of roses, citrus, and fresh-cut grass. Parties weren't his favorite thing. But the University politely *requested* that all staff and faculty be present for the University's end-of-term gala. Why the University bothered with the subterfuge baffled him. Everyone knew this evening was to raise funds from all the wealthy benefactors.

Gearing himself up to schmooze with donors and have endless conversations about the English department all evening, he pasted on a smile and went straight for the refreshments.

"Isn't it bad enough that we have to get all dressed up in the robes and then sit through the long and tedious graduation ceremony year after year?" Professor Allen chuckled as he walked up to Devin at the refreshment table. "But now we have to attend a party as well?"

This wasn't the first time they'd discussed their displeasure about the yearly event. Devin smiled at his colleague. "Not just attend, remember. We must hobnob."

An older woman stepped up to the punch bowl. Her light blue eyes and jewelry caught the light and sparkled. "Would you care for some refreshment, gentlemen?" She lifted the large ladle and began to serve up several small crystal cups.

"That would be wonderful, thank you." Devin nodded his thanks.

Professor Allen did the same.

"I think I'll go hunt for a corner to hide in until it's all over."

"Would you mind if I joined you?" His colleague raised one brow. "At least if we appear deep in conversation, there's a decent chance we won't have to join the crowds."

"Sounds like a great plan to me." Devin spied his desired destination. Clusters of university professors and donors were springing up as the room filled. His grip tight on his punch cup, he took purposeful strides toward the small alcove at the back of the room, hoping and praying that he wouldn't get distracted along the way.

Thankfully, he made it without disruption, and Professor Allen joined him.

The history teacher glanced at his pocket watch. "Five minutes down. Only three hours to go." He sighed and took a sip from his cup. "Every year, these things seem to go longer and longer."

"Indeed." Most of the time, Devin spent these types of events watching people. Their mannerisms and expressions. He passed the time making up stories for all of them. One could learn so much about human nature by watching people laugh with acquaintances in one breath and drop the façade as soon as they thought no one was watching. Ridiculous, really. What would people think if they knew what he thought? Not that the opinion of a lowly English professor would mean much to them.

Better just to stand here and do his best to look like he was enjoying himself. "Any exciting new developments in the history department?"

Allen laughed. "Well, history hasn't changed—at least last time I checked—but we *will* have a new addition to the department next year. What with Professor Sadler's retirement."

"Oh? Do you know the new chap?"

Allen shook his head. "Nope. And it's not a male either. We will have the first female professor in the history department." A frown flickered across the man's face.

"That's great." He didn't have to fake enthusiasm. He felt it through and through. Cheering for Eliza for so long meant he had a firsthand view watching her struggle and triumph time and time again in her field. He didn't hold the same views as some of the older staff who insisted women should only teach women and children. "Have you met her yet?"

"She's supposed to arrive next week. Her credentials and education are impeccable, so I am hopeful she will be an asset and not a *distraction*." Allen stressed the word with a wink. He was about the same age as Devin but seemed to have adopted the attitude several of his peers held about women.

Devin raised a brow. "The world is changing, my friend. For the better, if you ask my opinion."

"Come back and tell me that when you have women in the English department." Allen chuckled. "Although, as a young, single man like myself, you would probably love meeting someone with the same interests. I can't say the thought hasn't crossed my mind." The smirk on his colleague's face seemed somehow . . . lascivious. Devin looked away.

Every year, he learned a bit more about the people he worked with on a day-to-day basis. Sometimes, he enjoyed getting to know them better. But others . . . not so much.

Still, they were all weary from the end of another long year. He could excuse his friend's narrow thinking for now.

He wasn't in the best of moods and might say something untoward himself if he didn't watch his mouth.

Perhaps a change of subject would be best for both of them. "What are your plans for the summer?"

"You mean, when I'm not here?" Professor Allen pointed to the floor and then out the window. "I would love to take some time off to spend at the coast, but I have so much to prepare for next term since I'm teaching two new classes. I will probably have to settle for dreaming of the beach rather than going." He took another sip from his crystal cup. "What about you? Since you're the new head of the English department, my guess is that you'll be up here as much as I am."

Devin nodded and took a deep breath. "You are correct. My only plans at this point are to get prepared for next term."

Usually he loved the summer and the shorter hours he needed to put into work, but his responsibilities more than doubled when he became head of his department. He felt the pressure to make sure the department continued to operate at a high standard. And he hoped to progress the program forward as well. As he'd said to his friend, times were changing. There was a great deal to do.

Yet . . .

Eliza's request niggled at the back of his mind. Even with all the work piling up on his desk, he would love to go west and see her.

He blinked away the thought.

The huge grandfather clock in the large hall rang out the top of the hour. Soon there would be a raffle, and a string quartet would play so that people could dance.

"Looks like we've survived fifteen minutes so far."

Devin groaned. "It's going to be a long evening." He worked to mask his disappointment.

"I'm off for a refill. These dainty little cups don't hold much." Allen waggled his eyebrows at him as he walked away.

His colleague's words gave him a chuckle as he glanced down at his own empty cup. But then noise from the front entryway drew his attention. A group of people entering had caught the eye of almost everyone in the room. The crowd was pulled along with them like a moving carpet.

Probably one of the wealthiest couples in Pittsburgh. People always liked to *ooh* and *aah* over their costly attire for the shindig.

Devin suppressed a yawn. The night was going to drag on forev—

The crowd parted.

That wasn't just any wealthy couple. That was the Millses. And their granddaughter.

Eliza.

His heart picked up its pace, and he found his smile. What was she doing here? They never came to this event.

The president of the University held his glass of wine up. "If I might have everyone's attention, please." His voice boomed in the room with built-in resonance.

The large hall quieted.

"Thank you." He cleared his throat. "I have some wonderful news to share with you that should get our celebratory evening off to an incredible start."

All eyes were on the president.

"The Mills family has donated one million dollars for a new scholarship fund to be established."

Before he could say anything else, applause burst through the room, making Devin's ears pound.

The president said something else, but Devin's eyes were glued to Eliza.

The Mills family had vast wealth. He'd always known that. But a million dollars?

One. Million. Dollars. An amount that he couldn't even fathom.

Just given away.

As he watched Eliza receive the compliments of guests and laugh along with several other donors, the punch in his stomach soured.

The woman he loved with all his heart was so far out of his reach, she might as well be on the moon.

Turning to the window, he could feel a great crack splitting his heart in two. He clenched his jaw tight. He had no right to a broken heart. He'd promised her grandfather, after all.

But over the years, the dream he'd kept buried would spark to life and escape its prison. Obviously, his heart was a very poor warden.

"Devin?"

Lost in his own thoughts, he didn't register who had spoken his name until he felt warmth envelop the crook of his elbow. He looked down and spotted Eliza's hand resting on his jacket sleeve as though it belonged there.

"Devin? Are you all right?"

She was a vision in a navy blue dress, all sparkles and light. Her red curls had been tamed into some sort of swirl on the top of her head, making her look regal and elegant. How could he ever have thought he was worthy of her? He blinked at her several times, trying to get his bearings. "Yes. Of course."

"Why are you standing over here in the corner?" She laughed and shook her head. "Aren't you excited about the new scholarship fund?" She leaned in a bit and whispered. "And you don't have to endure the boring party by yourself . . ."

He forced himself to laugh along with her.

The string quartet began to play.

"Come on." She grabbed his hand. "I'd prefer not to dance with any of the old, stodgy professors. I think you should be my partner, and that way we can keep each other company and from boredom." Her matter-of-fact tone gave him little option.

Not that he would have ever denied her.

As soon as she was in his arms, he realized his serious error.

Somehow he had to rip the love he held for Eliza Mills out of his heart.

~~~~~~

TUESDAY, JUNE 13, 1916 • DINOSAUR NATIONAL
MONUMENT, CARNEGIE QUARRY, UTAH

Another delegation of wealthy tourists followed Eliza to an overlook of the bone quarry. The ring of hammers against rock echoed through the air. Puffs of dust and dirt dotted the area as men moved large piles of rocks from the south quadrant of the dig. Eliza's fingers itched to hold a chisel and hammer again. To unbury bones and stories of the earth.

But for now, she would be content sharing her knowledge with those eager to hear.

The group yesterday had stayed for five hours, asking question after question. She'd loved every minute of it. Getting to talk about the work was *almost* as good as doing it.

This group seemed just as eager.

On their walk out to the quarry, she explained the Great Dinosaur Rush that started decades before. She detailed some of the behaviors of Cope and Marsh—two paleontologists who had sought to outdo each other through sabotage and subterfuge—and it brought the expected gasps and horrified expressions.

Those two men lacked any vestige of integrity in their bitter rivalry to gain acclaim. The only good thing to come of their rivalry was the attention it brought to the fact that paleontologists were digging for evidence of great beasts.

She hated to admit it, but she wouldn't be here now if not for Cope and Marsh and their work.

Once everyone made it to the ledge and found a spot to gaze down at the work below, she began her presentation. "Welcome to the Carnegie Quarry here at Dinosaur National

Monument." While there wasn't much out here except the quarry, and the grueling travel by train and stage to get here wasn't ideal, she did her best to help all the visitors see the magic of the bones coming to life. Some days it was easier than others.

Hopefully today would be easy.

"You have probably heard of and seen *Diplodocus carnegii*, which has been on display in the Hall of Dinosaurs at the Carnegie Institute since 1907. Even though it was found in the Sheep Creek Quarry in Wyoming back in 1899, there wasn't space for it until the new Hall was built. Standing at nearly fifteen feet high at the hips and a gargantuan eighty-four feet long, our skeleton—which we lovingly call 'Dippy'—is only the beginning of what we hope to accomplish in the coming years at this quarry. We work so these great beasts can be displayed for all to see."

Taking a deep breath, she licked her lips. The air was dry and smelled of dust and rock. "In 1909, when Mr. Earl Douglass discovered the first bones that led to this quarry, he knew that he had come upon a great discovery. Since then, he has led the work here. If you're lucky, we might get the opportunity to speak with him today."

"Mr. Douglass is here? We've heard so much about him." The man in a pinstriped jacket and trousers adjusted his bowler as he scanned the quarry with renewed vigor.

Not exactly equipped for the terrain. Eliza pushed her opinions aside and smiled. "Yes, sir. He's here every day. He is most passionate about the work here."

One of the women stepped toward her. "Even though the bones seem large—one of them I can see clearly from here—the men are using small tools. Could you explain the process of extracting the fossils from the quarry bed?"

Her smile stretched. "Perfect question. I'd love to. If you will all follow me, please?" She led them to another lookout about forty yards away. "Over here, you can see the pile of rocks, dirt, and debris. When we know there is a good bit to dig before we get to the actual fossil, we can use larger chisels, hammers, and shovels to move those layers. But whenever a fossil is visible, we have to delicately chisel the rock and earth around it. Keeping it intact is always the top priority. That's where the small tools come into play, and it is time-consuming work. We chisel, brushing away the debris, check to make sure there are no cracks, then chisel away some more."

"Sounds tedious." The man in the pinstripes appeared a bit bored and shoved his hands into his trouser pockets. "Could we perhaps see some of the bones taken out of the quarry?"

"By all means. We will walk down and see what has been crated up this week."

The thundering of hooves echoed around them and the tiny rocks at her feet jumped and scattered. No one rode at a breakneck speed out here. What was going on?

A horse and rider came into view. Someone was in a hurry.

Eliza walked out to meet the rider and ensure he didn't go sailing off the bluff into the quarry. She recognized the young man who worked at the telegraph office.

"You've got a telegram, Miss Mills." He tipped his cap at her as he jumped off his horse. "My boss said it was urgent."

She stepped toward him to take the envelope. "Thank you." She pulled a coin out of her pocket. What could be so urgent? Could it be from home?

As she handed the boy the money, her heart sank. Had something happened to Grandfather and Grandmama . . . ? *O God, please let them be all right.*

"Thanks." The kid hopped up on his horse and hurried back the way he'd come.

She glanced at her little tour group. "I pray you all will excuse me for a moment." She nodded at them and took quick steps away to give her a small amount of privacy.

Eliza ripped into the envelope.

She unfolded the sheet of paper and read.

Dr. Masterson from England is coming out to quarry.
Please help him with whatever he needs. —Andrew Carnegie

Dr. Masterson. Her breaths came in short gasps. *The* Dr. Masterson.

What an honor it would be to have him out here! As she clutched the papers to her chest, her mind raced with all the possibilities.

She'd been studying everything the man had ever written. He was the top expert in Europe. Far exceeding anything that anyone in the United States had done—no matter how much Cope and Marsh and everyone since had attempted to show their superiority.

This could change her whole summer.

This could change—she swallowed—her whole life!

FRIDAY, JUNE 16, 1916 • JENSEN, UTAH

Those ridiculous dinosaur enthusiasts were ruining everything.

She lifted the field glasses again. Once her eyes adjusted, she scanned the horizon. From the quarry of the current dig toward the east and then north, she scanned back and forth.

They were getting too close.

Why did Earl have to find those stupid fossils here? No one ventured to this out-of-the-way place in Utah.

Everything would have been completely fine had they just left everything alone.

Lowering the glasses, she fumed. Stomping her right foot, she growled at the site. This was not supposed to happen. She tapped out a rhythm on the side of the glasses.

On the bright side, in the last few months, they hadn't progressed very far. But every inch mattered when they were headed in her direction.

For decades, she'd watched as every man around her got what they wanted. Her father. Brothers. Uncles. Nephews. The deacons at church. Mr. Earl Douglass. The list could go on. All the while, women—like herself—had to toe the line and do what was expected of them. Never allowed dreams or wishes. It wasn't fair.

If her parents had simply allowed her to do what she wanted, then they wouldn't all be in this predicament.

There was no way she would back down now. Not after all she'd gone through.

She looked through the field glasses one more time and calculated the distance. To her best guess, they were only 100 yards away. At most.

All right, it was time to up the ante. Her plans would have to change. But as sure as the sun rose each morning, she wasn't about to allow this little hiccup to sidetrack her.

If those fossil hunters knew what was best for them, they'd get out of her way, or she'd remove them. Permanently.

three

"Am twenty-six years old today. More than a quarter of
a century is gone and nothing accomplished yet of any
value. Have hoped to make my life amount to something
but have been disappointed so far. I realize if I am ever
to amount to anything I will have to start soon. I have
decided what I would like to do and what I would like
to make of myself—a teacher and a scientist."

~Earl Douglass

FRIDAY, JUNE 16, 1916 • ADAMS FARM NEAR JENSEN, UTAH

The clink of silverware on plates echoed through the hushed
room.

Eliza scanned the table. The family of six that was hosting
her for the summer had a lovely home. The fact that they had
a bedroom to spare when they had four daughters already was
a testament to their good fortune out here in the West. While
it wasn't nearly as wild and untamed as she'd expected, it was
still remote and lacked the growing populations of the East.

Back home, buildings seemed to be constructed at a steady
pace, expanding the city's borders. And there were always

48

plenty of voices from people on the streets, sidewalks, in the shops . . . even from neighbors.

Mills Manor sat on a good deal of acreage back home. She didn't even know how much. But they could still see their neighbors and hear them. But out here? There was no sign of a neighbor north, south, east, or west.

The quiet outside—little noise other than the rustling of the leaves in the wind or the song of a bird—had taken some getting used to. But it was the silence inside that startled her the most. Even in her massive estate in Pittsburgh there was always a hum of activity. Not only the servants, but Grandmama and Grandfather weren't quiet people. Every meal was filled with conversation.

She'd expected to arrive and need to get accustomed to a boisterous environment.

The Adamses were good people, their girls mannerly and smartly dressed. But Eliza didn't know them very well yet. Everything seemed to be a bit too proper whenever she was around. She'd heard the chatter and giggles multiple times as she approached the house. But they instantly ceased whenever she stepped over the threshold.

Time to change that.

She set down her fork and lifted her glass for a sip of water. "What are your plans for the summer, Louise?" She pointed her question to the eldest daughter.

The girl's gaze darted up from her plate and her cheeks pinked, but the sparkle in her eyes showed her pleasure in being asked. "Mama needs me to help with her shop, so I'm working every morning there."

Mrs. Adams had a shop. Wonderful. "I had no idea. What kind of shop is it?"

"Millinery." Louise beamed. "I'm trying to convince Mama to copy a few of your hats. They're so beautiful."

"And really, *really* big." The youngest piped up from her

chair. Then covered her mouth with her hand as she glanced at her mother.

Eliza giggled and dabbed her lips with her napkin. "They are large, aren't they, Mabel?" She shrugged. "But I love hats. My dearest friend in all the world back home often tells me that my hats are monstrosities. But he doesn't understand how much women love their hats."

"Is that your beau back home?" Mrs. Adams raised her coffee cup to her lips.

"No." Eliza lifted her fork and knife once again. "His father was my private tutor, so we grew up together. He loved English. I loved science. We both hated math."

The two middle Adams daughters laughed along with her. There. That was just what she'd hoped for. To see them relax in front of her. Eliza'd had enough stiff and stuffy meals to last a lifetime. "I take it you two don't like math either?"

The taller—Adelaide . . . or was it Eleanor?—scrunched up her nose as she shook her head. "Mama often has me help her with the sums for her shop. I don't like it at all. But I do like your hats."

The younger of the two bobbed her head up and down so much that her ribbons flapped. "They're not monsters . . . monstrosery—"

"Monstrosities." Louise helped her younger sibling.

"Monstro . . . sities." The girl held her chin up after saying it all by herself. "When I grow up, I want to wear one just like your green one."

Mrs. Adams looked ready to interject at any moment, so Eliza leaned toward the little girl and grinned. "It's my favorite too."

The older woman sent her a soft smile and then turned to her daughters. "Girls, it's time to take care of the dishes."

"Yes, Mama," they chimed in unison.

The four young ladies from age eighteen down to six stood and began to clear the table.

"You are very kind to indulge them." Mrs. Adams's voice was low as she laid her napkin to rest on the table.

Eliza wasn't ignorant to the fact this family had opened up their home to a friend of Mr. Andrew Carnegie himself and that it probably brought a great weight on their minds. "I don't see it as indulgence at all." She blew out a slow breath and looked from Mr. Adams—who hadn't said a word the entire meal—back to his wife. "You have been wonderful, gracious, and so very kind to host me for the summer. But rest assured, my expectations aren't ridiculous. For me, it is a blessing to simply have the opportunity to spend time with such a loving family. I'd love to be looked at as another member of the family. Nothing more. No special treatment."

The clock chimed and it was the perfect reason to exit. Mrs. Adams seemed to be speechless while Mr. Adams's mouth hung open. It all became clear. Grandmama had a hand in this. No doubt sending pages of instructions and requirements for her granddaughter's accommodations.

No wonder the family had done everything to the point of perfection since her arrival. "I best be off to the quarry. Thank you so much for another lovely meal." She hurried from the table, gathered her things, and strode out to her waiting horse. Every day, it had been saddled and waiting for her at the hitching post.

She'd have to come up with something clever and creative to thank this sweet family. Over time as she got to know them, surely she would learn their personalities and tastes. By the time her summer was over, the Adamses would be her second family.

The ride to the quarry was uneventful, and she made her way to the tent that had become her office of sorts. A place to get out of the intense sun and spread out maps and papers without the wind whisking them to Colorado.

It would be magnificent if Earl would invite her to be a part of the dig. Only time would tell if that would happen. He was a man who had high expectations. Everyone had to give their very best. Truth and honesty were of utmost importance to him.

She winced. What would he think if he found out that she'd written all those papers under a man's name? To Earl, that would be a lie. She couldn't bear the thought of disappointing a man she respected so deeply. Grandfather's frustration with her chosen profession, though he'd finally relented, was still palpable.

Eliza gnawed at her lip, her chest tightening. No. It was best if none of it came to light.

She'd simply have to work extra hard and do her very best. Whatever she could do to help him do this work and see his dream for this area come alive, she'd do it.

"Miss Mills?" A wife of one of the other workers peeked into the tent.

"Good morning. Mrs. Hawkins, is it?" One thing she prided herself on was remembering the spouses of the workers. "What can I do for you?"

"I just came to chat. I heard Earl telling my Jim about your work for Carnegie back in Pittsburgh. It's fascinating that you do this work too." She stepped toward Eliza and bit her lip.

Eliza caught that inquisitive glint in the woman's eyes. A thrill shot through her. She recognized that look. "Does paleontology interest you as well?"

The woman nodded. Then strode forward and held out her hand. "Please call me Deborah."

"Eliza." She shook the woman's hand and then perched on the edge of the makeshift table. "I love that you are excited about this science too. May I ask what brought on your interest?"

The younger woman's eyes sparkled. "Back in 1908, I was fifteen. I remember Mr. Meyer coming to town all excited because he and one of his hands found a bone that couldn't belong to any living creature we know of today. It was fossilized in the rock, he said, but clear as day. For some reason, I wanted to go find it and dig it up myself. I had this little thrill inside just thinking about it. The community buzzed about it for a while, but then, you know, the tragedy that happened to their family overshadowed his excitement and most people forgot about it, I guess." She shrugged. "But then the next year, Earl found this. That same insatiable desire inside me sprang to life. But by then, my parents wouldn't allow me to do anything of the sort. Told me my duty was to get married first."

Eliza sent her a smile. "Well, I've seen the way you look at Mr. Hawkins. It appears that part of the plan worked out all right."

Deborah leaned forward, her face radiant with a glow that could only be attributed to love. "It did. And I am thankful." She looked down at her hands. "But I haven't had any children yet, and well . . ." Her gaze snapped back to Eliza's. "I was wondering if I could help you out here. My husband said he's fine with it if you are."

Eliza could barely restrain from grabbing the woman and twirling her around, much the way she would Devin back home. Taking a breath, she tamped down most of her giddiness and smiled at the woman. "I'd love to have your help! I'm not sure there would be any funds to pay you much, but I will gladly pay you out of my own earnings."

Oh! To have another woman around! How wonderful!

Goodness. She hadn't realized how starved for friendship she was. Without Devin around, it felt like half of her was missing. Maybe she and Deborah could team up . . . especially if her next question had a favorable answer. "Did they ever dig up the bone discovered at the Meyer's?" As soon as the words were out, she regretted them. She should have asked about the tragedy of the family first. But she'd been holding it in ever since Deborah brought it up.

"No. The discovery was forgotten when the whole family disappeared. The grandparents. The parents. The children. All of them. Nowhere to be found. Food was cooking on the stove. Horses were saddled right outside the door. It was strange. They were never found."

"Who owns the ranch now?"

"A long-lost brother. He'd been the black sheep of the family for a good while but returned when the sheriff sent him word of what happened. He's not a rancher, but he's done his best to make his family proud."

Eliza could almost taste a victory. If those bones were still there . . . if she and Deborah could somehow be allowed to dig them up . . . imagine what that could do for the world of paleontology. Perhaps Dinosaur National Monument could even be expanded? They could have a visitor center and bring Earl's vision for the place to life. "Do you think you could go with me to speak to Mr. Meyer?"

"Of course." Deborah's eyes widened. "Do you think he'll allow you to look around and dig?"

"Maybe. But we won't know unless we try."

MONDAY, JUNE 19, 1916 • PITTSBURGH

Devin stepped over the threshold and closed the door behind him. "Dad?" His day had been full of meetings that had been exhausting and boring all at the same time. Some of the older professors seemed to enjoy talking simply to hear the sound of their own voices. He made his way through the small cottage he shared with his father and laid his leather case on the table.

"Back here!" His father's tone was full of the same joy he exuded every day. "How did the meetings go?"

Devin found his father in the little room off the kitchen. His favorite. Probably because it was full of windows and was the cheeriest room in the house. "Long."

"Sounds like you need to get away." Dad stood and walked over to him, handing him an envelope. As he stepped around Devin, he gripped his shoulder and squeezed. "I'm going to make some dinner. Are you hungry?"

"Famished, actually." Devin turned the envelope over in his hands.

Eliza.

Her handwriting sent his heart into a fast trot. He closed his eyes for a moment and steadied his breathing.

Dad began to shuffle around pots and pans in a cabinet. "She addressed it to both of us. It was sweet that she sent me a note in there too. My letter is on the table if you'd like to read it."

The clanking covered up the pounding of Devin's heart. It had been one thing to say good-bye to her and an entirely different thing to realize each day that she wasn't within walking distance. They hadn't been apart more than a few days since they were children. Each day that passed he told himself to push thoughts of her aside. After all, that was what he wanted. To let her go.

But now, she'd been gone for two weeks, and it had been awful. Pure torture.

"Are you just gonna stand there staring at it? Or are you gonna read it?"

Devin laid it on the table on top of the letter to Dad. "I'll read it after dinner." He had to do something about these feelings for her. If he allowed himself to get eager every time she sent word, he would never be able to let her go.

"You'll read it *now*." His father was beside him holding a skillet, his firm voice scolding. "You've been a complete grump since she left. It's going to take time for me to concoct something for us to eat anyway. Take them back to your room and read them."

He'd never shared his feelings for Eliza with his father. Hadn't told him about the promise he'd made to Mr. Mills. Then the pledge he'd recently made to himself.

"Son?"

He'd been standing there staring at the letters. He glanced back to Dad. "I don't think that's a good idea."

His father set the skillet down on the table and took a seat. "All right, sit."

He did as he was told.

"I've had an inkling for a while now that what you felt for Eliza was more than just friendship. But I wasn't certain until she left for this new job. You haven't been yourself." Dad pursed his lips and took a long, slow breath. "And now I see it written all over your face. I'm sorry I didn't say anything to you until now, I really had no idea that your feelings for her ran so deep. How long have you been in love with her?"

Devin couldn't move for several moments. Then he slumped forward with a sigh. There was no reason to keep it all inside any longer. It's not like his dad was the town gossip and would spread it around. Swiping a hand through his hair, he met his father's gaze. "It was a childhood crush—or so I thought—for many years." Memories scrolled through his mind in vivid pictures. "But love? Probably since I was about sixteen. There's never been anyone else that even remotely caught my attention. It's always been her. Naturally, it didn't help matters that we spent so much time together. I could never say no to her adventures. Or the chance to be with her a bit longer."

Dad chuckled. "You two have always been inseparable."

"But a few weeks ago, I couldn't sleep one night, and with all the tossing and turning, I finally got up and pledged to myself that I would let her go. It isn't good for me to be loving her with no chance of that love being returned. I've been dreading the day she comes to tell me that she's courting or worse—betrothed."

"Dev—"

"No. Dad. Please." He held up a hand. "I haven't ever said anything because I didn't want the lectures. I didn't want the sympathy every time you looked at me. Do you realize that each time she came to the university to see me—Every. Single. Time.—I had to brace myself? Thinking, it's going to be today. She's going to want me to share in her excitement that she's in love. My heart has been broken hundreds of times because I can't bear the thought."

The rush of words halted. He couldn't say anything else without choking up. All these years, he'd kept it all locked inside. Because it was the right thing to do. And now, he wished he could make it disappear.

"I wouldn't ever lecture you, son. Never. Not on matters of the heart."

He lifted his gaze to Dad's. There were tears in his eyes.

"Read the letter, son. Read the one she wrote to me as well. You should know that after all these years, she's already like a daughter to me. I love that girl. Love her passion for science. Even more, I love her passion for the Creator, and how she's grappled with many in the scientific world who try to deny His existence. You know I adore her. And you know I want you to be happy. I'd never stand in the way of that."

"Her grandparents would. Dad, I promised Mr. Mills I would never pursue her." At his father's frown, he shifted gears. "Besides, she's never once shown an inkling of interest in me other than friendship."

"Are you sure?" Dad tipped his head to the side. "Sometimes us Schmitt men can be pretty dense." He shrugged. "I didn't see that my own son was in love for all these years. And your mother definitely had to help me see that she cared for me. I had a hard time believing I was worthy." He stood and picked the skillet up. "At least go read the letter. As to the promise to Mr. Mills, we can talk more about it over dinner."

Devin pushed himself to his feet and stared at the envelope and paper underneath. With a nod, he snatched it up and marched to his room.

He sat in the straight-back chair at the small desk under the window. With stiff shoulders and a clenched jaw, he pulled the letter out, bracing himself for the words from Eliza. He refused to let them in. He couldn't. Wouldn't let them affect him. He was letting her go. He could do it.

Dear Devin,

How are things going at the University? Are you bored out of your mind yet from all the meetings and the old gents who blather on about how things used to be done?

He leaned back in his chair and laughed. She knew him better than anyone else, that was for certain. Relaxing a bit, he settled in to read.

I imagine you will have your work cut out for you to whip the old geezers into shape and help them to see the importance of molding the next generation. Or at least, teaching them about correct grammar usage. Which is of utmost importance too.

It would be tolerable to take English again if it was in your class. You've always been able to make all that interesting to me. Even literature, of all things! Which we both know wasn't my forte. But give me a book on geology or chemistry, and I'm all ears.

First, I have to admit that you were correct. It has been very difficult for me to not be near a city. The closest town doesn't boast much at all. It's a good thing I brought trunks of clothes, hats, and shoes—otherwise, I probably would have to send word to Grandmama to ship more to me.

But thanks to the new monument here (although there isn't an actual monument yet, just the quarry), people are coming by the stagefull, which is, thankfully, bringing in more business. Right now, it's saloons and places to stay. But it is a start to civilizing this little corner of the West. The Carnegie Quarry out here is magnificent. While some might only think of it as a hole in the ground, it is the grandest sight I've ever seen. So many bones! I feel giddy every time I see it.

Devin smiled. He could hear her voice as he read, and it lifted his spirits. Life without her was dull. Without color.

When I first met Earl Douglass, I thought I might faint with joy. Ever since his Apatosaurus *was shipped to the museum and assembled next to Dippy, I've wanted to meet him. I must report that he is very amiable. And not at all full of himself for his findings. In fact, he is very focused on his work and nonchalant.*

While I haven't done any of the excavating with Mr. Douglass yet—which would be a dream come true—I've had my hands full keeping the sightseers informed and answering all their plethora of questions. It is definitely the greatest job I've ever done.

I've had the privilege of speaking with Mr. Douglass a couple times. I must say that I completely agree with his vision for the monument. Instead of digging all the bones out, wouldn't it be grand to leave an exhibit in the rock so that people can see them? Preserved where they are, it would be an incredible education for the future generations.

But Mr. Carnegie wants to fill his Hall of Dinosaurs, and I don't blame him.

Perhaps over time, Mr. Douglass will convince the powers that be to see the great advantages to his vision.

If anyone could help convince people, it was Eliza. Perhaps he should suggest that to her in his return letter.

There have been so many visitors that it has been a learning experience to adapt my knowledge in talks for them. They have a great deal of questions! Each day, I feel I learn just as much as they do and go back to my room and make copious notes for the following day.

Speaking of rooms, I have the cutest little space at a nearby farm. The family is sweet and precious. Mr. Carnegie said that he wanted to get more housing built out here for the workers at his quarry—as many of them make do with tents—but there's only so much manpower to go around.

She filled the next two pages with all the stories she'd gotten to tell and the different people she'd met. Some were wealthy and famous people who'd come to see the great dinosaur bones. Others were simple folks who couldn't resist the pull of the great beasts in the ground. It sounded like Eliza enjoyed educating both groups equally.

When he flipped the last page over, he felt his smile slip. He was almost done with her letter.

Now to the most exciting news. One of the wives of the workers told me the most fascinating story about some bones that were found prior to Earl's discovery. We went out to the ranch and spoke to the owner. He's willing to allow me to hunt for the site of the fossils and even dig them out if we find them! Won't that be fantastic?

And just as exciting, Dr. Masterson is coming here. Can you believe it? Mr. Carnegie sent a wire the other day, and I must admit that I've been just a bit ecstatic over the news. You know how much I have loved Dr. Masterson's research and papers. He's the one who inspired me to write and submit my own in the first place. And to think, I get to meet him!

I know I teased you about coming to visit. I was genuine and earnest in my request, but I don't believe you took me seriously. So I'm going to ask again.

Would you please come out to visit? I'd love to share this excitement with you. And even if you don't find it interesting, there's nothing else for you to do out here, so you could bring all the papers you wanted to grade and every book imaginable to read. There's nothing to distract you. Although it can get pretty windy, and your dear books might get covered in dust.

I would beg and plead if I could. It would be nice to see a friendly face. You could even see the Rocky Mountains you've always dreamed of seeing on your way out!

Please? Would you do this for me?

I promise I won't ask anything else of you. At least . . . not this year.

Your dear friend,
Eliza

Devin looked up from the letter and stared out the window. He really had no desire to go stare at a wide trench in the ground. Then there was his schedule. All the meetings. All the planning that had to be done for the next term. The reorganization he had to do of the department.

He wasn't all that thrilled to leave Dad either. What if something happened to him while Devin was gone? He scratched his jaw and looked down at the letter again. If he said any of that to Dad, he'd get an earful about his pitiful excuses.

But the picture Eliza painted with her vibrant words tugged on him. Seeing an alligator fossil at sixteen was probably small potatoes to seeing mammoth skeletons unearthed in Utah. Beyond all that, there was Eliza with her joy and cheer. He missed his dearest friend. Pulling out a couple sheets of clean paper, he thought through his response.

Obviously he was going.

What other choice did he have?

Thursday, June 22, 1916 • Carnegie Institute

It should have been him! Why he'd been passed over for the prestigious job by some upstart in petticoats and feathers was beyond his understanding. It was as if Mr. Carnegie didn't care that *he* was the foremost expert on fossilization and the Jurassic period this side of the Mississippi River. The opportunity to study and be a part of the work at Dinosaur National Monument and show Earl who was the expert hadn't just slipped through his fingers—it hadn't even been offered to him.

In the beginning, he'd simply wanted what was owed to him.

The prestige. The fame. The accolades.

He'd already missed out on what should have been his in Utah.

This wasn't just about that joker-posing-as-a-paleontologist out at the quarry.

Now that woman was invading his realm and taking opportunities that should have been his.

Now, it was personal.

Besides, she was easier to deal with and more insignificant.

He stroked his jaw, his mind cluttered with thoughts. Mr. Carnegie, and anyone in the scientific community who supported that woman, needed to see reason. She was not qualified to explain the depths of evolutionary science. She didn't even believe in it! Was she going to tell some sort of antiquated Bible story and try to charm tourists and scientists alike with her poppycock ideas about creation? He scoffed, the sound echoing off the walls of his office. They'd come a long way in the past few decades. This was no place for a woman. Especially not a spoiled, rich one who always got her way simply because of who her family was.

Anger rippled through him. There had to be a solution. A way to expose her for the fraud she was.

His university friends were adamant against any sort of campaign to topple the annoying Miss Mills. Not because they didn't share his viewpoint. They did. But they refused to do anything to anger Mr. Carnegie and have their funding for various experiments and areas of study taken from them.

Cowards.

It was exactly as Darwin said, survival of the fittest. Conquer or be conquered. Kill or be killed.

He dropped his hand with the thought. How far was he willing to go? Agitated by the mess on his desk, he gathered the scattered essays from his final class and stacked them in an orderly pile. With deft movements, he set the desk to rights, the rhythm of order soothing his frayed nerves.

Murder was a bit extreme. Perhaps he was looking at this situation all wrong. She was in Utah for the summer. There was nothing he could do to stop her here in Pennsylvania. The idea turned in his mind and gained ground. Yes. That was the place to start. Another trip to Utah. To observe her and find ways to prove her presence was a disgrace to the scientific community.

Perhaps there was a way to kill two birds with one stone, since things in Wyoming weren't going as planned.

Shoving a few papers into his leather briefcase, he slipped the leather straps through the brass buckles and secured them with a tug. Smashing his hat on his head, he made his way back to his house. He had summer plans to make.

four

"Almost every day I hear of places where I want to go but cannot as I have no means of conveyance. I want to spend several months, or years perhaps, exploring the country around here."

~Earl Douglass

SUNDAY, JUNE 25, 1916 • JENSEN

It had been far too long since she'd arrived in Utah, and Eliza still hadn't made it to church. Goodness, she should be ashamed of herself. But there had been much to do, and she hadn't asked about local congregations or a way to get to them. The past two Sundays, she'd overslept and even missed breakfast. Her host family had been long gone by the time she awoke.

Something Grandmama would give her a serious reprimand over, if she knew.

Eliza smoothed a few flyaway hairs into place and stared at herself in the mirror. Her skin glowed with a slight tan. Just one more thing Grandmama would mention. However, out here in Utah, it was nearly impossible to keep one's complexion pale. She snatched her hat off the end of her bed and meticulously pinned it into place. It would have to do.

What she really wanted to don were her dungarees and loose work shirt so she could get out there and dig. Her fingers itched to pick up her tools and join Mr. Douglass in excavating the quarry. Catching the wayward trail of her thoughts, Eliza shook her head. No. She needed fellowship with other believers far more than anything else.

She hid her yawn with a hand and made her way down the stairs and out the front door. Mr. Adams had promised to leave her a conveyance so she could go to church rather than her riding the horse she usually took out to the quarry.

When she opened the front door, a smile curved her lips. A lovely horse and buggy awaited her.

But as soon as she left the shade of the front porch, the heat of the morning hit her in the face. Gracious, it was hot. The fan attached to her wrist would definitely get a great deal of use today.

As she climbed into the buggy and took hold of the reins, sweat ran down her back. If this was an indication of the rest of the summer here in Jensen, she might have to rethink her clothing choices for work.

While it had been important to dress well for the incoming crowds, the added weight of her fine clothing made the heat almost stifling. But Mr. Carnegie's expectations were high. Especially since she never knew when one of their visitors would turn up and introduce themselves as friends of his. Wealthy and the cream of the crop of society. Which even though Mr. Carnegie was one hundred percent sold out for his philanthropy and expressed that he didn't care about people's class and social status, he still reminded her how important it was to teach the next generation to use their wealth in an upstanding and gracious manner.

So her dungarees were still neatly folded in the trunk. For now. But perhaps, a few layers of her finery could stay at home from now on.

Eliza turned on to the main road that ran alongside the Adams's property, thankful for the slight breeze against her skin. One of the church options Mrs. Adams told her about was located on the edge of town, a mere fifteen-minute ride. She shifted the reins in her hands, grateful the horse seemed a gentle sort. Sending up a prayer of thanks for the generosity of her hosts, Eliza scanned the horizon, admiring the way the mesas stretched across the land. She'd never seen anything like the red, gray, and white rock that littered the terrain, and the vast horizons that stretched for miles. Back home, there was a lot more lush and green, a lot less dirt and rock. Rolling hills and trees shaped the country outside Pittsburgh, while here, it was rugged and wild. Though she was growing accustomed to the scenery, it still took her breath away.

"The heavens declare the glory of God; and the firmament sheweth his handywork."

The verse brought a smile to Eliza's face. "Today is definitely a day when Your glory is on display, Lord." She turned her attention back to the road.

Soon, the small white church Mrs. Adams recommended came into view. Nerves bubbled in her stomach. If only Mrs. Adams was with her, but since they had a family event several miles away, they would be gone all day.

Here she was. On Sunday morning. Venturing to church on her own.

Alone.

She'd never had to go anywhere new by herself. To make her own introductions. To try and fit in. Why, even at the quarry, she'd been expected and introduced immediately to Mr. Douglass.

It was unsettling to think about. Going someplace where she didn't know a soul. But heavens, she was twenty-seven years old. Just because she'd always had the advantage in society to be well-known and chaperoned to all events didn't mean she couldn't stand on her own two feet.

There couldn't be that many people out here anyway.

Farmers? Ranchers? Families from the little town of Jensen? How intimidating could that be?

By the time she reached the small building, her insides were in complete knots. The temptation to turn around and go back to bed was strong.

But no. She could do this. She *would* do this.

Her neglected Bible needed opening, and her dry soul needed a bit of refreshment.

When she entered the building, the pianist began an introduction to a hymn.

Taking a seat in a pew in the back, she dared not look at any of the curious eyes staring at her. As soon as she was situated, the rest of the congregation stood and began to sing.

> All the way my Savior leads me;
> What have I to ask beside?
> Can I doubt His tender mercy,
> Who through life has been my Guide?
> Heav'nly peace, divinest comfort,
> Here by faith in Him to dwell!
> For I know, whate'er befall me,
> Jesus doeth all things well,
> For I know, whate'er befall me,
> Jesus doeth all things well.

Eliza studied the back of the small crowd as they finished the hymn, and then everyone took their seats again. Her eyes widened. Not one of the women was wearing anything fancier than a bonnet. And here she sat with what Devin called one of her monstrosities on top of her head.

If the massive thing hadn't been seriously pinned into place, she might consider taking it off here and now.

And her dress. Granted it was the plainest one she owned, but it was a great deal fancier than any of the other attire in the room.

Heat rose to her face. She forced herself to swallow down the desire to escape. She was in church after all. The place where everyone was equal before God. It didn't matter what one wore, right?

A large man with a weathered-looking Bible in his hand frowned at the congregation as he read from the Scriptures. His voice boomed in the small space, as he emphasized a lot of negative words from whatever passage he was preaching from—he jumped from one to the other without giving any references. She flipped around in her Bible and finally gave up.

Eliza frowned. The way he spoke left her . . . beaten down. This service wasn't encouraging at all.

In fact, it made her enormously uncomfortable.

She flipped to the Psalms and focused on the soothing words instead. She'd already been on edge before coming in here, and his yelling wasn't helping at all.

But the more she focused on the page, the more her eyes drooped.

Perhaps she should have gone to bed a bit earlier last night. All she wanted now was to stretch out on the long wooden pew and close her eyes.

She blinked rapidly. That wouldn't make a very good impression, now, would it?

Lifting her gaze back to the preacher, she studied him.

If she saw him on the street, would he have the same stern expression? If she didn't know he was a preacher, she would say by first impression that he was an angry and unhappy man.

That wasn't fair. Was it?

How did someone know that a person loved God? By how they acted? How they treated people?

The more she watched him, the more she thought of him as grouchy and unfriendly.

You have no right to be so judgmental, Eliza Mills! After all, what would people say about *her*? Was she showing others that she knew God?

The preacher pounded the pulpit, and she jolted in her seat. Her hat threatened to shift, and she put a hand up against the weight. Good thing too, because then the preacher began to yell, and she jumped again. Gracious, it made her heart pound. Was it always like this?

She'd heard of these fire-and-brimstone preachers but hadn't experienced one firsthand. Her ears ached from the tirade of not giving in to sin, keeping their homes in order, and not associating with those of no faith.

But it must work for some people because there were lots of heads bobbing and several amens shouted from the pews.

Not for her though. The only thing it accomplished was making her restless.

She dipped her head back to her Bible and flipped through the pages to find some of her favorite verses. Perhaps if she spent the time memorizing more Scripture, it would be better for her mindset than the pulpit-pounding of this shouting man who grew angrier and louder with every word.

By the time she'd memorized all of First Peter chapter one, rustling sounded around her. Oh! The congregation was standing for a final hymn.

This time, she didn't even bother to sing along. But she prayed the whole time for her heart to still and soak in whatever it was that God wanted her to leave this place with today.

She kept her eyes closed until the final stanza and then lowered her head as a deacon prayed a benediction.

Anxious to be on her way, she had her Bible in her arms and the strings of her purse on her wrist before he said amen.

With a quick dash out of the pew, she hurried out of the small building. The Adamses' buggy was only twenty feet away. She picked up her pace. Freedom was so close.

A touch to her arm. "Miss?"

Eliza bit back a sigh. Obviously, she hadn't been fast enough. She pasted on a smile and turned.

Four ladies met her gaze. Where had they come from? And so quick?

Funny, she was inches taller than any of them. There were heels on her kid leather boots, and she was a bit over eight inches above five feet in her stockings anyway. But all of a sudden, she felt like a giant. And with the sun behind her, the shadow of her hat covered all of them. She fought the urge to giggle at thoughts of what Devin would say in this moment.

It wasn't the time nor the place for her to be laughing, but being able to find the humor in the situation helped her relax. "Good morning." There. That was pleasant enough.

"Good morning. We wanted to greet you and welcome you to our little church. I don't believe we've met?" The lady in blue studied her. "I'm Mrs. Elvira Manning. And you are?"

"Miss Eliza Mills." Funny. Their initials were the same.

The others introduced themselves, and she nodded at each.

"Where are you from, Miss Mills?" Mrs. Manning's pinched lips didn't give off a friendly welcome.

"Pittsburgh."

"Oh." The other three ladies actually spoke in unison, their eyes wide.

But Mrs. Manning wasn't impressed. Her eyes had narrowed the tiniest bit. "What brings you to our lovely town?"

Now this was a subject she could talk about. She smiled. "I

work for Mr. Andrew Carnegie. I'm here as a representative of the Hall of Dinosaurs at the Carnegie Institute to help people understand what is happening out at the quarry at Dinosaur National Monument."

Mrs. Manning stiffened. The frown on her face intensified. "So you are one of those evolutionists, are you?"

"Heavens, no." Eliza drew back as if she'd been slapped. "I believe in God as Creator and His Son Jesus as Savior."

Every eye studied her. Disapproving scowls deepened the lines on their sun-weathered faces.

"If that is true then what are you doing out there working with those . . . heathens?"

Heathens? Eliza arched an eyebrow at the way the woman spit the word. It was no secret that many in her field of study had chosen to follow Darwin's theory of evolution. So it was understandable why the woman would be skeptical. But just as many scientists were strong in their faith.

The disdain of these women coupled with the angry sermon . . .

Well, really. It was just too much. "That's an awfully judgmental thing to say, don't you think, Mrs. Manning? Aren't all men and women loved by God? Isn't it His desire that none should perish?"

The woman's chin lifted, her gaze sharpening into a glare. "We aren't about to allow a bad apple into our midst, spreading lies and the evils of science. I can see you don't belong here, Miss Mills. As God-fearing women, we will just choose to agree to disagree with you."

"But—"

"Good day, Miss Mills." The lead hen gathered her little group of cackling chickens with her.

What a mess! "Good day." She called it to their backs, but none of them turned or even flinched.

Lifting her skirt a bit to navigate the step into the carriage,

Eliza ran the conversation through her mind. As she took one last glance at the little church building, she shook her head. Never in her life had she seen or heard anything like it. Was this how some people thought Christianity should be lived out?

If so . . . well, no wonder so many didn't want anything to do with faith. Perhaps she should pen a letter to her pastor back in Pittsburgh. The difference between the service she'd just attended and what she'd grown up with was startling. How did one respond to such outright hatred and judgment? Was this what all preachers out West taught their congregations?

When she returned back to her home away from home, Eliza stepped down from the buggy and placed her hands on her hips as she studied it. Even with all her education, she had no idea how to take care of the horse or how to unhitch it. Without any other options available, she led the animal close enough so the water trough was in reach, set the brake, and tied off the reins. She'd have to apologize later.

Exhaustion and the urge to erase the happenings of the day overwhelmed her. When she entered the kitchen, she reached up and pulled the pins from her hat so she could remove it and relax her neck and shoulders.

An envelope on the table caught her eye with a note on top.

Eliza,

This came in the post for you yesterday, but it was late by the time we looked through it. We'll be back this evening. Hopefully your visit to church was a lovely one.

Lovely. Ha! But there was always next week. And a different church. As soon as she saw the return on the envelope, she plopped into the chair and opened it up. Devin had written!

Dear Eliza,

    Your letters found Dad and me both well and eager to hear of your adventures.

    In truth, you were correct in your assessment of my summer thus far.

    So, I have decided to acquiesce to your request and travel out West myself.

    It might take me a while, since I do intend to see the Rocky Mountains before heading your way. I will take the train to Denver, where I plan to stay a day or two, and then north and west to your beloved dinosaur monument.

Your friend,
Devin

She flipped the single sheet of paper over and stared at the blank side. Devin was a lover of the written word. Why such a brief letter? Why, she'd penned at least seven pages herself. Perhaps the dull and boring days surrounded by the University halls and gray-haired professors had worn him down.

It'd be depressing for her, that was for sure.

But joy pushed all other thoughts aside. Devin was coming! As the truth sank in, Eliza bolted from her chair and spun around the room.

Her best friend was coming. That was almost enough to erase this morning's catastrophic church attendance from her mind.

Almost.

Tuesday, June 27, 1916 • Mills Manor, Pittsburgh

"Your father tells me you're headed out West."

Devin sat stiff on the edge of the blue velvet chair. "Yes, ma'am." He hadn't been summoned to the manor since—

well, ever. Until today. And when he arrived, it was Eliza's grandmother who waited in the parlor. Dressed in black. He swallowed and his stomach sank. "Nothing has happened to Eliza—"

"Heavens, no." The woman's gaze snapped to his. Tears shimmered at the corners. "My apologies, son. I didn't realize how my summoning would affect you." She pressed a hankie to her nose, then lifted her chin a bit. "My dear Mr. Mills passed an hour ago. That's why I had to see you immediately."

Shock immobilized Devin for a moment. Eliza's grandfather . . . was dead? The poor woman! "I am deeply sorry for your loss, ma'am." And he was. Even though Mr. Mills was a powerful and stern man, Devin had many good memories of him with Eliza. Her grandfather had been generous to so many. Himself included.

Mrs. Mills twisted the handkerchief in her hands, giving Devin a tremulous smile. "It is providential that you are headed out West. This isn't news I can send to my dear granddaughter via letter or telegram. I certainly don't wish for her to hear about it in the papers once they reach her." Mrs. Mills leaned forward and touched Devin's hand. "It's a horrible thing to ask of you—to bring her such news—but you are the only one I trust."

He let that sink in for a moment. "You want me to tell her? About her grandfather?" As the weight of it hit him square in the face, he didn't want to think about how much this would hurt Eliza. She adored her grandparents.

Mrs. Mills's nod was slow. Sad.

And it broke his heart. But wouldn't it be better to come from him than from anyone else? As much as he hated to be the bearer of the news, he had to do it. "I will do whatever you need me to do, ma'am."

"You always were such a good boy. My husband thought the world of you."

He did? That was news to Devin.

"Don't look so surprised. He thought of you like a grandson." The look in her eyes softened. "He was proud of you. In fact, he was the one who recommended you to the board to become head of the English department." Her lips turned up into a sad smile. Then several tears slipped down her cheeks and she pressed the hankie to her face again. "My apologies." A muffled sob escaped.

Whatever the proper high-society protocol was at this moment, he really didn't care. He stood, stepped over to the settee, took a seat next to her, and wrapped an arm around the older woman's shoulders.

Several moments passed as her shoulders shook. Though silent, her grief filled the room.

When the tide of emotion passed, Devin stayed by her side, willing his strength to help hold her up if even for a moment.

She patted his hand on her shoulder. "Thank you, dear boy." With a deep breath, she straightened and lifted her chin.

He returned to his seat and tugged it closer so he could hold Mrs. Mills's hands. He hadn't ever been particularly close to her, but she'd been a steadfast presence in his life for as long as he could remember.

And she was now alone. Her husband of fifty years had taken his last breath. Her granddaughter was across the country. She had no other family. How would Mrs. Mills face the future now before her?

Wait a minute . . .

"Mrs. Mills, perhaps it would be best if we sent an urgent telegram and told Eliza to come home. You need her here."

Her hand came up quickly and sliced through the air. "No. I have given my granddaughter a hard time about her chosen profession all these years, and she has remained passionate. Oh, I wasn't against it, but if she couldn't take some pushback from the people who love her the most, the world would have eaten her alive. This isn't an easy time for women—wealthy or poor. Well, my dissent comes to a stop now that it's just the two of us. I refuse to take her away from this incredible opportunity." She pointed a finger at Devin. "It is your duty to ensure that she stays put. Understood?"

He knitted his brow. "Are you s—"

"Young man, do not argue with me on this." The fire was back in her eyes, and she straightened even taller on the settee. "I don't want her staying past the summer, but I can speak to her about that at a different time. Right now, I need you to break the news to her and bring her this note." She lifted an envelope from the table beside her and stared at it. "I wrote it as soon as he closed his eyes and I knew." Her voice sounded far off. She cleared her throat. "Make sure you wait for the appropriate time when she will be able to compose herself before having to speak with others."

"Yes, ma'am."

"She will need a good cry. And knowing Eliza, she will want to go out into the wilderness and dig and pound in the dirt for a while. Scream at the heavens and vent her grief. She's always been passionate in her emotions. Stay with her, please, keep her safe and from hurting herself. Don't allow her to think that I will wither up and die without her here. It will do me good to have these weeks on my own. I would like to be . . . *adjusted* to these new circumstances by the time she comes home."

"Yes, ma'am." But wouldn't she prefer to grieve with her granddaughter? They could help each other through this. He almost said so, but by the rigid set of her jaw, her mind was made up.

"I hear you're leaving tomorrow. Don't change your plans for me. The mountains are beautiful. Take a moment to revel in their grandeur for me." The sad smile was back, and she patted the envelope into his hand. "Now go. I'll expect a visit from you when you return."

Devin stood and kissed her wrinkled hands. Then he bowed and left the manor with a new weight on his heart and mind.

~❦~

WEDNESDAY, JUNE 28, 1916 • JENSEN

She slid the plate over to her husband, a new idea forming in her mind.

Waiting for him to die—even with his haphazard ways— was going to take too long.

Especially with all those people digging out at the quarry.

What she needed was a plan to delay the diggers and one to speed up the demise of the man in front of her.

Oh, he'd been fun and everything she thought she wanted at the beginning. Everything she'd fought her parents for. But she'd grown tired of his lazy ways and the fact that he refused to give her any money. He did enough to keep up appearances, but that was it. The man was a bum and stingy and it sickened her.

For ten years, she'd kept up the charade of dutiful wife while he did whatever he pleased, knowing that one day it would all be over. But her patience had reached its end. He wasn't going to get any more time than he deserved.

Which meant he should have been dead years ago.

Inwardly laughing at her own joke, she allowed her lips to turn up into a small smile. The man was an idiot. He had no idea what she'd been planning all these years. What she'd done to get what she wanted. And he would go to the grave in his ignorance.

The sweet taste of revenge was on her tongue.

But she'd have to be careful. There were eyes and ears everywhere.

She was a planner and could work around the obstacles.
Especially knowing that there was an end in sight.
She could do anything with that knowledge.
Anything.

❧

THURSDAY, JUNE 29, 1916 • DENVER, COLORADO

The air was stale with dust and sweat. Children whimpered
in their mother's laps, the heat too oppressive for them to
exhibit any stronger emotion. The once bustling and noisy
railroad car had slipped into a weary silence with each clack
of track against wheel.

Sweat trickled down Devin's temple, dampening his side-
burn. He longed to mop his face with his handkerchief, but
his shoulder was wedged between the rigid back of the train
seat and the burly man next to him. His hip ached from lack of
movement, pressed against the unyielding metal of the train.
He closed his eyes. Maybe when he woke up, they would finally
be at their destination.

"The Chicago, Burlington, and Quincy line is twenty minutes from Denver." The conductor's voice shattered the quiet
of the car, startling Devin out of his hazy state. "Once again,
the CB&Q line will be arriving in Denver, Colorado, in twenty
minutes!"

His announcement couldn't have come at a better time.
Thank You, Lord. The sincere prayer lifted to heaven.

Twenty minutes until he was free of this sweat-infested
torture chamber. He glanced out the window, watching plain
after plain whip by in a blur. When he'd decided to visit Eliza,
his imagination had run wild with the thought of seeing new
cities and states. He'd imagined great rolling hills easing into
grand snow-capped mountains. Big-horned sheep. Maybe a
bear or two.

Any thrill he'd felt died the second day out of Chicago after miles of unending prairie. How had he not known how flat the middle of the country was? It seemed like the horizon was one long line of flat land and cloudless blue sky.

Not that the heartland didn't have its charms. To be sure, the rippling acres of wheat brought to mind the opening stanza of *America the Beautiful* by Katharine Lee Bates. The spacious skies and amber waves of grain were breathtaking.

But Devin was ready for some purple mountain majesty. And a good long walk.

After all the miles traveled, he still hadn't formulated the best way to share the news with Eliza. She didn't need flowery words or prose. Nor did she need to be coddled. But if he simply blurted, "Your grandfather's dead," that would be about as caring as stabbing her in the heart.

The crowd grew restless and noisy around him as people shuffled their belongings and family members. Devin shoved the thoughts of Eliza aside. God would give him the words, he needed to trust in that.

The large man beside him snored and then snorted and shifted his weight even more into Devin's side. With a wince, Devin tried to dislodge himself from being the innards of a train-passenger sandwich, but the more he moved, the more the other man leaned into him.

A loud hiss and the screech of brakes startled the snoring man from slumber, and he shifted his weight an inch or two. Praise God! But then the man went right back to snoring. As soon as the train was fully stopped, Devin would have to maneuver around him.

All around Devin, people began to stand, groaning and laughing with fellow travelers. It seemed the aches and pains of train travel were universal. Relief was palpable as people donned hats, folded newspapers under their arms, and grabbed small luggage cases out of the roped storage above them.

Devin hadn't trusted his bag to storage. Instead, he'd kept it between his feet the whole trip. Not that there was anything precious in the bag, save a few changes of clothes and his shaving kit. But replacing those items would strain his already thin budget. And if he showed up with nothing, Eliza would just offer to help replace the items he'd lost. He wouldn't depend on her charity, no matter how kind it was. He could stand on his own two feet. And support his father.

He'd determined to pay off Dad's house—their house—this year, and it had taken every spare penny since his father hadn't been able to work for several years. Most days, his father was still sharp as a tack. Then others, he showed the effects from the stroke two years ago.

The shoulder holding him hostage moved, and Devin nearly wept. Feeling crept back into his arm and relief made him sigh. He pressed his fingertips into his shoulder and rotated it a few times, praying the stiffness would ease the more he moved. Standing, he clasped the handles of his bag in one hand and placed his bowler hat on his head with the other. Then he joined the slow shuffle of passengers exiting into Denver's Union Station. The noise was overwhelming.

"Watch where you're goin'!" A man growled the words at a mother with a young girl tucked close to her skirts. His gold ring glinted in the afternoon sunlight as he gripped his walking stick in his hand. "This is what happens when you mingle the masses!" His glare swept the crowd—including Devin. "People who don't know when to get out of the way of their betters!" He thrust his walking stick in front of him and rammed through the crowd, the scent of his foul cigar lingering in the air.

Devin approached the woman, glancing down at the little girl. Large blue eyes rounded with fear, and she turned her face into the plain cotton of her mother's dress.

"Are you all right, ma'am?"

The woman jerked away from Devin, her eyes narrowed. She held her daughter's hand in a white-knuckled grip. "We're just fine and don't need no help from the likes of you, fancy man!" She turned on her heel and disappeared into the crowd.

Devin's mouth dropped open. He was riffraff and lower class one minute and a fancy man the next. A small smile tugged at the corner of his mouth. Wait until Eliza heard about this. Wouldn't she laugh? The smile disappeared. He needed the next couple of days to settle his heart and mind. And to gather his courage if he was going to tell his best friend good-bye at the end of this trip.

A young boy around the age of ten caught Devin's eye. "Two bits to carry luggage to the famous Brown Palace, mister!"

He shook his head and pressed on. "But thank you."

"'Germany Pounds Britain as Battle of the Somme Rages On!'" three teenage boys shouted, waving their newspapers in the air.

Devin swallowed and searched the area for a way of escape. He needed fresh air and at least three feet between himself and another human being. Clenching his jaw, he pushed through the swarm of people and finally found the large wooden door leading out to the bustling streets of Denver.

He scurried down the sidewalk, sucking in great gulps of air. He found an empty bench and sat for a moment, dropping his bag by his feet. He took his hat off and ran his fingers through his hair. If Eliza were with him, she'd be laughing at his dramatic attitude. But then again, if Eliza were with him, he wouldn't be miserable at all. He'd be having the time of his life.

Frustration welled within his chest. This was the conundrum of Eliza Mills in his life. One minute, he couldn't wait to share everything with her, to hear her laugh, to make her smile. Then the next minute, his heart plummeted because he loved her, and he'd made a promise. If he could teach his heart that they were just friends and could always be friends, life would be simpler.

He'd done well thus far, not thinking about her every waking moment. It had been difficult. She'd traveled this way before him. Seen the same fields, sidewalks, and buildings. What had she thought when she got to Denver? Had she been as exhausted as he was right now? He smiled and shook his head. No. She'd still be full of life, ready to examine every inch of Denver available to them. Her zest for life was incomparable. Eliza made everything mundane fun. How he'd missed her light and joy these last few weeks.

But the separation had also been good. He'd spent many hours in prayer, chatting with his dad, and reading the Word. He needed wisdom in the coming days.

Devin swiped a hand over his jaw, wincing at the rough growth of hair against his palm. He needed a proper bath and shave to feel presentable again. And to get his head back on straight. Maybe getting to his boardinghouse and doing a bit of exploring would do him some good.

He picked up his bag and walked back toward Union Station, determined to find a streetcar to take him to a boardinghouse on Stout Street. A colleague back home had recommended it for its reasonable rates and close location to the train station. He had less than one day to explore what he could of Denver. It was time to make the most of it.

Bother. He didn't need a streetcar. He could walk. The exercise and fresh air would stretch out everything that had been crammed into the train car. He passed an older gentleman reading a newspaper on a bench. "Sir, could you perhaps give me directions to this address on Stout Street?"

"Oh yes." The man studied the paper for a moment and then smiled up at him. "Head over to 18th Street, and take it all the way down to Stout. Then you'll want to follow it away from the mountains. You should find it pretty quick."

Away from the mountains. Devin looked up from the man's gaze and took in the view. He'd been so focused on his own thoughts that he'd forgotten why he'd even come this way. "Thank you, sir. I appreciate it."

"Just remember the mountains are on the west. If you get lost, that's a good reminder." The older man chuckled and went back to his paper, probably amused by Devin's sudden awe of the scene.

"Thank you, again." He smiled and headed toward the direction the man had pointed him for 18th Street. Every chance he had, he kept stealing glances at the mountains in the distance. There were so many of them. Rising out of the plains in craggy, majestic beauty.

Breathtaking. That's what it was.

After two blocks, breathtaking began to take on a new meaning. Why was he so out of breath? Granted, he'd been walking at a much brisker than normal pace because he was eager to see as much of Denver as possible, but he was never winded like this at home. For a moment, he stopped and set down his case. He mopped his forehead and took several long, deep breaths.

"New in town?" A young man chuckled and tucked a newspaper under his arm.

Devin nodded. "Yes, I just arrived in on the train."

"From back East, are ya?"

"Yes." He wiped at his neck, his collar feeling all too tight.

"Well, you're standing on ground that is higher than most of what people back there call mountains. You're over 5,000 feet above sea level, my good fella."

"Is that why I'm out of breath?" Devin shook his head.

"Yep." The man shot a wide smile at him and then tipped his cap. "Have a pleasant stay in Denver."

"Thank you." At least he was almost there and then he could take some time to venture out toward the mountains. He took several more deep breaths and then leaned down to pick up his case.

But it was gone.

And so was the young man.

five

"I am getting where I do not fear, at least as I used to,
to go to the greatest depth one can reach in science."

~Earl Douglass

"Mr. Meyer, do you have any idea where your brother found
the fossils?" Eliza stood in her denims and long shirt outside
the barn with Deborah, hoping and praying he would know
which direction to send them in after checking his brother's
journals.

The older man was wiry and short. He ran his hand through
his white hair. "I read what I could of the journals and only
know that it was along the creek. But since it flows through
the entire ranch from south to north? That's a good deal of
acreage to cover."

She was afraid of that. But that was all right. They could do
this. "Do you mind if Mrs. Hawkins and I ride the creek bed
and see what we can find?"

He shrugged. "Not at all. Just let me know if you find something and where. I'll have my hands build a temporary fence so the cattle won't get in there and wreck your work."

"Thank you, sir. This means a great deal."

The man sent them a crinkly smile. His face seemed weathered and wrinkled from hours in the sun every day. "Selfishly, I'm glad you asked. I don't get many visitors out here, and the hands are always busy with the ranch. It's been a mite lonely all these years since I moved here from Dallas. What with all the rumors and all."

Eliza restrained a frown. Rumors? What rumors? She shook her head. No matter. She'd take his permission and run with it. Hopefully, she and Deborah wouldn't give Mr. Meyer any reason to take it back. "We're very grateful, and I'll make sure to check in with you on our arrivals and departures. Whenever that might be. We will have to work around my schedule out at the quarry, mind you, so there might be several late nights."

"Not a problem. I hope you find something. A little excitement and change of pace might be what these old bones need." He tipped his hat to them.

Eliza led Deborah back to their horses. "How long do you think you'll be able to stay today?"

"My husband decided to go visit his father about two hours south of here. So he'll probably be gone until well past dark." Deborah's grin lit up her face under her wide-brimmed straw hat. "I'm all yours for the rest of the day."

Eliza patted her saddle bags. "I've got water and food to last us for a week, so I think we're good to go, then." She laughed. All the excitement of a potential find bubbled up and she shivered, even though it was sweltering outside. "I think our best bet is to journey along the creek together. I'll take one side, you take the other. If there are fossils to be found, they will probably be within a deeper gulley that's been exposed over time. The creek down here by the house is shallow with only a foot or more of ground above the water."

Deborah nodded and they mounted their horses. "I'll keep my eyes open. I'm a fast learner. But you'll have to just keep talking me through what to look for. Maybe by the end of the day, I'll know what I'm doing." Her laughter rang out across the prairie.

"All right, well, let's go before we lose any more daylight." Eliza nudged her horse into a quick trot and headed toward the creek and hopefully . . . bones.

Later that night, Eliza made her way up the steps to the porch of the Adams's home. Everything in her body ached. Everything. Even her pinky toe.

She licked her lips and grimaced. All she could taste was dirt and grit from being blasted by the wind all day. Though they'd ridden along the creek for hours on end, they hadn't covered as much ground as she'd hoped. They'd spent a great deal of their time scrambling down the creek's banks to check out formations along the way, but none of it bore fruit. No magnificent fossils found. *Yet.*

As the old saying went, Rome wasn't built in a day.

Deborah was a quick learner. Still, they had a long way to go before they made it to the other side of the ranch. The Meyer ranch—one of the largest in the state—was made up of thousands upon thousands of acres.

She reached for the door handle, and it slipped out of her grasp as the door swung open.

Louise stood there, her grin wide. "I've been waiting for you to get home so I could hear all about it." Her voice was a low whisper—probably because the younger girls were asleep—but the enthusiasm still couldn't be missed.

Eliza stepped over the threshold and looked down at her clothes. "Gracious, I'm covered in dirt." She stepped back and tried to brush the loose particles off her pants and shirt.

"Don't worry about it." Louise tugged her arms and dragged her into the house. "I'll sweep again as soon as you head to your room." Leading Eliza into the kitchen, the younger girl uncovered a plate of food and tall glass of lemonade. "Here. Eat and tell me all about it. Where were you digging? Mama said it was on a local ranch?"

Eliza sat down and went for the lemonade first. Her throat felt full of grit. After several swallows, she picked up a fork and stared at the plate full of meat and potatoes. Her stomach growled. "The Meyer ranch. Do you know it?"

Louise's eyes went wide.

"What's wrong?"

The young woman's brown eyes glowed in the light as she glanced around the room, even though they were the only two present. Then she leaned closer to Eliza. "That place is haunted."

The words sent chills skittering down Eliza's spine. Haunted? Stuff and nonsense. She sat up straight and shook her head. "Maybe you have it confused with another place. It's a lovely ranch. Well kept up. Prosperous. Mr. Meyer is kind and generous."

"No, I'm not confused. That's the place. Mama wouldn't like me talking about it . . . but about ten years ago, maybe? I was still a little girl—" she looked toward the sink as if lost in thought—"the whole family disappeared. *All* of them. Mr. Meyer's parents. His brother and his wife. And all ten of their children. Just vanished into thin air. With food cooking on the stove, fires in the fireplaces, horses saddled and waiting at the hitching post. None of the hands saw anything and they all left because it spooked them so much."

While she'd heard about the family missing, Eliza was certain there must be more to the story. "But that doesn't mean it's haunted."

"Oh, yes, it does." Louise's head bobbed up and down, her eyes as wide as teacup saucers. "It took a good while for the sheriff to get ahold of Mr. Meyer's brother—the one who inherited

89

everything. He was a big-city kind of guy. The black sheep of the family since he didn't like to ranch. Well, he came out and was torn up something awful with losing his family like that. He decided to stay and fulfill his father and brother's wish—to keep the ranch flourishing. But weird things happen all the time out there. The new Mr. Meyer can't keep hands because of it. I think the longest any worker has stayed was just less than a year. Which is unusual for a well-paying ranch like that one."

Eliza leaned back in her seat. It *did* sound odd. But that didn't mean it was haunted. "There's got to be some explanation."

"There's only one explanation for it. It's haunted. Everyone around here knows it, even if they don't say it out loud. People give the ranch a wide berth. You shouldn't go back there anymore."

***

MONDAY, JULY 3, 1916 • CARNEGIE INSTITUTE

Nelson had spent a fortune in telegrams, but he at least felt prepared for the journey ahead. Research was key to accomplishing anything.

He hadn't done enough in the past and look where that got him. With only a few fossilized bones instead of a full skeleton.

Well, this time would be different.

He scanned all the replies.

Miss Mills, that little rich brat, was bringing in more wealthy donors by the week, and everyone raved about her. There was even a hushed rumor of her contacting a local rancher about digging on his vast acreage. On top of that, the quarry work was flourishing and full of fossils.

There were still several key factors that needed to be sorted out if he was going to turn this around in his favor. And without anyone to trust, he'd have to do all the work himself. At least until he arrived out West.

6666

KIMBERLEY WOODHOUSE

There were plenty of unsavory characters out there willing to do anything for a buck. Or so he'd been told.

If he played his cards right, he could smear Eliza out West whilst doing the same thing here at the institute. Then she could disappear. He didn't care where. As long as she was gone.

Then Mr. Carnegie would see his true value. He'd get sent out to Dinosaur National Monument and could help bring it to its full glory. It wouldn't hurt for him to increase his own recognition with another specimen for the Hall of Dinosaurs either. If his dig in Wyoming didn't pan out, he'd have to simply forge the rest of the bones. As curator, he knew what to do. The paperwork and evidence trail would be a bit more complicated.

A tragic accident could befall the supposed real fossils. *After* he'd made the plaster replicas.

Yes. That would be simple enough.

Mr. Carnegie was ignorant about what really went on. It wouldn't hurt him one bit. Besides, he'd backed the wrong people.

In the end, he'd pay.

They'd all pay.

MONDAY, JULY 3, 1916 • DINOSAUR NATIONAL MONUMENT

Looking out at the quarry, Eliza wished for one of her wide-brimmed hats. The sun was drilling down on them. And what she wouldn't give to be in a pair of dungarees and a loose-fitting shirt rather than all these layers.

If only she was back out at the Meyer ranch searching for the legendary fossils. Haunted or not, she couldn't wait to go back.

Sweat trickled down her back as she pushed the thoughts

aside and prepared for another set of questions from the twenty or so folks who'd traipsed out to the quarry today.

Perhaps it was time to start dressing the part. This whole immaculate, fashionable, and elegant attire for society folk simply wasn't practical out here in the dust, dirt, and extreme heat. And who cared if anyone thought different of her?

And truth be told, what better way to show people out here the reality of what was going on?

But as soon as she finished her frantic trek to the top of the bluff and turned to see the group behind her, she sighed. It was a vaporous dream to think that she could dress however she wanted. These people would look down their noses at her and not consider donating to the institute, which *was* the end goal, after all. No matter how practical her desires might have been.

Most of society's elite would never understand her desire to dig in the dirt, nor her comfort in men's clothes.

She restrained a frown. Could this be part of Mr. Carnegie's plan? Her family had quite a reputation among the wealthy families of Pittsburgh, and most of the people she met who knew Carnegie knew her family as well. That gave substance to what the workers were doing out here. Credence to her words. All because they had money.

But giving to the work shouldn't be based on all that.

What should matter was her experience and expertise.

Mr. Douglass's even more so. After a lifetime of digging, giving up everything, doing all he could to continue his studies, he deserved accolades and cheering and great respect for what he'd discovered here.

But the people who visited really didn't care about the sacrifices made.

Sad, but all too true.

The slow and steady progression of the tour group as they made their way toward her discouraged her rather than excited her like normal. Oh, what was wrong with her today?

It wasn't good for her to dwell on such things. Verse eight in Philippians chapter four came to mind. She definitely hadn't been focused on what was pure, true, or of good report.

This was what happened when she didn't get enough sleep because she was imagining herself finding a skeleton of great proportions out on the Meyer ranch.

No. That wasn't true. It was what happened when she didn't take the time to study the Word or to pray.

The enthusiasm she'd held for her work here had waned last weekend. And she wasn't sure why. Other than missing the comforts of home, the city, and her family. Even more than that, she missed Devin. She could discuss anything with him and all would be right with the world.

And then there was that church last Sunday. What a horrid experience. No wonder she'd felt out of place. Without those who supported her, or her and Devin's constant conversations, she hadn't been able to hash out her thoughts.

At least he was coming to visit. That would be wonderful!

The new group assembled closer to her, and a hush fell over them. She put on her best smile.

"Welcome to Dinosaur National Monument. On behalf of the Carnegie Quarry, allow me to share with you our excitement to have you here to see the progress."

She dove into her explanation of the history of the quarry, what kinds of bones they'd found so far, and what they hoped to accomplish.

A man in the rear of the group raised his hand.

"Yes, sir. Do you have a question?"

"I have to admit that this fascinates me. Would you tell us a bit more about how you transport all these fossils?"

She clasped her hands in front of her. "Excellent question. We make crates out of lumber, depending on the size of the fossil, line them with hay, and transport the crates via wagon and then the railroad to their final destination."

"But you must have to prep the bones somehow? Or do they just get cushioned in the crates?"

"Let me give you the basics." She did love it when the sight-seers enjoyed the details. She was extremely curious herself. "Once the fossils are clean of debris, we coat them in gum arabic. This makes them stronger—we don't want to break any priceless, fragile fossils in their long journey. That wouldn't be good." She made an exaggerated scared face and some of the crowd laughed.

"Then we paste tissue paper along the bone segments to prevent the next layer of plaster-soaked burlap from sticking. If the bones are extra-long—which, because these are dino-saurs, that happens regularly"—another silly face followed by the audience's laughter—"we essentially make a very large splint for them inside that plaster-soaked burlap layer to help stabilize them for travel."

Another man in the front raised his hand. "How do the people on the other end figure out the puzzle of how to put it together? Or do one of you go with each shipment of bones?"

"Even if we went with the bones, I'm not sure we would remember everything accurately for each skeleton. That's why the bones are sketched and photographed before we even dig them out of the ground. We do a crude bit of assembling here to see what we've got. While every dig team probably has their own way of doing things, most of the time, each piece is num-bered on the sketches and then in the crates. It helps to reduce the guessing on the other end, but as you probably know from newspaper articles over the years, mistakes are often made. Sometimes it can't be helped when so many different animals are found at one dig site. We try to do the best we can when we first discover the bones and also do our best to rectify any mistakes as quickly as possible."

"Is there perhaps a better way to do it? Seems like it could get confusing if a lot of fossils are shipped at once." This came from the young, stylishly dressed woman at the front of the crowd.

Several other hands raised. Eliza nodded. "It can be. Especially since it's rare that complete—or I should say, almost complete—skeletons are found. Sometimes it takes many years before we understand the whole beast. For instance, a lot of times, skulls aren't found with the body. It might be a long time before we find another specimen with an intact skull so we know exactly how the animal looked."

Another man, off to the side, lifted his hand. "How do you know it's a fossil and not just a bone-shaped rock or something else?"

Eliza giggled. "You want to hear a fun test?" She pulled a small fossil out of her jacket pocket and leaned down to pick up a rock. "Obviously, we have scientific testing we use on each fossil after it's found to validate what it is, but on first sight, there is something we do that you might find a bit odd."

Everyone's eyes were riveted on her.

"Did you know that if you lick a fossil it will stick to your tongue, but if you lick a rock, it won't stick?" Eliza suppressed a giggle as people drew back in disgust.

"But be warned if she asks you to try it"—a warm voice somewhere behind the group sent tingles up her spine—"getting the fossil off your tongue afterward might be a bit of an issue. Don't ask me how I know." The tall, familiar figure stepped around the sightseers.

"Devin!" She dashed to him and jumped into his arms.

six

"There will never be another so faithful and true. None like her can charm away pain."

~Earl Douglass

Holding Eliza in his arms after weeks without her melted every bit of resolve Devin had to keep his distance.

After a long hug, he pushed her back and kept his words low. "We have an audience, Miss Mills."

She straightened her hat and clapped her hands together. "Everyone, this is my dearest friend in all the world. We've been the best of chums since we were children, and I was so excited to see him, I lost my manners for a moment."

Several in the little group reassured her that they didn't mind and understood. Eliza made her way back to the front of the group and continued the rest of her tour. Devin crossed his arms over his chest as he watched her talk and gesture, drawing her audience in with her wide smile and expert storytelling. He pulled his handkerchief out and wiped at his forehead, grimacing at the amount of sweat running down his face. This heat was brutal. How did they manage?

Within the next twenty minutes, she'd finished up with the tourists and sent them on their merry way. He braced himself. Should he tell her about her grandfather now? No. Maybe once they left the quarry and she didn't have to worry about taking care of people.

Fanning herself as she walked over to him, she grinned. "I'm so glad you're here!" She threw her arms around him once again, and he couldn't resist hugging her back. As he held on, he didn't care about the heat anymore. In fact, nothing mattered.

This time, she was the one who pulled back. "Well . . . tell me all about your trip. Did you get to see the mountains?" She slid her hand through the crook of his arm and led him down a path.

"I did." He groaned. "But let's just say my little visit in Denver didn't start off all that pleasant."

"Oh dear." She angled her head toward him. "What happened? Did you have trouble with the elevation?"

He tipped his head back and forth and released a chuckle. He could at least laugh about it now. "You could say that. I was anxious to get to my boardinghouse since I only planned on staying there a day and wanted to explore as much as I could. But in my rush to walk the mile from the train station, I found myself out of breath and set my bag down. A seemingly nice young man spoke to me and explained the elevation, then he left. And so did my case."

She stopped and released his arm, a hand flying to her mouth. "Oh no!" Then her hands went directly to her hips. "I sure hope you went to the police."

"I did." He crossed his arms over his chest and studied her posture. "It amuses me that you still enjoy mother-henning me." He waggled his eyebrows at her and laughed.

She swatted his arm and relaxed. "Oh, stop. *Some*one has to look out for you."

Devin rolled his eyes and let out a laugh. Soon Eliza joined in, and the tension eased from his shoulders. They continued to walk away from the hustle and bustle of the quarry.

"So? What happened?"

"Sadly, all that transpired from my visit to the police were reminders to not trust anyone, to keep my eye on my belongings, and then a couple wasted hours as different policemen came and went, listened to my story, and wrote it all down numerous times."

"I hope you didn't lose anything too valuable?" She bit her lip. "I'm so sorry this happened. All because you came out here to visit me."

"Clothes and my shaving kit. All of which I was able to replace. Don't worry." He wouldn't tell her how much that cost. She wouldn't understand living on a budget.

Eliza looped her arm back through his, her expression relaxing. "Well, I'm very glad that you are all right. I would hate for anything to have happened to you."

"I'm fine." But the way she looked at him—with care and concern that no other woman had ever shown him—melted his resolve again. Oh, how he'd missed her. "It seems like you are doing well with your work here."

"I am." She squeezed his arm. "Although, you were right. I told you that in my letter and I'm sure you would love to hold that over my head for all eternity, but I'm freely admitting it—I miss the city. I miss good food. I miss being able to go to a museum or the theater. And I miss pants."

"Ha!" The guffaw came out louder than he anticipated. "Pants? Are you serious?"

"Oh, very." She led him to a boulder to sit. "At home, I could venture out on my own and not have to worry about what I wore. Men's pants are much easier to work in. Cooler too."

He missed her in pants too. Not that he would say that out loud—

Stop it, Schmitt!

He grit his teeth. Ever since he'd arrived and she'd thrown herself into his arms, all his good intentions had flown out the window. He straightened and determined to do better. *Again.* "I can imagine they are much easier than your skirts"—he pointed to her head—"and those crazy hats you love so much. Although, I have to admit, that one is about half the size of the ones you usually wear. It boasts half the birds, bows, and baubles too."

She laughed along with him. "So I like big hats." She shrugged. "With all your teasing, I thought you liked them."

Answering honestly wasn't an option. Truth be told, he liked her in anything. Because she was Eliza. Beautiful, red-headed, green-eyed, exuberant Eliza. "They're fine." There. That was noncommittal. "You look lovely no matter what."

"You have to say that because you love me and you're my best friend." She swatted at his arm. "But I'll take it."

He loved her. *That* was the understatement of the day. Of the year. He folded his hands in his lap and looked out toward the horizon. "Well, you have me for a couple weeks. What shall we do?"

Her eyes lit up and she grabbed his hands. "Oh, it's going to be grand having you here. I have a tour group tomorrow. But on Wednesday, we're not open for tourist groups—even though people will sometimes still come—so I won't need to answer questions. I plan on wearing my dungarees and giving you a full tour of the quarry. We can hike all over and have a picnic. How does that sound?"

Then after a nice day, he'd give her the note from her grandmother and tell her about Mr. Mills. The responsibility settled over him once again. Eliza was going to be heart-broken.

"That doesn't sound good to you?" She tapped his shoulder.

Devin blinked, shaking away his thoughts. "Um, sorry. It sounds perfect." And it did. Even though he'd have to break both their hearts. Something in the rock wall across from them caught his eye. "What do you think that is?"

They stood and went to examine it.

"Huh." Eliza studied it and got really close to it. Taking out her chisel from a loop on her skirt, she pulled the smaller rock from its wedged environment. "It's been painted." She handed it to him.

"How old do you think it is?" The markings didn't make sense to him.

"Nothing ancient. Probably within our lifetimes." She shrugged. "You found it, you should keep it as a keepsake." She tucked her chisel back into her skirt and darted back up the path. "See if you can keep up, Schmitt."

Perhaps he should simply enjoy this last time with Eliza. When the time came, he could be a rock for her. The steady friend he'd always been. When he left . . . he'd tell her good-bye. Oh, she'd think it would simply mean until she returned to Pittsburgh, but Devin would deal with his heart later. There wasn't any harm in making some beautiful memories with her one last time and helping her through a difficult time.

Right now, it was good to see her so happy and in her element.

He would simply have to wait until he returned home and rip his heart in two then.

❧

WEDNESDAY, JULY 5, 1916 ⸰ DINOSAUR NATIONAL MONUMENT

The morning sun wasn't nearly as brutal as it had been the past few days. Of course, that might be because she had finally gotten her wish and had donned her favorite pair of men's pants.

She'd even dared to loosen her corset under the loose-fitting man's work shirt. The shirt was long, almost to her knees, but that seemed a bit more decent since there were sure to be other men around. Exposing her legs for everyone to see wouldn't be good.

Devin had seen her in trousers for years. He'd probably seen her in her undergarments when they were children, although she couldn't remember for certain. They had spent lots of time in the swimming pond behind Mills Manor as kids.

She smiled. What would she have done throughout her life without Devin? He knew when she was nervous or overwhelmed. He tolerated her dragging him around on one adventure after another with a steadiness and humor she'd never seen in another man. And he always rejoiced with her, no matter how large, small, or ridiculous. Eliza let out a sigh and cinched her pants around her waist, ensuring they would stay in place.

If only she could feel as comfortable around everyone else as she did with him. Not having to live up to society's expectations. Just being herself.

She chuckled. Grandmama would give her such a lecture if she knew her granddaughter's thoughts. But her grandmother wasn't awful about it. She simply wanted to make sure that her granddaughter understood the world's expectations of someone of her station.

And how those expectations kept society running.

As she laced up her worn hiking boots—also men's—over her thick socks, she ruminated over her life. At twenty-seven years old, Eliza felt like she had a pretty good handle on things. She knew what was expected of her. But she longed for something . . . more.

What it was, she couldn't put her finger on, but that was another reason she loved exploring. The more adventures she took, the more education she gained, the more experiences she logged in her memory, the more she searched for that . . . *thing*.

Devin's father had drilled into her Paul's words about being content in whatever circumstances he was in. Eliza worked at taking those words to heart, she did. In all her exploring, she'd been content. More than that—she had been ecstatic. But there was always something wanting . . . like she hadn't found exactly what it was she was supposed to do for the rest of her life.

Wait . . . what? She straightened. There was no doubt she loved paleontology. It was an incredible science. She'd been obsessed with digging fossils out of the dirt since she was ten. But even with all the papers she'd written on the subject, all her studies, her degree, her job at Carnegie's museum, and now out here at Dinosaur National Monument . . . what was she *supposed* to do with this love she had for the science?

She'd enjoyed all of it. Still . . . something niggled at the edges of her mind. Like she wasn't doing exactly what God wanted her to do.

But what was that?

Eliza blew out a breath. Even if she sat here all day, she wouldn't figure out the answer. So she stood and headed for the door. Mrs. Adams had promised to help her pack a picnic for her and Devin today.

An hour later, she led Devin down the path into the dug-out quarry. He'd dressed for the occasion as well, favoring lighter fabrics for his shirt and pants to survive the hot Utah sun. His dark hair was covered with a wide-brimmed hat. He looked more relaxed than Eliza had seen him in a long time.

Good. He deserved a break.

As always, he was the gentleman and carried her bag. While it didn't contain an anvil, it did have some tools and their picnic. She couldn't help but smile and cover a laugh.

"Where are you taking me today?" But instead of the whining young kid's voice from their childhood, his masculine tone held a hint of amusement.

"You know where we're going. Don't you want to see what they're doing here? It's amazing. They've already dug tons of fossils out of the ground and shipped them back to Pittsburgh."

For the next couple hours, they hiked together through the quarry. As she showed him the bones visible in the rock, he seemed eager to see more.

He'd always been supportive of her desires and this work that she loved. But today seemed . . . different. It gave her heart a little thrill.

She pointed to several more that had been marked just in the past couple days. "I can't wait to see what they pull out of this quadrant. It looks to be a wealth of fossils."

Devin stepped back and studied the wall. "You know . . ." He paused and looked back to her and then the wall. "I've always been interested in this because you love it. But it's never been overly exciting to me. But this"—he shook his head and brushed his fingers over the rock—"*this* is truly remarkable. I can see why you fell in love with this science. It makes so much sense to me now."

She wanted to spin around, but she refrained. "You mean, after all these years, you finally understand my weird fascination?"

With a laugh he turned to her. "Yes, I think I finally do." His face turned serious. "Now, if I could just get you to see the importance of great works of literature. Perhaps we could read *Moby Dick, The Odyssey,* and even *Hamlet* while I'm here, and we could dis—"

"Don't say it." She made a face as if she might vomit. "That would be torture for me and you know it."

Devin pressed his lips together, but she could see the smile he was attempting to suppress. "Which would also make it tortuous to me. You are *not* a good sport when it comes to studying subjects you don't like."

She stomped her foot. "That's not fair. Your father made me study everything, and I made it through." Oof. Now she sounded like a whiny debutant. But she *would* make her point.

"Eliza"—he laughed harder—"have you forgotten that I was there for all of your schooling? You came up with excuses on a daily basis for why grammar, literature, and even the higher maths weren't necessary for what you wanted to do with your life."

"But all those subjects were *booooring*. And I'll have you know, I haven't used one bit of any of that in the last ten years. So there."

They burst into laughter. Oh, it was good for her soul to have him here. No one understood her like Devin.

As she led him back to the top, they reminisced over stories from their childhood. All the projects his father made them do together . . . all the ways she tried to convince her tutor to switch subjects.

"For a science person, you sure did find a lot of creative ways to challenge his methods."

She grabbed her large sack from him and pulled out a checkered cloth. "Here, help me spread this out. And then you can catch me up on how he's doing."

They laid out the picnic and sat down on the ground. Ham sandwiches, apples, cheese, pickles, and lemonade. Her stomach growled.

They filled their plates.

"Allow me to say the blessing?" He lifted his eyebrows at her.

"Please."

After a quick prayer, they both dove into their food. Hiking around in the fresh air always made her ravenous.

Devin swallowed down a big bite of sandwich. "Dad's still as sharp as ever—most of the time. But I can tell he's wearing out a bit. The stroke a couple years ago, while mild, slowed him down. I'm sure you've seen it."

She nodded. "I meant how is he doing the last few weeks since I've been gone?"

"Oh." His ears turned pink. "He's tutoring a bit this summer to help those kids who are a trifle behind in their studies. You know, after he completed your schooling, he floundered a bit and taught here and there. He never wanted me to say anything to you, but he struggled to find his place. He kept doing whatever he could to support us, especially through all my collegiate education. And thanks to your grandfather's generosity, we made it." He made an odd face that she couldn't decipher. Opened his mouth. Shut it. "There's something . . ." He looked away.

"Go on. What is it? About your dad?" Now he had her worried. "You said he struggled to find his place?"

Devin blinked several times. "Um, yes. He did. But once I was hired at the University, his doctor suggested he slow down a bit. He didn't, and that was when he had his stroke."

She hadn't really considered what Mr. Schmitt had gone through once she was off to college and he no longer worked at Mills Manor. "I'm so sorry. I didn't realize—"

"You have nothing to apologize for. Dad wanted it kept private, and I respected his wishes. But now he's accepted the fact that he's not as young as he once was, and he keeps telling me that he'd like to be around to see his grandchildren."

"He will be a wonderful grandfather." There was that look again. What was going on with Devin?

He cleared his throat. "I think so too. Anyway, the tutoring keeps him busy enough, but also allows him to get more rest. Which he knows he needs. He didn't marry my mother until he was thirty-four, and then I didn't come along until he was forty. So he's led a long and full life. Hard to believe he'll be seventy years old in a couple years."

What a blessing to have had these two men in her life. "I'm so very thankful for both of you. I don't know where I'd be without you."

"Oh, you'd still be digging in the dirt, of that I'm certain." He smiled and took a sip of his lemonade.

After they devoured their lunch, she packed up the dishes and the cloth and stuffed it all back in the bag. "Let's go stash this in one of the tents and we can explore some more."

"Wait a second . . ." He narrowed his gaze at her, but his eyes twinkled with merriment. "You mean to tell me that I didn't need to haul that thing around with us for the entire morning? We could have left it up here?"

She set the bag down and giggled, running away.

"You did that on purpose!" He gave chase.

"Well, I missed the old times!" She dashed around in a large circle and then came to an abrupt halt when she spied a group of ladies watching them. Frowns covered their faces. Eliza put a hand to her chest and sobered, using her best tour-guide voice. "I'm sorry, the monument isn't open for any guided tours today."

The woman in front looked all too familiar as she stepped closer. "We didn't come for a tour. We came to speak to you." Her words were cold.

"Oh. I'm sorry." And then it hit her. The woman was from that church she visited. Several of the others looked like her little group. What were they doing here?

Eliza braced herself. "Mrs. Manning, is it?" If she remembered correctly, there were four of them in the woman's group on that awful Sunday morning. Now there were seven.

Mrs. Manning crossed her hands at the wrist, her mouth pinched as if she'd tasted the juice of a lemon. "After meeting you a couple weeks ago, we spoke to our reverend about how we could bring you back into the flock." Her voice took on a snide edge. "He suggested we hadn't learned enough about you yet. But now . . ."

"What do you mean, bring me *back* into the flock?" Who *was* this woman to think she could speak to Eliza in this manner? She straightened and all of grandmother's training came to bear in her posture and expression.

The woman huffed. "Seeing you dressed like this"—she waved a hand at Eliza's pants—"and running around like a child. With a man chasing after you." Mrs. Manning put a hand to her throat and shook her head.

All the women with her did the same.

"It's *ungodly*. That's what it is." A woman from the side spat the words.

Mrs. Manning lifted her chin a little higher. "Yes, it's ungodly. Disrespectful. Unladylike. Indecent." She cleared her throat. "We came out here to offer to mentor you—as it says in Titus. To lead you back onto the path of righteousness. You stated you believed in the Creator and His Son Jesus as Savior . . . well, instead of finding you here as a wandering sheep, we can see with our own eyes that you are just as heathen and lost as the rest of those awful evolutionists."

Eliza's mouth dropped open. A heathen? Lost? Fury burned in her chest, but before she could respond, Devin spoke up.

"Doesn't Scripture tell us not to judge one another?" His calm but firm voice came from behind her. Then he stepped up to stand beside her. "Matthew chapter seven says, 'Judge not, that ye be not judged. For with what judgment ye judge, ye shall be judged: and with what measure ye mete, it shall be measured to you again. And why beholdest thou the mote that is in thy brother's eye, but considerest not the beam that is in thine own eye? Or how wilt thou say to thy brother, Let me pull out the mote out of thine eye; and, behold, a beam is in thine own eye? Thou hypocrite, first cast out the beam out of thine own eye: and then shalt thou see clearly to cast out the mote out of thy brother's eye.'"

"Are you implying that we are *hypocrites*?" The leader of the pack screeched the last word and sneered at Devin and then back at Eliza. "And *this* is the quality of man with whom you choose to keep company? He clearly has no morality in him. How dare you!"

This had gone far enough. "How dare *you*!" Eliza stepped closer. "This is the godliest man I've ever met. And he knows the Word of God better than y—"

Devin's hand on her arm calmed her a bit. "There's no need for us to argue like this. If we are all believers, then we are brothers and sisters in Christ." His touch grew firmer as she tried to inch forward. "This is not how we should be speaking to one another. Shall we start over?" He reached out his right hand in greeting.

"No. We shall not start over." Red-faced and shouting, the woman gripped her handbag. "We shall report back to our reverend and call a prayer meeting for the salvation of your wicked souls." She turned on her heel and marched away.

"Disgusting," one of the women threw at Eliza.

"Heathen," another threw out.

"Ungodly." Another clucked her tongue at her.

As Eliza watched the little passel of women storm away, the anger inside her swelled. "Can you believe that?" She pressed a hand to her forehead. "Because I'm wearing pants?"

"Oh, there was much more to it than that." Devin gripped her arm. "You need to ignore them. Somehow shake their hateful words from your mind."

Well *that* was easier said than done. She pulled her arm from Devin's grasp. "All I wanted to do was go to church! Find a good congregation to worship with. But then . . ." She started pacing, allowing every ugly and hateful thought to surface. "Those awful women, their hateful attitudes, are why some people don't want to go to church. Who could stand that kind of unfair and untrue judgment?"

Who, indeed. Even as she spoke the words, hurt sliced through her. She dropped to her knees and caught her breath on a sob.

Devin came to wrap his arms around her shoulders.

She turned into his chest. "Oh, Devin, I'm certain they will spread the word about me throughout town." She closed her eyes against the stinging tears. "What will Mr. Douglass think? And what if . . . what if Mr. Carnegie finds out?"

He didn't answer. Just held her in his arms as she cried.

~~~

WEDNESDAY, JULY 5, 1916 · JENSEN

The full moon tonight was high in the cloudless sky. Most people were fast asleep. Perfect time for her to sneak out and get things moving in the correct direction.

Word had reached her of some lady dinosaur digger thinking they could find bones out on the Meyer ranch.

It infuriated her to no end.

She needed to stop the work out at the quarry, not have them expand elsewhere.

Especially not out on that ranch. That would only make things worse.

Perhaps if she started some rumors of her own. Planted a few seeds that this new woman wasn't trustworthy. That would surely get people up in arms.

Their town was still small and the locals who had been there a long time were adamant about honesty. She'd seen several people shunned over the years when they weren't aboveboard in their practices.

They still had plenty of riffraff. Which aggravated all the upstanding citizens who looked down their noses at everyone else.

The rumor mill was a powerful tool. Might as well use it.
But first, she had tools to steal and poison to place.
She wasn't about to let anyone else near that gold.
It was hers.

seven

"I am too light and trifling. If I had a burden for the souls of my fellow men that I should have I would not be so trifling."

~Earl Douglass

WEDNESDAY, JULY 5, 1916 • ADAMS FARM

Eliza had invited Devin to meet her host family for dinner tonight. At the time, she'd had no idea how rotten the day would be. And now, with puffy eyes and a tear-stained face, she'd have to put on a smile and introduce him to the whole family.

It wasn't a bad thing. She adored Devin and the Adams family. But just then she would have preferred being alone.

As she and Devin rode their horses back to the Adams's home, he must have picked up on her misery. He hadn't spoken a word since they'd left the quarry.

He knew her all too well.

"I'm really glad you're here, Devin." She turned and offered him a half-smile. "Thank you for coming out."

"You're welcome."

Silence surrounded them once again, and that was all right. Dinner was sure to be full of questions now that she'd gotten the girls to open up to her. And Devin would evoke a fair share of curiosity, especially from the girls. Hopefully he would take the attention off her.

But the words from those awful women kept needling her mind. She pushed them away. *No.* She would not allow them any more presence or thought.

Devin sighed beside her, and she turned her face to him. "Everything all right? That sounded like some heavy thoughts were tumbling around that mind of yours."

"Yeah." Another sigh.

Coming from him, that meant something weighty indeed.

He looked at her. "I know we've got this dinner ahead and I didn't want to make things harder for you, but there's something I need to tell you. It is of great import." His jaw was tight, his eyes serious.

"All right." Maybe he didn't feel comfortable having dinner with strangers. Had she bothered to even ask if he wanted to, or had she once again dragged him along for whatever she wanted?

"Your grandmother asked me to come see her before I left."

"Oh?" Maybe this wasn't about dinner after all. Even so, she should work on being a better friend to him.

"It's a—"

"Eliza! Eliza!" Louise and Adelaide ran toward them from the fenced-in yard. "You're here!"

She sent a look to Devin and leaned over. "Sorry. I didn't realize they would be waiting for us."

He directed a smile at the welcomers. "It's all right. We can talk later."

"Louise, Adelaide." Eliza steered her horse toward the gate. "I'd like you to meet Mr. Devin Schmitt. He's my oldest and

112

dearest friend." Her horse stopped at the fence, and she dismounted. She handed the reins to Louise, who hadn't moved, said a word, or even blinked since she caught sight of Devin. Eliza leaned close to the girl's ear. "Louise."

"Oh!" Louise glanced down at the reins in her hands and then back up at Devin. "It's lovely to meet you, Mr. Schmitt."

"Please. Call me Devin." He dismounted and removed his hat. As he approached the sisters, he nodded at each one. He handed his reins to Louise as well. "Thank you for taking such good care of Eliza."

Adelaide giggled and twirled. "It's wonderful having her here, she tells us such wonderful stories about digs and fossils and the museum. Don't you just love her stories?"

Devin looked over the top of the girl's head to Eliza. The twinkle in his eye warmed her. "Oh, yes. I love her stories. Always have." He turned to the other sister as he followed Eliza toward the house. "How about you, Louise?"

But the eldest girl just stared at him.

Adelaide grabbed her arm. "What is wrong with you? Come on, I'm starved." She took the reins from Louise and wrapped them over the hitching post.

Louise shook off her sister's hand, her face turning bright pink. She turned on her heel and ran into the house.

Eliza tucked her hand into the crook of Devin's arm. "Looks like you have an admirer."

His eyebrows danced up and down. "Oh good. I've always wanted one of those."

She giggled and squeezed his arm. Amazing how he could lift her spirits no matter how low they were.

They walked up the porch steps, and he opened the screen door for her.

"Mrs. Adams? We're here." Eliza led him to the kitchen to meet her host. Introductions and pleasantries were exchanged and then the large group settled around the table.

At first, the Adams family was as quiet with Devin as they had been with Eliza her first couple of weeks at their house. But the awkwardness gradually melted away as Devin asked questions of Mr. and Mrs. Adams and then each of the girls.

To their credit, the four sisters kept their manners, being gracious and sweet. Every time Devin asked Louise a question, she blushed before answering.

Her wide eyes and soft smile as she watched him made Eliza smile to herself. Why *wouldn't* the eighteen-year-old be smitten with Devin? He was a very handsome man. And brilliant.

He took that moment to glance at her. The intensity of his blue eyes sucked her in and made the rest of the room disappear. He was entertained by her host family, but she also saw concern and care for her in his gaze. They'd shared so much over the years. She could never ask for a better friend.

As Devin looked back to Mr. Adams, Eliza's heart screamed for the connection to return. Now that Devin was here, she felt whole and complete again. Why had she ever thought leaving him was a good idea?

Mr. Adams pointed his gaze at her. "Eliza, have you heard about the trials Mr. Meyer is enduring?"

She blinked and focused her attention on her host. "No. Is Mr. Meyer all right?" She'd hoped to go out to the ranch and survey more of the creek after church again.

Mr. Adams shook his head. "He's lost more than four dozen animals. They don't have any idea how or why yet, just found them dead on his ranch."

"Horace, dear." Mrs. Adams tilted her head toward the youngest daughter. "Perhaps we should have this discussion later."

"You are right, my dear." He straightened and took a sip from his glass.

Eliza understood Mrs. Adams's reaction, but she needed to know more. "When did this happen?"

"This morning." He cleared his throat. "Mr. Schmitt, Eliza tells us that you are the head of the English department at your university. That is an exceptional achievement for a man so young."

"Thank you, sir."

The two men discussed higher education as Eliza pondered what she could do to help Mr. Meyer. Losing that many animals was devastating, no matter how large your herd was. The man had been so kind to her, she wanted to do something. But what?

A loud pounding on the front door startled her out of her thoughts.

"I'll get that." Mrs. Adams stood and walked toward the door.

As soon as Eliza heard her name, she pushed from the table to find out what was happening.

Charlie—one of Earl's right-hand men—stood on the threshold with his hat in his hands. "Miss Mills, I'm sorry to disturb your dinner, but Mr. Douglass said that you made the most recent inventory of all the tools."

"I did." She turned halfway toward the stairs. "Do you need it?"

"Yes, miss. It appears someone came in and stole a bunch. Mr. Douglass said it would be easier to go through the inventory now so we know what's missing."

~~~

SATURDAY, JULY 8, 1916 • JENSEN

Dear Dad,

I pray you are doing well and enjoying some time to your-self. I hope you've received my other letters with news of Denver, the Rocky Mountains, and my arrival here in Utah.

I won't rehash all that, but I need to ask for your prayers. By the time you get this, I'll soon be home again, but I know that God hears all our prayers and isn't constrained by time.

Several difficult circumstances have happened out here, and they have prevented me from telling Eliza about her grandfather. My hope is to be able to have some quiet time with her tomorrow after church and give her the note from her grandmother.

Beyond that, I told you how I've been feeling the need the past few months to let Eliza go. On the train out here, I thought I'd done a pretty good job of preparing my heart to tell her good-bye.

Not that I don't want to be her friend anymore. But it's more symbolic than that. The fact that I love her so deeply makes it difficult to see her and act the way we've always acted.

When she was gone for a few weeks, I thought it was good for me. I thought that I was building a healthy wall around my heart. But as soon as I saw her again, it all flew out the window.

I've even convinced myself that enjoying this time together isn't wrong. That it's my last chance. So I'll say good-bye when I leave.

I'm struggling, Dad. In a much larger way than I ever imagined. The more time I spend with her, the more I long to be with her.

Since you are the only one who knows about my feelings for her, I covet your prayers to stay strong. To be willing and able to say good-bye when I have to. To allow her to be free.

I would never want to stand in the way of her dreams. Though her grandfather has passed, I still feel beholden to the promise I made him all those years ago. I am thankful that when I leave, she will still have several weeks here. It will make it easier to say the true good-bye.

I pray you are doing well. I wish you could see the quarry—it truly is a thing of magnificence. A reminder of the awesome power of God.

I'll see you soon.
Love,
Devin

He set his pen down and reread the letter as it dried. Just getting the feelings out on paper and asking Dad to pray was healing. But he still had to make it through these next few days.

Days that he dreaded and looked forward to all at the same time.

Holding Eliza as she'd cried, being able to comfort her simply by being with her, had stirred his heart as never before. Though helpless to do anything for her, he'd wanted to gather her in his arms again the moment she'd left them.

He sighed and looked back at his letter, folded it, and slid it in an envelope. He would seal it and mail it later. Right now, he needed to get to bed. He was accompanying Eliza to a new church tomorrow morning.

She'd been so wounded and angered by those women's words that she wanted nothing to do with a church out here. But he'd finally convinced her to go again, that not all churches out West would be like that one. They both knew how much she needed the fellowship of other believers and hearing the Word preached. They both needed it.

If she neglected it now, it would be far too easy to continue down that path.

So Devin had asked around in the little town this morning and had met with the pastor of a small country church. The man had been knowledgeable and kind. Not a hint of judgment against those who worked out at the quarry. Which was a good first step.

Perhaps while Eliza gathered her strength to go back to church, he could gain his own strength to be Eliza's friend. *Just* her friend.

That would be a miracle in and of itself.

~~~~~

Sunday, July 9, 1916 • Jensen

The jitters seemed to have invaded Eliza as she walked up to the sprawling, ornate ranch house. "I thought you said we were going to visit another church?"

"We are." Devin stopped in the path and smiled down at her. "They are meeting in one of the family's homes while they save up money for their building. They were meeting in the barn, but with the warm temperatures, the smell is not all that conducive to a church service."

She met his gaze. The sparkle in his blue eyes calmed her quaking spirit. "I can imagine. I'm glad we will meet inside the house." The way he looked at her made her feel like she knew who she was. She'd felt so protected and safe in his arms, even as she'd shed ridiculous tears over the words of those women. He hadn't scolded her. Hadn't ridiculed her. Hadn't said a word. Just let her cry. How was it possible he'd become even *more* wonderful in the weeks they'd been apart?

"What?" His brow crinkled. "Why are you looking at me like that?"

"I'm just thankful for you. And nervous." She clasped her hands over her Bible and stared at the house. "What if they are like the last one?"

"Come on. Have you ever—in all your travels—met another church group like that last one?"

"Well no, I've *heard* of them but have never experienced it. Let's also remember, it only took *one* group to make me feel like this."

He tugged at her elbow. Eliza let him turn her toward him. "Eliza"—his voice was low and gentle—"you can't let their words control your actions. You aren't responsible for their behavior. Only for yours. Don't let the cruel behavior of a few women shake your whole faith."

Conviction pricked her heart. He was right. "All right." She bolstered herself with a deep breath. "I'm ready."

When they walked into the home, several people were milling about, trying to find their seats. But they all turned and greeted Devin and Eliza with smiles. Eliza let out the breath she didn't realize she'd been holding. Already the atmosphere felt different. Less stiff. More hospitable.

"Welcome! We were just about to get started." A woman in a light yellow dress rushed over to them. "Here's a hymnal." And she led them to a comfortable settee near the front. A man brought a couple more chairs from another room of the house and placed them behind the settee.

Wooden chairs filled every available space around the several couches that filled the massive room. A large stone fireplace was the focal point of the room. Children sat on the floor at the front with several older young people behind them. In the corner sat a lovely grand piano, and a young woman— probably not more than twenty—began to play.

A man in a vest, tie, denims, and worn boots stepped to the front of the fireplace. "Open to page fifty-seven, if you will, and join in."

Devin held the book open and flipped to the correct page. The man up front sang out in a strong baritone voice:

Be kind to each other,
The night's coming on,

When friend and when brother,
Will surely be gone!
Then, 'midst our dejection,
How sweet to have earned,
The blest recollection,
Of kindness returned.

When day hath departed,
And memory keeps,
Her watch, broken hearted,
Where all she loves sleeps,
Let falsehood assail not,
Nor envy disprove,
And trifles prevail not,
Against those whom you love.

Nor change with the morrow,
Should fortune take wing,
The deeper the sorrow,
The closer still cling!
Be kind to each other,
The night's coming on,
When friend and when brother,
Will surely be gone.

The words washed over Eliza's soul, bringing tears to her eyes. That was the kind of love she was looking for in a church. Genuine love and care for one another. She tugged a small handkerchief out of her handbag and dabbed at her eyes, then glanced around the room.

Several others were wiping at their eyes. Sniffles and amens rippled through the small group.

The man up front cleared his throat, clearly moved by the song himself. "It was our joy to celebrate the homegoing of Mr. Vickers this past week. I know he impacted practically every person in this room. This was his favorite hymn and I thought it would be very fitting for us to sing it together this morning." He flipped several pages in the book. "Now let's move a few pages over. 'He Hideth My Soul'"

As the group began to sing, her heart rejoiced and sent another thank-you to heaven. She'd have to express her appreciation to Devin for spurring her to try another church.

> A wonderful Savior is Jesus my Lord
> A wonderful Savior to me
> He hideth my soul in the cleft of the rock
> Where rivers of pleasure I see
>
> He hideth my soul in the cleft of the rock
> That shadows a dry thirsty land
> He hideth my life in the depths of His love
> And covers me there with His hand
> And covers me there with His hand
>
> A wonderful Savior is Jesus my Lord
> He taketh my burden away
> He holdeth me up and I shall not be moved
> He giveth me strength as my day

As they sang the chorus again, more tears burned at the corners of her eyes. She'd been trying to deal with everything in her own strength. Once again. Why couldn't she rest in her Savior? His salvation was perfect. And that was all that truly mattered.

Everyone took their seats as the song leader and pianist took theirs.

A youngish-looking man—he didn't seem to be much older than Devin—stood up at the front with his Bible. "I notice we have a few people visiting our fine church family this morning. I'd like to extend a warm welcome to you. My name is Peter Stevens, and I'm fortunate and blessed to be the pastor here." He nodded and smiled at each person in the room. Which took some time. But it was clear these people loved him as much as he loved them.

"When I received the telegram requesting my wife and I to journey out to Utah, I have to admit I was a little hesitant. We'd always lived near family. And always near the city."

Many chuckles filled the room.

"Since we are celebrating one year of fellowship with this wonderful group of people today, I'd like to ask the elders and deacons to come forward at this time so that we can pray over the future of God's church here in Jensen."

Several men maneuvered their way to the front, and Eliza found she didn't want to close her eyes. The pastor and those men all knelt down at the hearth. A good many of the men around the room got out of their seats and knelt at their chairs. She'd never seen anything like it.

Reaching over to Devin, she grabbed onto his hand and bowed her head.

The most heartfelt and beautiful prayers she'd ever heard came from those men. They weren't flowery or full of big theological words. They weren't high and mighty and booming so that everyone could hear their voices. Most of the time, she had to strain to hear. But the humility and yearning expressed by those men was amazing.

By the time they were done praying, a good thirty minutes had passed. But there wasn't a dry eye in the room. It could have gone on for hours, and Eliza would have been happy. Never had she heard such anointed praying. It was like they were right there, at the throne of grace.

The pastor opened his Bible and read from John chapter one. One of her favorite passages of all time. He read a few verses and then taught on them in a very conversational manner. He even asked questions of the group. And people answered! She'd never seen such a thing in church.

Devin had opened his Bible and laid it across both their

laps. When she glanced down, it was almost intimate that he shared it with her. She'd been so caught up in the pastor's teaching that she hadn't even thought to open hers.

As the pastor taught through the whole chapter, she found herself mesmerized. It was a familiar passage, and yet it seemed fresh and new.

In that moment, she was hungry for the Word. Hungrier than she'd ever been.

He wrapped up the service, challenging each of them with the Great Commission in Matthew 28.

A renewed vigor for her faith swirled inside her.

As they left, it seemed like every person there greeted them. It was warm and loving. She'd never remember all the names, but she couldn't wait to come back next week.

Devin helped her back up into the carriage and took the reins. "I would ask you what you thought, but I can tell that you liked it."

As the horse went into motion, Eliza turned a bit to see him better. "I did. Very much."

"Sounds like maybe you've found yourself a good church here now. That's the best thing. Especially if you're going to stay permanently."

His smiling face couldn't squelch the doubt that crept into her spirit. Permanently? "It's a wonderful church. And I will gladly attend while I'm here. I am in desperate need of spiritual growth, that's for certain."

"Uh-oh." He peered at her. "I know that tone of voice. What's wrong? Was there someone you didn't like? Did someone say something ugly to you?"

"Heavens, no. The church was wonderful. The people were lovely." She bit her lip. "But it has made me rethink what it is that I am supposed to be doing. I mean . . . he challenged us with the Great Commission at the end. How is my digging for dinosaur bones going to accomplish that? Have I been selfish all these years? And you heard what those women said out at the quarry. They don't think it's godly for me to be doing it. What do other people think?"

One side of his mouth tipped up in a smile. It was a smile she knew all too well. "Scripture also tells us that we are to do our work heartily as unto the Lord. Are you doing your work heartily for Him?"

"Yes . . . at least . . . yes, I think I am."

Devin tipped his head a bit. "Really? You think? You're one of the most cheerful people I know when it comes to your work. There are plenty of days I don't have the right attitude about my job. But I'm convicted to do my very best for His glory. Just like teaching English and literature can be honoring to Him, so can digging for dinosaurs."

This work that she did . . . she was more passionate about it than anything else she could be doing. Goodness, Devin's father always had a hard time keeping her focused on her other studies from the time she was little. But he did help her understand so much about paleontology. He'd bribe her with getting her other work done by telling her he had a new book, paper, or interesting find to report to her.

It worked every time.

In the few conversations she'd had with Earl the past few weeks, she knew he was a man of faith. Even though he still wrestled with many things. What scientist didn't? Especially when it came to dinosaurs or when they lived. But his passion for the work and for the Bible continued. Several times, she'd heard him quote Scripture to the other workers.

But he didn't seem to be attending church anywhere. At least from what she'd heard.

The battle between science and faith was real. Overwhelming at times.

But she wasn't in this to prove when the dinosaurs roamed

the earth. She wanted to show people how awesome the Creator was for bringing these beasts to life.

Devin elbowed her gently. "Penny for your thoughts?"

"They're worth far more than a penny, Mr. Schmitt." Their long-standing joke was fun to keep running.

"Okay then, how about a dollar?"

"That's more like it." She straightened. "There is so much that I don't understand about dinosaurs. And that's all right, because I will continue to dig and learn." With a swallow, she looked at him. "I love what I do. And I don't think that's going to change."

"Good to hear." He released the reins with one hand and patted her knee. "It would be a pity for you to give up when it's something you love so much." His voice had turned serious, and he snapped his head forward.

She watched him for several seconds. The lines of his jaw were hard, and she could see him clenching. What had changed his mood?

"Are you all right?"

"I'm great." His face softened. "Why don't we go back to the quarry? I've got a few questions I would love for you to answer." He smiled, but it didn't quite reach his eyes. "As long as you are okay with delaying lunch a bit."

"I'm starved, but I think I can manage."

He didn't respond, just kept driving.

When they reached the quarry, he set the brake and then hopped down. He reached up and helped her down from the carriage. Her stomach did a weird little flip as she took his hand. She must be hungrier than she thought.

They headed down the path, but she stopped in her tracks and gasped. "What happened?"

Tables were overturned. Tools were scattered. And worse, the pile of debris they'd removed from the fossil wall was now covering everything.

Two of the tents were on their sides. Two more were slashed.

And in paint, several words had been scrawled.

Blasphemers.

Go Away.

eight

"Sometimes it seems more pleasant to live in hopes of something better coming than to witness the realities of life."

~Earl Douglass, quoting his wife, Pearl

Sunday, July 9, 1916 • Dinosaur National Monument

All the joy of the Sunday service and meeting fellow believers had evaporated. Devin couldn't believe the mess in front of them. Toolsboxes were overturned, their contents strewn across the rocks and dirt. The tent flaps fluttered in the wind, revealing the chaos inside as well. It was as if a tornado had cut through camp and scattered anything that wasn't pinned down throughout the quarry.

Then there was the paint. A horrible brownish-red smeared across the cream canvas, spelling out cruel phrases. Devin clenched his jaw as his gaze traced the phrase, *Go away!* Anger rolled in his stomach, and he turned from Eliza, trying to hide just how angry he was. On her behalf. What was their world

127

coming to that vandalism was an acceptable way to show your disagreement with someone?

Lord, I know You tell us to pray for our enemies. I need Your help to do that now. It's hard when enemies seem to come from the very place that is supposed to be about loving You and others.

The vandals had to be those women who had lambasted them yesterday. How could people who called themselves believers do such a thing?

Then again, Eliza had been worried that rumors would fly after yesterday's debacle. What if someone had heard the story and decided to do this? It seemed far-fetched but not beyond the realm of possibility. At this point, he really didn't trust anyone. How could he leave Eliza here in the midst of all this?

He knew all too well the stories of the lengths people went to sabotage one another in paleontology. Could this just be another example of that? If so . . . who would do it? Maybe he should speak to Mr. Douglass about it.

Devin made his way back to Eliza. Her shoulders were hunched tight, her lips pinched. But it was the sheen of tears in her eyes that broke his heart.

"Eliza . . ." He touched her elbow. She was trembling. Without another word he slipped his arm around her shoulders, and she turned into him, face pressed into his waistcoat. After a moment, she pulled away and swiped at her eyes with the back of her hand.

"Someone really doesn't like us, do they?" Her laugh was shaky.

Devin offered her his handkerchief. "Someone is a coward."

Eliza wiped her face and shook her head. "I've had a lot of struggles in my chosen profession. I always knew it wouldn't be easy, but the sense of purpose I felt . . . It always seemed God-given. But now . . ." Her gaze flicked back to the word *blasphemer* splashed on the side of a tent as she pointed to it. "What . . . what if I'm wrong?"

Devin shoved his hands into his pockets. Never in his life had she thought she'd misheard the Lord in regard to her passion for His creation. The confident smile, the joy that usually shone from her face when she was here at the quarry . . . all of that was gone. How could she even think that these people were acting on God's behalf?

"You can't let the crazy actions of deluded people shake your foundation."

Eliza shook her head, refusing to meet his gaze. "You don't understand." She walked toward a pile of empty toolboxes. Devin followed her, picking up various chisels, brushes, and shovels out of the dirt. They worked in silence for a while, making their way around the camp. The longer they worked, the more Eliza's statement pecked at him.

She said he didn't understand. Maybe that was true. He didn't face a lot of opposition in his job at the University. Unless it was an old-timer resistant to a schedule change. Some had gotten surly when new books were proposed for curriculum. But no one had ever called him a blasphemer.

He picked up a hammer and twisted it around in his hands. He'd seen one like this in Eliza's grip hundreds of times as she tapped against a chisel, working to free a fossil from the earth. The pleasure she felt in exploring treasures of the earth was contagious. Even if he didn't share her passion for the work, he could share her happiness. And she'd taken so much of the criticism leveled at her in stride. Even when several scientists at the museum protested her hiring, Eliza merely smiled and worked twice as hard to show she was smart enough and qualified for the job.

Devin tossed the hammer in the toolbox and carried it to the wagon where they'd been stashing all the tools. First, the tools that were stolen. Now this. And not even a day apart.

He slid the toolbox into the bed and then walked toward the tent on the far left side of the quarry. He'd seen Eliza enter it a few minutes before.

She was there, bent over the square table in the middle, furiously scribbling something on a piece of paper. She looked up with a small smile, then went back to her paper. "We will need buckets, turpentine, rags, brushes, and a few other things to get the worst of the paint off the tents. A couple can be sewn back together, the others will need replacing. I needed to write it down before I forgot."

Devin nodded. "I think we picked up all of the tools."

"Good. If we missed any, the men will know when they go to dig tomorrow morning since they'd just compared the inventory with what was still here last night. Thank you for your help, Devin. I know this wasn't what you had in mind for your Sunday afternoon." Eliza folded the paper and slipped it into the pocket of her skirt, along with the pencil.

"I'm happy to help however you need me to, you know that."

She continued as if he hadn't spoken. "I need to go out to Mr. Sanders and see if he has some of these supplies available. If not, I'll check the general store."

"Sounds good. I can—"

"No, Devin. It's fine. I can get this clean by myself."

Devin rocked back on his heels. "What do you mean, by yourself?"

"Just what I said." She finally looked at him and Devin's heart sank.

Her face was free of any emotion. His best friend was retreating into a shell and trying to block him out of her pain. Well, he wouldn't let her.

"Don't shut me out. I know you're hurting." He kept his voice low and soothing. "You don't have to face this alone."

Eliza shook her head. "I do, though. All my passion and ambition have brought me to this point. What if it's some sort

130

of sign that I've missed the Lord? That I'm not actually where I'm supposed to be?" Frustration laced every word. "How can I honor Jesus and say I'm following Him when even people in the church think I'm some kind of irreverent woman, rebellious in the face of God?" She crossed her arms, looking out of the open tent flap at the quarry.

Lord, help me. Help Eliza. How can I encourage her that You have her in the very palm of Your hand?

He rubbed his face, hoping words of hope and comfort would come. But his mind was blank.

"See? Even you can't argue with me." Eliza gave him a sad smile. "I think maybe I've been too stubborn in my pursuit and haven't listened to God. It's time to figure out what the Lord really wants me to do. Grandfather has made plenty of comments over the years, and Grandmama pushed against me almost every step of the way."

He winced, and his heart clenched at the mention of her grandparents. He walked toward her and grabbed her hands, holding them tight in his. His voice cracked. "Eliza, I have watched you dig in the dirt and come to know Jesus more deeply through studying His creation. You have a God-given love of this earth that saturates everything you do. When you talk about it to people, your face lights up. They do as well."

Tears slipped down her cheeks. She shook her head and opened her mouth, but Devin freed a hand and covered it. Her eyes widened. But he refused to back down.

"How many men and women had trials and tribulations when they followed the will of God for their lives? Thousands, millions throughout history! Think of those who died for Jesus because they loved Him and believed in Him. I'm sure they felt discouraged and were tempted to quit because so many people opposed them. Even believers who haven't died for Jesus still face struggles and persecution." He dropped his hand to her shoulder. "I know you've faced battles in your work before.

Most of them simply because you're a woman. This is just one more battle. And not just as a woman, but as a child of God. Don't give up."

Eliza closed her eyes for a moment. Had he pushed too far? Been too preachy? At last, she opened her eyes and sighed. "But how am I preaching the gospel, Devin? How is anyone learning about Jesus and His love through me digging in the dirt?" She stepped back and his hand fell back to his side.

"That's true." He tossed around how to answer the enormous question she'd put before him. "But think about all these tourists who come to see these bones. All the visitors who came to the museum. Think about the men at this dig who hear you talk about the glory of God's creation every day. Your enthusiasm and love for God and what He has made is infectious, Eliza. And I pray when you get alone with the Lord, He will remind you of these things as only He can. Promise me you will wait on Him and not make any hasty decisions." Devin smiled at his friend, praying she would be encouraged.

She chewed the corner of her lip, a sure sign she was at least considering what he'd said. Finally she nodded and gave him the first genuine smile he'd seen since they encountered the mess. "I promise. And thank you." Eliza leaned forward and kissed his cheek. "Thank you for being my friend."

Devin nodded, his cheek burning where her lips had brushed his skin, and his heart sinking with the reminder of what he still needed to tell her. He pushed the thought aside. Right now, they had a mess to finish cleaning. "Let's go get those supplies."

Eliza nodded and they made their way out of the quarry back to the small wagon. Devin glanced over his shoulder at the camp and those horrible words still blazing in the sun. *Lord, I hope Eliza will hear Your truth over the loud lies of the devil.*

After a quick change of clothes, gathering what supplies they could find and a lunch of what they could grab to eat in the wagon, Devin and Eliza were back at the quarry. The afternoon flew by as they baked under the hot sun, but he was determined to help her move past the vandalism.

Earl and his wife had helped for several hours, but it was clear the event had affected them both as well.

Once the last tent was set to rights, Devin went in search of Eliza and found her sitting in the dirt surrounded by tool chests with the inventory list in her lap.

"Hi."

She looked up at him with a dirt-streaked face. "Hi." The single word held the weight of the world.

"A lot of tools were damaged, weren't they?"

"Yeah." The sigh she released with her answer was long. "I'm determined not to shed any more tears over it, but after yesterday's theft and then today . . ." She shook her head. "I'd like to go hide for a while."

He squatted down beside her and placed his elbows on his knees. "What else needs to be done?"

"Nothing. We've done all we can do. Earl is going to shut the quarry down for a bit. No more visitors. They're going to speak to Mr. Carnegie and the authorities about ways to keep the site more secure, and a lot of the tools will have to be shipped to us."

Devin turned to look toward the sunset. "I hope they can find whoever did this and prevent them from doing it again."

"Me too." She scribbled something on the paper and then got to her feet, brushing all the dirt off her. "It looks like I have a few days off from my work here, which will be good. I've been wanting to show you the Meyer ranch." The smile that appeared was good to see, even if it was forced. "Who knows? Maybe you'll help me find the legendary fossils that the original Mr. Meyer said were there."

"That sounds great. Another adventure." As they walked back to the wagon, he knew.

It was time.

"What? No sarcastic reply?" She poked him and a real smile lit up her face.

He didn't say anything until after he helped her up to her seat. "Eliza . . ."

She studied him, the brief moment of joy slipping from her face. "What is it?"

He pulled the envelope from his pocket and gripped it tight. "There's no easy way to tell you this. No matter how hard I tried to find the right words . . . there are no *right* ones for a time like this."

She flicked her gaze down to the envelope and back up to his face. "What is it?" The hesitancy in her eyes gripped him like a vise.

He hated that he was about to bring her pain and heartache, but he had to tell her. "The day before I left, your grandmother summoned me to the manor. I went to see her, and she gave me this to give to you. I've tried to wait for the right time to tell you, but the longer I wait, the more I realize there is no correct or good time." He set the letter down and gripped both of her hands. "Your grandfather passed away that morning."

She gasped and stared at him as her head slowly shook back and forth.

"Your grandmother didn't want to tell you via telegram. And she didn't wish for you to find out via the papers. That's why she asked me to be the one to tell you."

Eliza trembled and tears pooled in her eyes. "He's gone?"

"I'm so sorry." He barely dipped his chin in answer.

Her grip on his hands tightened. "I can't believe it." The tears streamed down, leaving white paths in the dirt on her cheeks. Her trembling increased. "Could you . . ." She bit her lip. "Would you . . . read the letter to me, please?" She sucked in a huge breath and blinked several times as the tears multiplied.

He released her hands and picked up the envelope and

opened it. More than anything, he wanted to hold her right now. He pulled out the single sheet of paper and unfolded it. As he held it in his left hand, he reached his right hand over and covered both of her hands again. She latched on and squeezed—holding on as if her life depended on it.

He inhaled and cleared his throat.

"Dearest Eliza,

Your precious grandfather closed his eyes moments ago. I know his last breath will be coming soon. He developed a chest cold two days ago, and when he finally allowed me to summon the doctor last night, the news wasn't good. I haven't slept a wink since then, wanting to spend every moment he had left by his side. The shock of his departure hasn't hit me yet, and I'm sure that great tears will be forthcoming, so that's why I wanted to write you now.

He loved you so, my darling. Our greatest gift has been to raise you.

Last night he told me that he could die a happy man knowing that you were carrying on the Mills legacy. That you were a fine paleontologist, and he hoped you have the chance to share and teach with thousands of others about this science that you love so much.

With that, he added several things to his will. One addition is that he is giving a substantial sum to the Carnegie Institute for the Hall of Dinosaurs. He wants you to thrive and prosper with your work.

The rest of the details can wait until you return home, but please finish your work there this summer. It will take me some time to grieve my wonderful husband, and that is something I wish to do alone. You know how much I need my privacy, especially during difficult times. It says nothing about how much I miss you and love you, simply that I need to tread through my emotions with God alone as my guide.

Navigating this life without your grandfather will take some getting used to since I have never been on my own.

I will look forward to your return at the end of the summer with eagerness and great joy, my dear.

With all my love,
Grandmama"

Thursday, July 13, 1916 • Adams Farm

Eliza's pillow was soaked with her tears, and no matter how hard she tried, she had barely slept since she heard the news. She'd never suffered this kind of loss before. When her parents died, she'd been too young to understand.

The thought of never seeing her grandfather again, never hearing his voice, never feeling his whiskers against her forehead as he hugged her was almost more than she could bear. What must Grandmama be feeling? They'd been married for fifty years.

As strong and courageous and *stubborn* as her grandmother was, she deeply loved her husband. The past few years, Eliza had noticed her powerhouse of a grandmother slow down and become a bit . . . frail.

More than once in the night, Eliza determined to pack up and go home. Then she'd roll over and hear Devin's voice in her head telling her that her grandmother was adamant Eliza finish out the summer at the quarry.

She gave up on trying to sleep and sat up in her bed, pulling her knees to her chest. Her grandmother was very private. She asked for time to grieve on her own. The least Eliza could do was grant her that.

But staying out at Dinosaur National Monument no longer held the same appeal.

She longed for home.

Longed for the museum.

And having Devin here after an absence made her realize she didn't wish to be away from him either.

She scooted to the edge of the bed and placed her bare feet on the floor. The wood planks were smooth and a bit cool under her toes. A nice reprieve from the heat of the day.

At the window, she stared out at the stars.

Nothing had seemed quite right since she came out here.

She leaned her forehead against the glass.

If she'd never left, she would have had those last days with her grandfather.

She would have never gone to that judgmental little church. Or been subjected to the wrath of those women.

Without her drawing those people's unwanted attention, the vandalism and theft probably wouldn't have happened either. The quarry wouldn't be shut down.

The darkness of her thoughts swirled, overwhelming her to the point where she couldn't breathe. She gripped the ledge of the window and inhaled sharply.

Wallowing in the horrible things that had happened wasn't helpful. So . . .

What good things could she count? She bit her lip as she thought of Earl Douglass. Had she stayed in Pittsburgh, she wouldn't have met one of her heroes.

She wouldn't have seen the magnificence of the quarry and its plethora of fossils.

She wouldn't have had the opportunity to search for more on the Meyer ranch.

The ranch!

What if she actually found an intact skeleton in the creek bed? And why not? With Deborah and Devin by her side, they could bring it out piece by piece. When they were done, she would bring it back to Pittsburgh and place it in Carnegie's Hall of Dinosaurs in honor of her grandfather.

She closed her eyes. Yes. She could do that. For him.

Some of the pressure in her chest eased. Devin was right. God had given her good things and good opportunities in life. Maybe that was why the loss of them hurt so deeply. Especially Grandfather.

Weariness washed over her, and she pushed away from the window. As she climbed back into bed, she pulled the sheet over her and sank into the mattress. She couldn't push her puffy eyes open if she tried.

God, it hurts. You understand this kind of pain better than anyone so I'm coming to You with my aching heart. Please comfort Grandmama in this time of grief, and show me what You would have me do. And please, Lord, if there are fossils on the Meyer ranch, I need Your direction. I also need help forgiving those who said such ugly things and whoever did the damage out at the quarry, because in my flesh, I don't want to.

The clatter of pots and pans downstairs registered in Eliza's brain as something important. But she moaned and rolled over. Her head pounded and her eyes were so heavy.

But then she heard Devin's voice downstairs. No matter how many other voices were in the cacophony, his stood out. Because she knew it.

She lifted her head so that she could listen.

When she heard her name from his lips, she forced herself to rub the sleep from her eyes and sat up.

The pounding only worsened. As she padded over to the washbasin, she caught a glimpse of herself in the mirror.

Her eyes were puffy and almost swollen shut from crying, her hair a matted, tangled mess, and her skin was splotchy and red.

This was going to take some work.

She washed her face and hands and soaked a cloth to place over her eyes for a few minutes. The clock in the hall chimed and she gulped. She had sent Deborah a note the day after receiving the news, delaying their planned excursion to the ranch. She had gotten a very kind response, which included Deborah's plans to stop by the general store each day in about an hour's time, if Eliza ever felt up to meeting her there. And she still had to dress, eat breakfast, and pack a lunch.

If only she'd gotten more sleep last night.

But then the reason for her lack of sleep hit her in the middle of her chest.

She lay back on the bed and placed the cool cloth over her eyes, fighting the swell of tears that threatened to swallow her whole and drag her into an ocean of grief.

Grandfather was gone.

"Go find me a dinosaur, Eliza."

Those had been his last words to her as she'd boarded the train west. While he'd never completely approved of her work, in the last couple of years he'd softened more and more toward it. Probably because, as Mr. Carnegie confided in her, he worked to wear the old man down.

She smiled toward the ceiling and lifted the cloth off her eyes. According to Grandmama, Grandfather *had* changed his mind. The least she could do was grant him his last wish.

Dressing quickly, she grabbed a couple extra hankies just in case she couldn't stop the tears later. She would go now and work to find something out at the Meyer ranch. It would give her purpose and something to keep her occupied while the quarry was closed.

When she made it down the stairs, the family was all around the breakfast table. Devin was with them.

He immediately stood and walked over to her, dropping a kiss on her cheek. "Are you all right?" His words were low and just for her. Tears hovered again at his care. He'd always been so considerate of her and her feelings.

She nodded and pasted on what she hoped was a congenial face. "Thank you." They walked over to the table together. "I'm sorry for my tardiness this morning. I'm glad you all went on without me."

Mrs. Adams reached over and squeezed Eliza's hand. "It's all right, dear. Grief is a difficult path to navigate."

Eliza blinked rapidly. She would *not* cry over breakfast, even if her hostess's kind understanding warmed her hurting heart. "If you don't mind, I am going to meet Deborah in a short while. Might I take something to eat on the way? And I know it's a great imposition, but I was hoping to pack a lunch as well."

Mrs. Adams stood and laid her napkin down. "It's not a problem. You grab what you want. Louise was gracious enough to pack a lunch for several people this morning when Devin arrived and said you would be gone all day." She turned to her eldest. "Louise, dear, please fetch the basket."

"Thank you, Mrs. Adams." Eliza picked up the cloth napkin from her place at the table and opened it up. Inside, she placed two biscuits, cut them open and slathered them with butter and jam, put them back together like little sandwiches, and then wrapped them all up. She turned to Devin as Mrs. Adams and Louise came from the kitchen. "Are you ready?" She peered up into his blue eyes.

"Whenever you are." His grin broadened.

Eliza felt her stomach twist, and she pressed a hand to her middle. What was *that*?

Louise broke the moment as she handed the basket to Devin and fluttered her eyelashes as she smiled. "It was so nice to chat with you this morning, Mr. Schmitt."

He dipped his chin at her. "My pleasure."

"Thank you." Eliza aimed the appreciation at Louise, but the young lady had eyes for no one . . .

. . . but Devin.

THURSDAY, JULY 13, 1916 • JENSEN

The newspaper crinkled as she folded it in half. She tossed it on the table and picked up her coffee cup. Taking a drink, she relished the warm liquid sliding down her throat. It was almost as satisfying as the headline she'd just read.

Vandals and Thieves Play Havoc at Carnegie Quarry!

At least someone else had taken up her cause to stop the work at the quarry. This would help her a great deal. Now, if she only knew who it was, she could meet with them and perhaps join forces.

No. That was too risky.

But it was good to know that others wanted the work stopped as well. Who cared about the motivation, as long as it slowed down those fossil hunters?

The descriptions in the paper had portrayed a mess.

As she sipped her coffee, she rolled around the words the vandals had used.

Maybe she could use some of the same verbiage. That way, the other party would know someone else believed in *their* cause. Which just might stir them up some more.

Adding a bit of fuel to the fire couldn't hurt, especially if it played out in her favor.

According to the article, cleanup was supposed to take at least a week. That gave her a bit of extra time, now, didn't it? Movement in the back of the house told her it was her moment of opportunity.

She went to the stove and added the arsenic to the pot. All of it this time. For over a week, she'd been testing it in small amounts, enjoying the suffering it caused.

"I've told you not to touch my newspaper!" Her husband growled as he stomped up to the table and snatched it from in front of her plate. He wobbled a bit, and his face was pale and gaunt.

"Still not feeling well, dear?" She fetched his breakfast that she'd kept warm on the stove.

"No. And I'll ask you to keep your mouth shut and let me eat in peace." He plopped into the chair and grabbed the fork from her hand.

She clamped her lips tight. This would be the last time he ever told her to keep her mouth shut. As she poured him a cup of coffee, she smiled and sat back down in her chair.

How had she ever thought he was the love of her life all those years ago? What a fool she'd been. He'd done a fine job of wooing her and acting one way, then turning into a different person as soon as they came home from the church.

He sipped his coffee, ate his breakfast, and read his paper.

She stood and went to grab her bonnet.

"Where are you going?"

"Out. It's no business of yours." For the first time in her married life, she didn't care what he thought.

"Why, you—!" His usual roar sounded pathetic as he tried to come to his feet . . . and failed. "What—what did you d—?" His head hit the table with a loud *thunk.*

She walked out the door, climbed into the buggy, and grabbed the reins.

For the first time in a very long time, she took a full breath and smiled.

What a lovely day.

nine

> "Am preparing a preliminary paper giving a brief diagnosis of all my new species. Some have been in my collections six or eight years and are yet unknown to science."
>
> ~Earl Douglass

THURSDAY, JULY 13, 1916 • JENSEN

"You've hardly said a word. Are you sure you're up for this?" Devin brought his horse a bit closer to Eliza's. The ride into town had been peaceful and quiet so far. Two things he greatly appreciated. But the puffiness around Eliza's eyes told the story she wasn't telling. Usually she started off quiet, and then her emotions would explode out of her. He wanted to be there for her when it happened.

"I am." The emotionless expression she sent him grew into a slight smile. "Don't worry. I don't think I'm ready to pitch a fit. Yet."

He chuckled. "I only called it pitching a fit that once. And you were twelve."

"I know. The memory made me smile though and I needed that."

"But"—better to get it out now rather than in front of people—"everyone needs to vent at some point. I know you, and if you don't go storming up a mountain today ready to lasso the clouds down to earth, I'll be worried."

Her lips curled as she narrowed her eyes. "Devin Schmitt. There is no need for me to storm up a mountain."

"Okay. How about hammer a rock to smithereens?"

"That's more like it." She lifted her chin as she faced forward once again.

Oh, how he loved her. "Good. And if you need to yell and holler at anyone, give me fair warning so that we can go into the wilderness somewhere, and no one can hear us. Then I'll let you yell at me for as long as you want."

Her shoulders shook with a silent laugh. "You're a good friend, Devin."

"I know." As they reached the outskirts of town, he winked at her.

They tied up their mounts in front of the hardware store and then Devin held the door open for Eliza.

Barely five steps into the store, Eliza exclaimed, "Deborah!"

Devin stepped up beside the two women.

Mrs. Hawkins's head snapped up from whatever she was studying on the counter. Her cheeks flushed pink as she gave them a grin. "When I heard that you were ordering yourself tools, I decided that I wanted to have my own as well. So I had Mr. Wayne order the same for me." She gripped Eliza's hand. "This is so exciting!"

Eliza's smile actually reached her eyes as she hugged her friend. "You know, I love that you are so enthusiastic about this. It really helps right now."

"I'm sorry about your grandfather." Mrs. Hawkins leaned in and whispered.

"Thank you." To her credit, Eliza held it together as she walked up to the counter to speak to the proprietor. "Mr. Wayne, I received word you have my order?"

"Yes, Miss Mills." The burly man walked over to a large floor-to-ceiling shelf and pulled down two brown-paper-wrapped packages. "One is for you. One is for Mrs. Hawkins." He peered at the other woman over Eliza's shoulder.

The women paid for their purchases and Devin reached over and grabbed both. "I'm assuming these go into the bag you're going to have me carry?"

Her laughter rang out in the store.

A wiry woman stepped in front of Eliza. "Did I hear you were going out to the Meyer ranch?"

"Yes." Eliza held out her hand. "Miss Eliza Mills."

The woman studied her and then took the offered hand. "Melissa Friedman." She pulled something out of her draw-string purse. "I was going to mail this. Would you mind delivering it for me?"

"Not at all."

"Thank you, Miss Mills. It was a pleasure to meet you." The woman walked to the counter, and Devin escorted his two companions out to their horses.

Eliza sent him a questioning glance and then looked to Mrs. Hawkins.

Once they were on their way, Deborah brought her horse closer. "That was Mr. Meyer's sister."

"Sister?" Devin tugged his hat down a bit lower. "When Eliza told me the story about how the ranch is haunted, no one said anything about a sister. Just the two brothers."

Deborah sighed and her shoulders slumped. "That's because she was disowned by their father."

"Whatever for?" Eliza looked ready to pounce. "She seemed like such a mouse of a woman. Why would any good and decent father do that?"

145

"It's a long story." Deborah lifted her canteen and took a sip. "Ford Meyer came out here decades ago when there was nothin' but rocks and dirt . . . oh, and the river. He built himself the ranch and worked it, adding to it for years. His two sons, Jasper and Lucas, were as different as night and day. Jasper loved the ranch. Lucas didn't. Now Ford and his wife—I've forgotten her name—had a hard life out here. They lost nine babies before Jasper survived. They were going through the alphabet naming their children. Lost another baby after Jasper, and then Lucas survived, then Melissa. Since Jasper wanted to run the ranch, they sent Lucas off to school to do whatever it was he wanted to do. He ended up getting a job in Dallas and stayed out there in the big city. Everyone in town thought of him as the black sheep.

"Then there was Melissa." Deborah paused and licked her lips. "Her family was the wealthiest around, so she couldn't marry just any old ranch hand. There was a large dowry, I've heard as well. But then she had to go and fall in love with Horris Friedman. She begged her parents to allow her to court and marry Horris. But her father said he was nothing but a gold-digger and a bum. The fighting went on for over a year. But her parents wouldn't budge.

"One day, she rode out to the ranch with Horris and informed her parents that they were legally married. It was clear Horris thought that was his ticket. He was married to the daughter of the wealthiest family in all of Utah. But Ford Meyer wasn't about to be swindled. He cut them both off. Disowned his own daughter."

Devin swiped a hand across his jaw. How did people treat their own flesh and blood with such hatred? He glanced at Eliza. She was leaning close to Deborah, her hand on the other woman's arm, completely engaged with this topsy-turvy tale. He had to admit it had captivated him as well.

"Wow." Eliza shook her head. "I can't even imagine."

"Now, I don't know all sides of the story, but I know that every time I see Mrs. Friedman, she looks miserable. She had been so in love that she was willing to go against her parents' wishes, just thinking they would eventually come to love the man too. But he must have put up an awfully good charade for her because her father was correct. He was out for the family's money. Rumor has it that he doesn't allow Melissa to spend any money, but he gambles and carouses all over the place."

Devin puzzled to fit all the pieces together. "So what happened to the family?"

"They just up and disappeared. Vanished into thin air. The senior Mr. Meyer and his wife. Jasper and his wife and all eight of their children. The sheriff and solicitor had to track down Lucas because the will said that he would inherit. Lucas never loved the ranch, but he seemed so devastated once he arrived that he took it over in honor of his family. It hasn't been easy either."

"They never found any trace of the family?" Devin couldn't fathom how all those people could simply disappear.

"Not a one."

"Louise Adams told me that everyone thinks the ranch is haunted—that's why the family disappeared, and why bad things seem to happen out there."

Deborah scratched her nose and weighed her head from side to side. "There are a lot of rumors, but that's the most popular one."

"Do you think the rumor about them finding dinosaur bones is real?" Devin had been raring to ask that.

"I think so. I remember Jasper being so excited about it. It was all he talked about for weeks. But not long after, they all disappeared. That was . . . 1908, I believe? Then Earl found the bones out where the monument is now, and no one said anything else about the Meyer ranch. But plenty of people believe the other rumor that Ford came out here with a load of gold. Some of the mishaps out at the ranch have really been just hands that hired on so they could search for hidden treasure." Deborah rolled her eyes.

"What about Melissa? She seems so . . . lost." Eliza stopped her horse and Deborah and Devin did the same.

"The only way she inherits anything is if her brother sells. Horris has hounded the man for years to sell it since he doesn't even like ranching. But Lucas refuses. Honestly, Lucas doesn't look any less miserable than Melissa, but most people believe that he feels he's paying penance for not being here for his family." Deborah placed a hand on her hip. "If you ask me, I don't think Melissa cares much about the ranch or the money. But she regrets marrying that man, I can tell you that much."

<hr/>

Thursday, July 13, 1916 • Meyer Ranch

The morning had passed in the slow and tedious work of surveying every inch of the creek bed. At places, it was only a yard or two wide. Others, it was almost ten yards wide. Those were the places that took a lot more time.

It hadn't been quite ten years since Jasper Meyer had the excitement of finding fossils. A lot could happen in that timeframe, but Eliza had checked and there hadn't been any flash floods that would have greatly changed the landscape. Still, they hadn't found anything yet and it was discouraging.

Devin rode back toward her from the quadrant she'd assigned him to search. He shook his head as he came near. "I double-checked the whole area and don't see anything."

"Same here." Eliza released a sigh. "Let's cross the creek and check in with Deborah."

"Sounds good."

Though the other woman had been within sight and probably earshot as well, they crossed the creek and dismounted.

Deborah was crouched over something. Using a small hand shovel, she was carefully displacing dirt. "What do you think, Eliza? Is this something?"

A little thrill shot up Eliza's spine as she crouched down next to her friend and studied what she'd found. Then she stood and surveyed the creek bed around them. There was a good-sized rock layer under several inches of mud and dirt. Probably at least twenty feet by forty feet long.

Devin stepped over next to her. "I know that look. You're thinking there's something under all this mud."

"Yep." She continued to scan the area. She held back her excitement. It was Deborah's first dig—she didn't want to get her hopes up just yet. "While the slope isn't as steep as down closer to the ranch house, it intrigues me. Obviously when the creek swells, its depth covers this whole area, thus the mud."

"What do you think?" Deborah called from where she'd been digging to get to the rock layer.

Eliza made her way over and leaned in close. "That, my friend, looks like a fossil." She waved at Devin. "Quick, bring me my shovel, you should grab yours too." Her heart lifted. *Thank You, God. I needed this little bit of encouragement today.*

Devin ran over with the shovels.

Eliza stood and marched about twenty feet down the creek bed where it narrowed. "Devin, you start down here. The goal is to get all the mud and dirt off this rock layer so we can examine it. Go all the way up the slope until you reach the grass line. That should be the end of the rock layer. Deborah and I will work from up there and make our way to you."

"On it, boss." He winked at her again, his smile stretching wide.

It warmed her heart and gave her a bounce in her step as she walked back.

For the next hour, they shoveled in relative quiet since it took a lot of energy to heft the mud and throw it away from their site. The more of the stone layer they uncovered, the more excited Eliza became. She leaned on her shovel at one point to catch her breath and couldn't believe what was before her eyes. Fossilized bones for certain. But they'd have to wait until they removed all the mud before she could analyze it for size and species.

"Go find me a dinosaur." Instead of producing massive tears like they had last night, this time Grandfather's words made her smile.

Devin looked up and caught her eye. He grinned and nodded. He knew. How wonderful to have him here to share this discovery. No matter what it was, she would be happy. Hopefully, Mr. Meyer would allow them to continue digging. They might have to temporarily reroute the creek, which he might not like. But she wouldn't know for sure until she saw what was here and then asked his permission.

Another hour later, they all stood back huffing and puffing and surveying their work.

"That, my friends, has got to be a dinosaur. It's larger than any other animal."

Deborah clapped her hands together and jumped up and down. "I knew it, I just could feel it in my bones! Pardon the expression." She giggled. "I'm so excited!" She ran over to Eliza and grabbed her hands.

After they hugged and rejoiced together, Eliza went over to Devin and hugged him.

"What? No spinning or twirling? I'm disappointed."

"We're standing on a thirty-five-to-forty-degree slope, silly. If I started twirling around, I'd surely end up in the creek." She hugged him again, and he beamed at her.

What would she do when he had to go back to Pittsburgh? It wasn't the same without him. Could she ask him to stay?

Probably not. Not with his job. And she'd never want to put that at risk. But that would mean weeks without him. The thought didn't settle well.

"What now, boss?" Devin stood next to her as they stared at the layer of rock together.

"Well, I should speak to Mr. Meyer and get his full permission now that we've found this. Then, tomorrow, that means we can divert the creek and start excavating the bones."

Deborah reached over and hugged her around the waist. "Thank you, Eliza. Thank you so much, from the bottom of my heart." She put her hand to her throat. "I never knew true joy could come from this."

Her friend was correct. There was nothing like a new find. The excitement of the dig. The hope for what they might uncover. The eagerness to see if it was an intact skeleton and what species. It was the reward of days and months of what often seemed like fruitless labor.

"Miss Mills."

Eliza whirled around and spotted a group of . . . one, two, three, four, *five* people walking toward them. All of them dressed in their finery—probably wealthy tourists. The man in front looked familiar. He'd been out at the quarry multiple times, if she wasn't mistaken. "Yes? How may I help you?" Her brow dipped low under her wide hat as she studied the approaching group.

The man out in front stepped down the creek bank toward her and held out a hand. "I'm Dr. Finley Masterson." His British accent was strong. "And these two lovely couples are the Stansons and the Bufords. We all must get back to New York and since the quarry was closed, I've hunted you down. I hope we're not intruding?"

She held her breath and stared at the man. "*The* Dr. Masterson?"

"One and the same, I'm afraid." He removed his hat, folding the well-worn brim back and forth.

"Forgive me." She extended her hand in greeting and shook his. "Mr. Carnegie told me you were coming. You'll have to excuse our appearance." She glanced down at her attire. "We're in the middle of a dig."

"Not a problem." Dr. Masterson smiled. "Again, we don't wish to interrupt, but there were a few more questions we wanted to ask before we headed back East, and we simply had to find our knowledgeable guide."

<hr />

THURSDAY, JULY 13, 1916 • MEYER RANCH

Devin clasped his hands behind his back as he followed along with the small group listening to Eliza.

After the past few days, she'd lost a bit of her confidence. That spark of exuberance that always came out when she talked about what she loved hadn't been there. Then he'd made it worse by sharing the news of her grandfather's passing.

Devin let out a breath. Their time out at the ranch today had been good for her, but she was subdued. Grief colored every smile. Every glance. Not that he blamed her. Not at all. He just wanted to help her, soothe her sorrow, comfort her.

The thought of leaving her now, when she was vulnerable in her mourning and struggling out at the dig was almost too much to bear.

He hated even thinking the thought, but selfishly, it was true. Even during the cleanup and emotional aftermath it had been so wonderful to just be with her again. In a couple days, he'd have to say good-bye.

He shook his head. This habit of getting lost in his morose thoughts needed to stop. Right now, Eliza needed him. Dr.

Masterson and his friends had taken them by surprise. And while Eliza usually handled these types of situations with grace and humor, today, she looked a bit lost.

The panic that crossed her features as the group closed in was unmistakable. Not only was she unprepared for guests, but she was out here in her men's shirt and denims.

Devin eyed Dr. Masterson's friends. Their clothes, while practical, spoke of finery and wealth. He prayed they would not be offended by Eliza's clothing and would understand how necessary what she wore was to digging out fossils.

Thus far, no one had commented. They were fully focused on Eliza and her work at the quarry. He made his way toward the group and found a place just off to the side, next to Deborah, who was taking in the conversation with wide eyes.

He couldn't blame her. Dr. Masterson's friends were asking some intriguing questions. Things he'd never thought of before. And he'd been hanging out with Eliza for two decades.

Amazing how much he still had to learn about her work.

The woman up front twirled her parasol and raised a hand. "Might I ask what you believe about the age of the dinosaurs? My father is a preacher back East and doesn't like the fact that we donate to the Hall of Dinosaurs exhibit at Mr. Carnegie's museum. I keep thinking that there must be an explanation that will appease my father and help me to understand these things as well."

The woman had obviously married well, since just the hat her husband wore probably cost more than every suit Devin owned.

Eliza gave the woman a small smile and cleared her throat. Her gaze flickered to Devin, and he gave her an encouraging nod. Her grin grew and she straightened her shoulders a bit more. "There was a paper written several years ago that talked about the *Iguanodons* found in Belgium."

The husband piped up. "I remember reading about that. More than thirty were found, correct? Almost completely intact?"

"Yes!" Eliza's face lit up with genuine delight for the first time in a few days. "More than one thousand feet deep on a coal bed." She stepped a bit closer. "Coal, as we know, comes from plant matter. But something has to happen for the vegetation to not decay back into the soil. This kind of event, along with time, and with heat and pressure, turns that vegetation into coal." She clasped her hands in front of her, eyes bright as she warmed to her subject. "Now what would address your question is the fact that these dinosaurs were fossilized and an integral part of the coal and surrounding sediment. Had they simply died after the coal was already there, they would have decayed—not fossilized. For them to be in the midst of the coal bed the way they were found seems to imply that they were in the same kind of event that also caused the vegetation to turn into the coal seam."

The woman nodded. "Like the flood?"

Eliza smiled. "A flood is definitely what I was thinking and what this paper spoke about." She lifted a finger. "Now, many different religions and cultural histories speak of a global flood. That could be the explanation for it. Which would also help us to understand many of the mysteries we face when we find these fossils."

Devin nodded along. She was doing a great job at explaining, while not making anyone feel that he or she was wrong. It must be incredibly difficult to do such a thing. Especially when it was such a divisive topic.

"She's remarkable," Deborah whispered, and Devin smiled.

"I think so too. I've always admired her ability to help someone understand a challenging subject such as this without making them feel small."

Deborah looked up at him, her wide-brimmed hat shielding her eyes from the blazing July sun. "Exactly! I've learned so much in such a short time."

The other woman in Dr. Masterson's party spoke up, cutting off their conversation. "I have had a hard time believing that the earth is millions of years old. Especially since we only have record of man for not even ten thousand years."

"Then I take it you don't believe in evolution?" the man next to Devin asked.

The woman turned and studied him. "I don't believe we came from monkeys, if that's what you're asking. No. But I would like to understand this at a greater depth."

In that instant, an argument broke out. With the evolution-question man throwing insults at anyone who believed like the woman did. Then that woman's husband joined in and threw insults back.

What rude behavior! He'd had the impression when they arrived that they were all friends. But the way they were bickering was more like enemies. And it was getting out of hand.

Dr. Masterson put two fingers to his lips and whistled.

The crowd stilled.

He crossed his arms over his chest. "I don't believe this is the way civilized human beings should be behaving. Personally, I'd like to thank Miss Mills for the lovely tour and for answering our questions."

"Yes, thank you." Parasol woman nodded primly.

"As to your questions about the age of the dinosaurs, I would like to say that it is something we are still working on." The tall man looked at each person in his small group. "There are many things we don't have answers to yet. But that is why we dig and why we study, is it not?"

Several nodded.

"What you, my friends, are hearing from Miss Mills today is history in the making. The Carnegie Quarry is one of the most magnificent I have ever seen. We should be commending our fine teacher, Miss Mills, not starting quarrels."

The two men who were the most outspoken appeared thoroughly chastised. Devin couldn't help but grin.

Dr. Masterson stepped a bit closer to Eliza. "Miss Mills, I would love to have your insights on that paper. It sounded to me as if you were well-acquainted with it. Would you perhaps know the author?"

Eliza's face turned pink and then a deeper shade of red. She blinked several times. "I—that is—I . . ."

"Are *you* the author?" Dr. Masterson sounded captivated. "I've been wanting to meet the author ever since I first read the paper."

Eliza's eyes flashed to Devin. Sending him that silent plea for help. He grinned at her and mouthed, "Go on. Tell him." She'd looked up to Dr. Masterson for so long, this would be wonderful for her.

"I . . ." She licked her lips. "That is . . ." She bit her lip and then held a hand out. "You remember my dear friend Devin Schmitt. He's the author of the paper."

Every head there did a swift jerk in his direction.

His face flushed as quickly as his heart sank. He'd told her plain and clear that he wouldn't play any part for her. And then she pulled this.

Dr. Masterson glanced at Eliza, then at Devin, the expression on his face unreadable. Finally, he stepped up beside Devin and shook his hand. "What an unexpected pleasure, Mr. Schmitt. I would love to speak with you in more detail about the paper. Perhaps we could have dinner together? Or lunch?"

Devin opened his mouth to respond and quickly correct Eliza's fib. There had to be a way to fix this mess. Then he noticed the pleading and shimmer of tears in Eliza's eyes. No matter what she did, he couldn't expose her deception right now. So he snapped his mouth shut, pulled his thoughts together, and met the paleontologist's gaze. "Perhaps. Feel free to settle the details with Miss Mills. I've got to go. Excuse me."

He turned on his heel and marched away. To where, he didn't know. But at this point, he had enough fire in him to walk all the way home to Pittsburgh.

ten

"It is hard when a man has toiled all his life with unflagging energy and enthusiasm to be cut off when he had gotten where he could make his efforts count, yet the loss is not his. It is to his family and to science."

~Earl Douglass

It took several minutes for her to dismiss the group. It felt awkward and unnerving to hint for everyone to leave. Especially Dr. Masterson. But he said he would come back tomorrow, which was wonderful. She could talk to him then about a time to meet. For now, she had to find Devin.

What had she been thinking to lie like that? Especially when he told her that he didn't feel comfortable pretending to be the author. Maybe in the early years when she'd first asked him—but that was a long time ago.

Her gaze darted across the horizon, hoping to catch a hint of where he'd gone.

The expression on his face right before he walked off gave

158

her a brief glimpse of how much she'd hurt him. He looked tormented.

She'd done that.

And that did awful things to her heart. She'd always cared for Devin. Loved him. In the way that friends and family do. But something about their interactions of late had her feeling . . . different. And she didn't know what to do about it.

Was it because they hadn't seen each other for several weeks? They'd never gone that long before without seeing one another. Perhaps it was the news of Grandfather's death. A fresh wave of grief crashed over her. She still couldn't believe he was gone.

Oh no. The fact that Devin had been asked to be the one to tell her. That must have been a horrible burden for him to bear. And then she had to go and do this.

It wasn't grief that had put Devin in this precarious position. She knew, no matter how convenient it would be to blame it on Grandfather, this was all her own insecurity.

As she rushed out along the long grass following where he'd gone, she could barely see him in the distance. Gracious, he was moving fast.

She picked up her pace and began to run as fast as her corset would allow. At this point, she didn't care about how much dirt caked her shoes or the bottom of her pants. She didn't even care about what people said if they saw her running after a man. All she cared about was apologizing.

When she was within shouting distance, she hollered at his back. "Devin! Please stop. Devin!"

When he kept on, she yelled again. "Devin! I'm sorry!"

Still, he didn't stop. There was nothing to block her voice. He was deliberately ignoring her. And she couldn't blame him.

So she ran harder. "I'm sorry." She cried the words now. Why wouldn't he stop?

She finally caught up to him and latched onto his arm. "Devin. Did you hear me?" She gasped and watched his face.

It was dark and stormy. Hard.

Unforgiving.

"Please." She put a hand to her chest, heaving for each breath. "Devin, I'm sorry." The tears couldn't be stopped at this point.

"I heard you." He didn't look at her.

"I—"

"After I specifically told you that I didn't want to play a part for you. You don't *need* me to do that. And yet you went ahead and did what you wanted. You lied, Eliza. And not just about yourself. You lied about me."

His words cut her like a knife into her heart. Quick. Sharp. To the core.

She licked her lips, her heart hammering in her chest. Devin had never been this angry with her before. The distance between them was a stark contrast to the warmth she'd felt just a few hours before. Still, he deserved an explanation, even if he didn't want one. "I didn't know what to say. And I wasn't sure if Dr. Masterson thought the paper was brilliant or if he thought it was terrible . . . I was scared."

"Oh, I see." He laughed at her and waved his hands out in front of him, but it was anything but joyful. "You didn't want the man you've looked up to all these years to hate your paper, so you thought it would be fine for him to think that *I* wrote a bunch of drivel!"

"It wasn't drivel!" The words shot out of her before she knew what she was saying. And in that moment she admitted the truth: She didn't have a leg to stand on. He was right. She'd been completely selfish. Worried about herself. Insecure.

Devin shoved his hands in his pants pockets, shaking his head. "That's my point! Nothing you've written for publication is drivel." His words were only a tad bit softer. "You're brilliant, Eliza. I don't know why you can't see it, but you are. And the fact that you can't see how incredibly selfish that was for you to go against my wishes . . . well, I'm furious." He turned away from her and then swung right back around and stepped closer. "Just because you're doubting yourself and can't see the forest for the trees doesn't mean that you should hurt the person who loves you the most!" His eyebrows drew tight together. "I know the last week has been upsetting in so many ways. But Eliza . . . we've been friends our entire lives. I've always been there for you. Always. I can't"—he clenched his jaw—"I can't even look at you right now." And he turned back around and paced in a circle.

"You're right." She lifted her arms up and then let them come crashing down. "I'm sorry, okay?" What else could she say?

Once more, he whirled on her and stepped right up to her until their faces were inches apart. "You always have gotten away with doing your own thing, Eliza. And most of the time, I'm along for the ride. Encouraging you and cheering you on. But how—pray tell—am I supposed to have an intelligent conversation with a paleontologist about a paper that I know nothing about?" His blue eyes bored into hers.

She opened her mouth to argue back because that was what she'd always done, but no words would come. The heat of his anger came off him in waves. But she found herself unable to move or even blink.

Her stomach did that weird flipping again, and a shiver raced up her spine. What on earth? It was brutally hot out here today. But she was caught up in his gaze.

For a moment, she thought God had stopped the sun like He did in the book of Joshua. Then, she flushed from head to toe as she thought for sure that Devin Schmitt was about to kiss her.

That idea was the best one yet.

She actually wanted him to.

He licked his lips.

A second passed.

Then another.

She held her breath.

But he shook his head and stepped back. "I can't keep up this charade, Eliza, and you know it."

What was he talking about? Blinking away the image of him kissing her in her mind, she focused on his words. But she still missed his presence. Right there. With her. What had just happened?

"You're going to have to fix this with Dr. Masterson. I'll meet with him, but *you*. Are going to have to. Fix. This."

❧

THURSDAY, JULY 13, 1916 • DINOSAUR NATIONAL MONUMENT

The quarry was beautiful. He'd never seen the likes of it, not even in his old digging days. Envy sliced through him. Earl Douglass had hit the proverbial mother lode of fossils.

All *his* discoveries paled in comparison to this.

Still, Douglass was a respected man of science now. All thanks to the bones here.

Being able to see various dinosaur skeletons emerging from the ground as if coming to life? It stole breath from his lungs. This was where he was meant to be. Not stuck in some museum, working for a man who didn't know the difference between *Diplodocus carnegii* and a *Brontosaurus*.

He ground his teeth together. The ignorance was insulting.

Every time they received bones at the museum, he cringed whenever he saw where they'd been found. Every skeleton that Mr. Carnegie raved about would bear Dinosaur National Monument and Douglass's name on a placard.

Carnegie wasn't terrible. He had given him the job of head curator for the Hall of Dinosaurs, and that was something.

Even though he should have had his name on the displays *and* been appointed curator. He'd poured himself into the work for Carnegie for more than two decades. Just because the man had money didn't mean that he should be the one making these kinds of decisions.

Why, the note the philanthropist dropped on his desk before he left practically begged Nelson to set things straight.

Well, now that he was here . . . perhaps he could wreak a little havoc. Opportunities for revenge were plentiful out in the middle of nowhere.

And someone else obviously didn't want the quarry and its workers here.

The newspaper had quite the write-up on the vandalism, theft, and the fact that the quarry was closed for the time being. Even though many headed out on the train were anxious to see the site, himself included, there were obviously dissenters.

Not that he would want any of the priceless fossils damaged. No. He just didn't like anyone else getting his credit.

Especially Miss Mills. That rich socialite didn't have any right to be there. And to hear that not only was she giving tours but had helped with actual excavation and preservation of select skeletons being shipped back to Pittsburgh . . . well, it made his blood boil.

He turned away from the quiet quarry and shoved his hands into his pockets. What if he ruined her good name here as well? He already had someone playing a part. Why not get his money's worth?

A smirk twisted his lips.

He could hire some other men to do a little dirty work. Men who loved money above all. No need to dirty his hands.

The idea took root and expanded in his mind. It was almost too easy to think about her demise. She'd be humiliated and would go back to her big mansion and leave his Hall of Dinosaurs alone.

Then, he would be there, ready to step in and show the world what a real paleontologist looked like.

His name would be on all the placards. *His* name would be behind the Hall of Dinosaurs. *His* name would be synonymous with the greatest discoveries of all time.

⁓

THURSDAY, JULY 13, 1916 • JENSEN

Back at the boardinghouse, Devin chugged down three glasses of water in rapid succession. He'd marched around the Godforsaken desert landscape to work off his temper. But when he almost passed out from the heat and lack of food or water, common sense finally knocked into him, and he headed back here.

He caught a brief glimpse of Eliza on his way back but refused to acknowledge her. He couldn't.

Because he'd almost kissed her. Even in his anger, he loved her with a passion he couldn't comprehend.

But she didn't see it. How could she? She didn't see *him*.

The facts were the facts. He'd been her pawn for all these years. She'd ask him along, and he did whatever she wanted.

She'd used him. And this time was the worst. He'd told her no. But she did it anyway!

It didn't matter that she'd just found out that her grandfather had passed. That was just another excuse.

He winced.

That wasn't fair. She loved her family and *was* grieving.

He refilled his glass one more time and worked to get his temper under control. But Eliza had a way of getting his emotions in high gear. She was under his skin and in his heart and throughout his mind.

He'd almost caved at the end. The look in her eyes had almost been his undoing. Like she'd never seen him before and didn't know what to do with his anger. To be honest, he hadn't known what to do with it either.

But they'd been standing so close together, and he'd *wanted* to kiss her. It didn't matter how angry he'd been. In that moment, he'd wanted to give in to his desires.

Devin marched to the bathroom to splash cool water on his face. He had to get rid of these thoughts. For years, he'd kept things bottled up. Under control. No one knew.

Who has really been playing a part, after all?

His chest hurt with the thought. He'd just laid into Eliza about it . . . but he'd had his own charade going for more than a dozen years. What a hypocrite.

Earlier today, his attitude had been completely different. And for once, he'd actually enjoyed himself digging and seeing the fossils in the rock show themselves. So just because she had a lapse of judgment, he had to go flying off the handle? What was wrong with him?

He shifted directions and went in search of clean clothes. He needed a bath to truly rid himself of all that transpired today. His anger with Eliza, and his anger with himself.

In the bathing room, he filled the bath with lukewarm water and dunked himself. It took him more than thirty minutes to scour and scrub his skin. He had dirt covering every inch of him, it seemed.

The harder he scrubbed, the more he visualized removing Eliza from his heart.

That was the crux of the matter. He loved Eliza. Wanted a future with her. But he'd made a promise to her grandfather. And he was a man of his word.

A little voice in the back of his mind wanted to argue. *But her grandfather's dead. Who cares about your promise anymore?*

"I do," he said to the empty room. Even though he'd rather give in to that voice. What he would've given to kiss her. Just once.

He plunged himself back under the water to try and wash the thought from his mind. Staying under for several seconds, he couldn't erase her from his thoughts. She'd looked as eager as he had been.

Could that be true?

He surfaced again and shook his head. It didn't matter. He'd given his word.

He pulled his weary body from the tub and dried off. His anger was spent. There was nothing left but shredded pieces of his heart. Again.

After dressing, he emptied the tub and then headed to his small room and pulled out his Bible.

The words blurred on the page. He couldn't focus. Couldn't think of anything but Eliza. Once he'd allowed his anger to boil over, his long-buried passion had gushed out with it. There was no way to put it back in its enclosed and locked-up space.

God, I can't take this anymore. I love her. I've loved her for so long, I don't know how to stop. Or if I even can. I've failed at my pledge to let her go. I'm sorry, Lord.

He closed his eyes and pictured her panic-stricken face when Dr. Masterson asked her about the paper.

Compassion replaced his anger. He rubbed his face with his hands.

Bother. He couldn't allow her to be embarrassed. If he couldn't convince her to tell the paleontologist the truth tomorrow, then he would play along with the charade. For one day. That was it. Then he was leaving.

He couldn't allow himself to feel anything for her anymore. No matter what, he'd have to stand strong.

He shook his head. Like that would happen. The only thing that had worked was when thousands of miles separated them.

Lord, help. I don't know what to do. Why is this so hard?

In that moment, silence filled every crevice of the room and his mind. Then . . .

Tell her the truth.

Where did that crazy thought come from?

But then it reverberated in his heart. All these years, he'd kept it all bottled up inside. Well, maybe it was time. So he could truly let her go. He could tell her and leave. That way she'd understand why he couldn't be at her beck and call anymore. It hurt too much. And he knew Eliza—she'd never *intentionally* hurt him.

He'd get it all out in the open and she'd finally understand. Then they could put all this behind them.

Once and for all.

───────⁓───────

THURSDAY, JULY 13, 1916 • ADAMS FARM

As her horse made its way back home, Eliza tried to sort through her thoughts and feelings. But everything was such a jumble. Between her grief, shame, aggravation, and fluttering heart, she was certain the world must be upside-down.

Tomorrow, she needed to tell the truth. Somehow mend fences with Devin. Then get back to digging. Deborah would be waiting for her first thing in the morning.

As she rode up to the house, she tugged a bit on the reins. "Whoa." Mr. Adams always told her to leave her horse tied to the post, and he would take care of it. So she dismounted and went about unbuckling the straps that held the picnic basket and her bag of tools.

But a corner of something white was sticking out of the basket. That was odd.

She opened it up and found a piece of paper.

As she unfolded it, she gasped at the scrawled note:

Stop digging on the Meyer ranch and at the quarry or I'll bury you with all the other bones.

eleven

"My plan is to spend the summers in the fields collecting fossils . . . and the winters in describing the new finds."

~Earl Douglass

Eliza was tired. Her heart. Her mind. Her body. Everything was just plain old tired. Thank heaven the quarry was still closed. And she wasn't meeting with Deborah until later. Right now, sipping coffee on the front porch with the Adams women laughing and chatting around her was as much as she could manage.

Especially after finding that note. She should probably show it to Devin. As if he needed one more thing to plague him in addition to what she'd done to him the other day. Still, she longed for his presence—mad at her or not. He would know what to do.

She took another sip of her coffee and worked to still her swirling emotions. Right now, she should be ecstatic that she'd

168

met Dr. Masterson. That he wanted to discuss one of her papers! And she should be even more ecstatic about the fossils out at the Meyer ranch.

Instead, all she could think about was her best friend.

With a shake of her head, she released a huff. She'd made a mess of things.

Horse hooves pounding the packed dirt silenced all conversation. Eliza narrowed her eyes. Was that . . . Devin? It was. Her shoulders tightened as he slowed his horse to a trot, then stopped at the small barn on the edge of the Adamses' property. A minute later he emerged and made his way toward the porch.

She put her mug on the small table next to her and stood. Her palms slicked with sweat as he made his way up the stairs and toward their group.

"Good morning, ladies." He nodded at each one, connecting with Eliza last.

Her breath hitched. All traces of the anger seemed to be gone. Hope sparked a tiny flame in her heart. Perhaps they were all right after all.

"I'm sorry to interrupt, but would you mind if I borrowed Miss Mills?"

Mrs. Adams stood and gestured for her daughters to follow her lead. "Not at all. Let's go in, girls, we can start our lunch preparations."

Eliza watched them slip past her, noticing the longing look Louise gave Devin. But he seemed to not notice. His bright blue gaze was trained steadily on her. Her heart skittered into a faster pace.

Once the group was out of earshot, he touched her elbow, leading her to the now-vacated chairs. "I truly don't want to make things more difficult for you." His face was etched with deep lines. He was tired. And serious.

She'd done that to him. Guilt flooded her and she felt the

169

heat rise to her face. They sat and Eliza pulled out her hand-kerchief, needing something to occupy her nervous hands.

"But I can't meet with Dr. Masterson and pretend I've written a paper I know nothing about. I think you need to come with me."

She swallowed against the lump forming in her throat. "So . . . you're going to tell him you didn't write it?" Biting her bottom lip, she considered the possibilities. Dr. Masterson would know that she'd lied. What would he say?

He huffed and studied her for several seconds. Then palmed his face and let his hand fall. "No. I'll play your little charade this once. I'm not out to embarrass you in front of the man. I know how much you admire him and have wanted to meet him. It's not my place to burst your bubble and take you to task. But remember, I don't know what I'm talking about. I need you there. And I need you to somehow give me a crash course on whatever it was that you wrote so I will not appear the fool when I'm speaking with him."

Relief washed through her. "Thank you, Devin. I know I don't deserve it. But thank you." She looked down at her hands, which had been twisting her handkerchief into a knotted mess. "Are you still mad at me?"

He shifted his gaze to the mountains in the distance. "No. And I apologize for my outburst of anger."

"It was justified."

Releasing a short half-laugh, he turned back to her and their gazes connected. "Yes, it was. You've seen my temper over the years, but nothing like that." His words had softened along with the crease in his brow.

Staring into his eyes, Eliza started. Oh. . . . So that was it.

These unexpected feelings were because she was attracted to him! In a very real—a very strong—way. It hadn't just been in the heat of an argument. Or when he'd held her when she cried. Or when he'd simply looked at her. Her heart had known. Her stomach had known. All the crazy flutterings, flippings, and uneasiness.

She had a crush on her best friend.

The thought was ludicrous.

But then it wasn't.

"I'm sorry I'm the one that made your temper flare. It was wrong of me. It was selfish. I allowed my pride to get in the way. Please forgive me? I feel horrible for the position I've put you in."

He tipped her chin with his knuckles. Teasing in his eyes. "Don't do it again and I guess I can forgive you." He lowered his hand and stepped away, but she still felt the warmth of his touch zipping through her. "Like I could ever stay mad at you."

"Hey, that's my line." She smiled. Usually, it had been Eliza's temper that had gotten them into a tiff. She'd always said it when they worked things out. Usually when she had to apologize for flying off the handle at him. Gracious, what a horrible friend she'd been all these years!

"I stole it." He shrugged. "But it's true. I guess I understand now why you said it so much."

"Our friendship means the world to me, Devin. I hope you know that."

He blanched a bit and the warmth slipped from his face as he dropped his gaze to the ground. "I do. You better get back to the girls. But I'll meet you at the Meyer ranch in a bit. I wish I could read the paper, but you'll just have to fill me in on the high points as best you can."

Eliza frowned. Had she said something wrong? Why the sudden shift in his expression and posture?

They stood and walked toward the porch stairs. Movement out of her periphery snagged her attention. Why was the front door open? Her gaze connected with Louise, whose face was in the open crack. The young woman gasped and pushed the door shut.

Had she been listening all that time? How much had she heard?

"Hello? Are you paying attention?" Devin waved his hand in front of her face.

"What?" She blinked. "Oh. I'm so sorry. I got lost in thought for a moment. Yes, I'll be sure to fill you in. We are meeting with him on Monday for lunch."

He dipped his chin at her and walked toward his horse. His broad shoulders filled out his suit coat.

Images of Devin through the years floated through her mind. His thick, wavy hair used to fall over his forehead before he tamed it to look the part of a university professor. His blue eyes had always held a smile and sparkle for her, whether they were studying together or out in the dirt digging.

The way he looked at her had always made her feel special. That's what friends did, right?

But there was so much more to it. At least, for her now.

And she longed for more than just friendship with him.

She'd never cared to explore a relationship with a man. No one had ever stricken her fancy—never. She'd never had a crush. Never even entertained the idea of a suitor because she thought every man was after her family's money. And to be honest, every other man seemed boring and only concerned about their own lives and wealth.

Every man except Devin.

Why hadn't she seen it before?

Deep in the back of her mind, she compared everyone to him. Oh, she'd acknowledged that some men were handsome and appreciated their looks. But that was as far as it had gone.

Why?

Because she had Devin. Her best friend. The best-looking

man, in her opinion. The only person who knew everything about her. The most caring and compassionate man she'd ever known. She'd never longed for anything else other than him.

Her heart shifted into a faster rhythm. Her mouth went dry. Her insides couldn't decide which way was up.

Devin was completely different. Always had been.

He was her favorite person.

She swallowed against the lump in her throat . . .

She loved him.

And he was leaving in just a couple days.

***

FRIDAY, JULY 14, 1916 • ADAMS FARM

Devin stepped off the porch of the Adams's house and walked to the barn, hoping the shade and water were helping his poor horse. This insufferable heat was about to do both of them in. As much as he hated leaving Eliza, he wanted to get back to Pittsburgh and its cooler summers.

"Mr. Schmitt," a soft voice called after him as he entered the barn. He turned and saw Louise Adams enter behind him. She closed the barn door and leaned against it.

"Is everything all right?" He studied her.

Her chest rose and fell in rapid succession, and she pushed off the door and stepped toward him. "I wanted to make sure *you* were okay." Her voice was breathless. "Everyone knows you and Eliza had a terrible falling-out."

"That's why I came here today. Don't worry, everything is fine now." He sent her a big smile to ease her concern.

But her face lifted, and her eyes widened. Sending her own smile back, she stepped toward him again.

Oops. He hadn't meant to encourage her in *that* way. But apparently, he had. He retreated a couple steps and held up

173

his hand. "I need to go, Miss Adams. But I appreciate your concern."

The smile slipped, and she bit her lip. "Can I pack you a lunch or anything? Where will you be today? I could bring it to you."

"That's very kind of you to offer, but I believe Eliza has everything we need. Thank you." He made a wide circle around her to reach his horse and rushed out of the barn as if his pants were on fire.

Once he was outside, he mounted and urged his horse to a fast gallop. He didn't dare look back, for fear that would encourage her.

It seemed his admirer was getting brave.

Now how was he supposed to deal with this?

Saturday, July 15, 1916 • Jensen

A little poison here, a little poison there.

Who cared? She'd make death quick. These people didn't need to suffer like her husband had.

With the quarry closed for now, she only had a small window of opportunity. Might as well cause as much chaos as she could right now to keep everyone scrambling.

She didn't need a plan for chaos either. Which was thrilling. All she needed was the end result. There were a number of ways to bring that about. Wouldn't it be fun to find out which one worked?

Smiling, she carried her basket of flowers back toward town with the poison tucked safely underneath.

One job done for the day.

Only two more to go.

Who would die first?

MONDAY, JULY 17, 1916 • MEYER RANCH

Eliza practiced what she would say to Dr. Masterson today as she rode out to the Meyer ranch. A few hours of chiseling away at some rock should help her mind. It was all over the place.

The way Devin had looked at her again . . . she hadn't been able to stop thinking about it the last couple of days. Why, she'd almost thrown herself into his arms! If she wasn't careful, her stomach would fly away, there were so many butterflies taking up residence.

She'd risen early and written up a hasty list with a few short notes for him to read over before meeting with Dr. Masterson. At least it covered the high points he needed to know.

She needed to tell him how much she appreciated him. For everything. But with all these new feelings swirling, she was afraid of saying too much. Especially if they weren't in private.

She slowed her horse as she rode up to the gate of the Meyer ranch. It was shut and appeared to be locked. Two men stood there with rifles. Their faces were streaked with dirt and sweat as if they'd been in the sun a good while already this morning.

"What's your business?" one man barked and then spit on the ground.

The threatening note came back to mind. She shook it off. "I'm Eliza Mills. Mr. Meyer has given me permission to dig on his property."

The man nodded. "Yeah, we were told you'd be coming."

The other man opened the gate.

As she rode her horse through, she questioned the first man. "What's going on?"

He shifted from side to side for a moment, considering her question. "Mr. Meyer will have to tell you that, miss."

The gate was shut behind her and she urged her horse forward. When she made it to the creek, Devin was there standing beside his horse.

She dismounted and hurried over to him. "What on earth is going on?"

He wiped his forehead with a handkerchief. "Not only were more of Meyer's animals killed, but seven of his hired hands were found dead this morning."

"*What?*" Had she heard him correctly? "*Seven?*"

"Yeah. The sheriff asked me to stay here because he wanted to question both of us as well. It sounds like they might be suspicious of Meyer. But I have no idea why. Other than the fact that it's his land." His attention shifted to something behind her.

She turned and looked. The sheriff and two others with badges on their chests walked toward them.

The sheriff eyed her. "You're Miss Mills."

She swallowed. "Yes, sir."

"Meyer said you're out here digging for fossils?"

"Yes, that's correct."

"Have you seen Mr. Meyer be violent toward his workers?"

What? She frowned. "No. Never. He's a very gentle man. Quiet. He seems weighed down with grief every time I speak with him. I don't think—"

The sheriff shook his head, cutting her off. "I can't go on feelings, miss. I know exactly what you're saying. I'm the one who went and found him when his whole family disappeared. Too many awful things have happened on this property. I don't believe in ghosts or hauntings or whatever else the people might say, but it does seem like something dark hangs over this land."

She managed a nod.

"I'm sorry to tell you this, but your digging will have to

halt for a little while. Just until we can clear up whatever has happened here."

From where Eliza was standing, he didn't look a bit sorry. But maybe she was judging him a bit too harshly. "But—"

"No buts, Miss Mills. At first glance, the doc is pretty sure that these people were poisoned." His dark eyes darted between Eliza and Devin. Was the man waiting for one of *them* to confess? "He's not sure how or why, but that means there's a murderer on the loose."

"I'll help her gather her things, Sheriff." Devin laid a hand on her arm. "Please let us know if there's anything else we can do to help."

As he led her away, she had no words. People were poisoned? Is that what happened to the animals as well? A chill raced up her spine. She'd made a grave mistake. "Devin, wait."

"What is it?"

"There's something I should have shown you. I think I probably need to show the sheriff."

His jaw clenched. "What is it?"

She reached into her bag strapped onto the horse and pulled out the note.

As he read it, his face hardened. "We need to show the sheriff right now." He turned them around and marched over to the man. "Sheriff!"

The lawman faced him.

Devin got there before she did and handed over the note.

The sheriff lowered it and looked at her. "When did you get this?"

"Thursday. I think"—she dared a glance at Devin's hard face—"I think someone must have put it in our picnic basket while I was out here. This was the only place I was stopped, and it had to have been after lunch."

"Was anyone else with you?"

"Mrs. Deborah Hawkins has been helping me dig, but she wouldn't do something like—"

The sheriff folded the note and slipped it in his pants pocket. "Best not to make assumptions, miss. You need to go on back home, and we will handle this." He rocked back on his heels, his mouth pulled down in a tight frown. "I don't know what is happening in this town, but people have lost their minds. We've got vandalism, theft, dead animals, and now dead people."

The back of her neck prickled. "With that note . . . do you think I'm safe? That *we're* safe?" She gestured to Devin. "And what about the Adams's farm?" The thought of that precious family being in danger made her feel sick.

"Now, Miss Mills, thinking about every wrong and evil thing that could happen helps no one. Mr. Adams isn't shy to speak up if anything goes wrong. Best thing you can do is go home and let us figure out what in tarnation is going on around here."

"Yes, sir."

She walked back to the horse with Devin beside her. Silent. Brooding.

They mounted and rode out of the ranch's gate.

Once they were a good ways down the road, she got up the nerve to break the silence. "Aren't you going to say anything?"

He shook his head, his lips pinched in a tight line. "We can talk about the threatening note you neglected to tell me about for *four* days later. Right now, we should get cleaned up and prepared to meet Dr. Masterson."

"But—"

"No buts, all right? I'm tired, and I need to read through the notes you brought me so I know what I'm talking about." He shook his head again. "And then we need to talk. It might not be pretty."

He urged his horse ahead a few feet, and she was forced to stare at his back. Even from this angle, she could see how tense he was.

What a horrible mess. But in her haste to keep him from worrying, she hadn't thought everything through.

It was clear now. From the expression on the sheriff's face, and Devin's, they thought the same thing.

Someone wanted to scare her or get rid of her.

But why?

twelve

"There is only one thing that bothers me much . . . I do want to be worthy of her and do not want her to be disappointed."

~Earl Douglass

MONDAY, JULY 17, 1916 • JENSEN

Eliza's head pounded.

After leaving the Meyer ranch, she stopped in to see Deborah on her way to the quarry, only to find that she was sick. When she filled her friend in on what was happening, the poor woman had cried, she was so disappointed that they couldn't dig for a while.

Then Eliza went to see Earl. After a long discussion, she still couldn't convince him to open the quarry to the public again. To make things even worse, the sheriff had stopped in and told Earl about the note she'd received. Since the head of the dig didn't wish for any destruction to come to the priceless fossils, he wanted Eliza to take a few days off, telling her that she needed to grieve her grandfather anyway.

180

Not what she'd hoped to hear.

Her fingers itched to be doing something.

Now, she was at lunch with Devin and Dr. Masterson. This should be a wonderful thing. But it wasn't. She needed to face facts. Wherever she went on this trip, disaster seemed to follow.

A pat on her shoulder brought her back to the moment. She smiled at Dr. Masterson and tried to focus on what Devin was saying.

Devin patted her shoulder again. "Yes, sir. We've been the best of friends since we were children."

"Ah. Well, I understand now how Miss Mills knows so much about your writings."

Devin's smile didn't reach his eyes, and he took a sip of his coffee.

Their food was brought out to them, and Eliza couldn't even remember ordering. But she dug into her meal anyway. It was delicious but sat like a brick in her stomach. With a sigh she put her fork down. Maybe a refreshing drink would help. She sipped her lemonade, smiling as Dr. Masterson joked and talked about the abundance of poorly written papers. Normally that would have Devin speaking up, but instead, he laughed along.

He was holding up his part of the bargain. And surprisingly well.

"Are you at a university?" Dr. Masterson studied Devin.

"Yes. University of Pittsburgh."

"I'm well-acquainted with it. In the paleontology department?"

Her heart jumped. They hadn't discussed what he would say if this question came up.

"English." Devin quirked an eyebrow.

"English? That's . . . interesting. What made you decide to teach English instead of paleontology?"

"Seeing all the poorly written papers."

Laughter rounded the table.

Before Dr. Masterson could say anything else, Devin set his cup down on the saucer and leaned back in his seat, looking the part of the scientific academic. "What will you be studying next, Dr. Masterson?"

The older man leaned forward, an eagerness in his eyes. "Frankly, I want to do a study into the formation of coal. That's why I was so fascinated with your paper."

"Oh? For what purpose?"

The man leaned forward even more. "To be honest with you, the dinosaurs found in the coal seam. The Belgium find fascinates me."

"Yes. That's what my paper was on."

Devin wasn't having any trouble with this conversation.

"I'm a recent believer. And I was under the impression that Mr. Douglass might be? And you as well, Mr. Schmitt?"

"I am." Devin smiled. "So is Miss Mills."

The paleontologist glanced her way and nodded. "Wonderful." He cleared his throat. "As you know, it's difficult to have our viewpoint of the world and its Creator in this field of study. Mind you, the big shift has taken on great speed since Darwin's book. I was a great proponent of it. But something was always missing."

Eliza sat up a little straighter. This great man, this man of science, had grappled with the age of the dinosaurs too!

"The *Iguanodons* in Belgium are a key to our understanding of the truth. I believe that coal can be made from vegetation at a much faster rate than millions of years. I'd like to run some experiments on it."

"That's marvelous!" She clapped her hands together. "That's exactly what I thought when I"—she barely caught herself— "read the paper." Her enthusiasm waned. Why couldn't she simply tell the man the truth? This was *her* paper they were discussing. A topic she was most passionate about. And now, it put a foul taste in her mouth. All because of her own insecurities. She pasted on a smile. "Thank you for sharing that with us, Dr. Masterson. I will eagerly await your findings."

Devin nodded. "Yes, we will."

"It's been lovely to share with you both about my faith as well. Thank you for that. I have been . . . hesitant to speak to people about it. But I do believe that God is growing me in this area."

A man brought a telegram to Dr. Masterson. He gave the deliverer a coin. "Excuse me, this must be urgent." He tore into the envelope and read the note. As he stood up, he sent them a smile. "If you will excuse me. My wife has gone into labor, and I must return to New York, where she's waiting, posthaste."

"Congratulations!" Eliza stood and walked over to shake his hand. "It has been an honor, sir."

"You, as well, Miss Mills. Keep doing the fine work that you are doing." Dr. Masterson turned to Devin. "Wonderful to meet you, Mr. Schmitt. If I'm ever in Pittsburgh, I shall look you up."

Devin took the man's offered hand and shook it. "Thank you, sir." He glanced at Eliza, a frown pulling at the corners of his mouth.

They took their seats again as the good doctor left. Eliza relaxed her shoulders. "That wasn't so bad? Right?" But she couldn't even convince herself of that. Guilt pecked at her, unrelenting.

"As long as he doesn't come looking for me in Pittsburgh." Devin shook his head. "You need to tell the man the truth, Eliza. Especially after he told us he was a Christian. Good grief, he's not going to think less of you, and you know it."

"But I lied to him."

"So did I." Devin widened his eyes at her. "And I hate that. So let's fess up now and you can correspond with him."

She bit her lip. "I have to admit, when I couldn't talk about the topic as the author of the paper, it lost all joy for me."

"See? We just need to tell him the truth. We should have done that from the beginning." He set his napkin down on the table. "We can probably catch him at the train. Come on"—he grabbed her hand—"let's go together."

"I don't know." Why was she worried? She loved what she did. "What if he doesn't respect the paper like he did when he thought *you* wrote it?"

"Eliza." He leaned in close. "You are the most fascinating conundrum. You have such confidence and fervor, and then you doubt yourself. Why?"

She couldn't answer. Especially with him so close. Her heart was attempting to pound its way out of her chest.

He squeezed her hand, giving her a warm smile. "You're the smartest person I've ever known. Look, I know you've always had to worry about whether people liked you or respected you for who you are rather than your family and their money, but I think it's time for you to stand up for your work. You're amazing and Dr. Masterson has the right to know that."

~~~~~

Monday, July 17, 1916 • Jensen

"Dr. Masterson!" Devin called out to the man on the platform. Thank heaven he hadn't already gone.

He turned. "Mr. Schmitt." He looked puzzled. "Did I forget something?"

"No"—he turned to Eliza—"but we've got something to tell you." He nudged her with his elbow.

Her jaw dropped a bit, then she snapped it shut.

"Go on," he encouraged.

But she wouldn't speak. What was wrong with her? This was the perfect opportunity. He widened his eyes at her. "Eliza?"

184

She seemed frozen.

Well, he wasn't having it. He clenched his jaw and turned back to the paleontologist. "Dr. Masterson, we have to confess that we've lied to you."

"Oh?" The man frowned.

"Eliza wrote the paper. All the brilliance you talked about, it was all her. I'm just an English professor." There. It was out. And it felt like fifty pounds had been lifted from his shoulders.

The man's frown deepened. He set his case down and his lips pinched together. "I see." He looked back and forth between them. "And why did you feel this lie was necessary?"

Devin shifted his gaze to Eliza, silently pleading for her to speak up. To share some of her story. Perhaps the good doctor would be understanding.

She licked her lips. "I'm sorry, Dr. Masterson. I've had to fight over the years for the opportunities in this field because people think I've only attained them because of my family's name and wealth. When you were asking all those questions, I got nervous. I wasn't sure whether you liked the paper, agreed or disagreed, or thought it was rubbish." She peered down at her shoes.

"So you thought it would be all right to throw your friend to the wolves because he could handle it? Just in case it didn't play out in your favor?"

Devin winced. Harsh words.

"No . . . well, that is . . . yes."

"This is why you wrote it under a false name. Your fear keeps you from spreading your wings, Miss Mills. And that greatly disappoints me."

Her head snapped up at that.

Devin hurt for her. He hadn't expected the older man to react this way, but at least it was all out in the open. Over time, they could mend fences.

Eliza lifted her chin. "I'm sorry for lying to you, sir."

His mustache twitched over his thin lips as he glared at her. "My greatest requirement is honesty, because, as I assume you know, so many in our field built their reputations on lies and falsehoods. You've only proven that you are just as bad as they." He turned. "Good day to you both."

"But . . ." Her word deflated like a balloon.

Devin took a deep breath and faced her. "Let's go." They couldn't do anything else here and he wanted to get her away from people in case she fell apart.

"I don't understand . . ." Her whispered words were ragged. "Why did he react that way?"

"We let him down. The man is under a lot of stress. His wife is having a baby, and I'm sure he would like to be there as soon as he can."

She scowled. "So much for telling the truth."

MONDAY, JULY 17, 1916 • ADAMS FARM

Devin drove the Adams family's extra buggy back to their home.

Eliza stared at her hands, folded in her lap. For the last ten minutes, neither she nor Devin had spoken.

What had just happened? She'd never imagined Dr. Masterson would react as he did. She sighed. "I'm sorry, Devin. This mess is all my fault. You warned me and had every right to be upset with me."

"You're forgiven." He turned his face toward her, and his smile was real. "Besides, I could never stay upset with you, and I'm leaving the day after tomorrow. I don't want there to be any bad feelings between us."

"Thank you. Me too." If only he knew the turmoil he caused her now. They'd had so much chaos to deal with that she still hadn't taken the time to examine her heart. But the thought of him leaving was awful. "I guess I can't convince you to stay a bit longer?"

His wry laugh held no humor. "I should be convincing you to come back with *me* now. There's far too much danger for you here."

Why did he have to remind her? "I guess it might be a good idea for me to go home. I mean, the quarry is closed to the public right now. Earl doesn't need me out there. I can't dig out at the Meyer ranch." Her shoulders slumped. She really was of no use here. "Maybe you're right. I should pack up and go home."

Without accomplishing anything.

Devin was quiet for a moment. "You could help your grandmother through this difficult time. I know it would be good for you both."

She nodded and stared off into the distance. Her trip out West was a bust. "I should probably tell Earl about the fossils on the Meyer ranch, so he can explore that area later."

"That's a good idea. He'll be thrilled, I'm sure, at your discovery." The chipperness in his voice sounded forced.

"He will." But the discovery would then be someone else's. She shook her head. It didn't matter. She didn't need credit. All she'd done was make a mess out here anyway. It was time to salvage her dignity and go home. "I'd like to speak to Mrs. Adams, and then would you take me out to the train station? I might as well make arrangements so that I can pack."

"Of course." He reached over and patted her knee. "I'm glad you're coming home."

She met his gaze, covered his hand with her own, and squeezed. "Me too." And she meant it. At least she wouldn't have to deal with Devin's absence and what that would do to her heart.

They drove up to the Adams's home, and the sheriff was on the front porch.

"I hope he's waiting to give us some answers." Devin set the brake, hopped down, and came around to assist her.

The sheriff walked off the porch and over to them. "I'm glad I caught you. Mrs. Adams said you were at lunch."

"Yes, sir. Is everything all right?" *Please let the news be good.*

The sheriff dipped his chin. "It is. We arrested Mr. Meyer just a little bit ago."

She jerked back. "Whatever for?"

"For the murders and all the other chaos that's been happening out on that ranch all these years. Apparently, that's been his cover while he's been hunting for his father's gold."

That didn't make one bit of sense! "I don't understand. Did he confess to this? That doesn't seem anything like the man I spoke with."

"Well, no, he didn't confess. But his sister's husband brought the accusation forward last week. Horris is now dead. And when we confronted Lucas, he didn't deny it. One of his hands brought some hefty accusations against his boss as well." The man rubbed his jaw. "And his sister substantiated the rumors that Ford Meyer came here with a lot of gold. Which also disappeared when the family did."

"How does that prove that Lucas Meyer did it?" Devin scratched his ear and studied the sheriff. "Seems to me that's a bit of a stretch. Besides, the note that was in Eliza's picnic basket told her to stop digging. Why would Meyer write that when he seemed excited when she found the fossils? Why would he even allow her to search there in the first place?"

Eliza's gaze snapped back to the sheriff's. But instead of answering, his brow furrowed. Then he shrugged. "But if we do have the right man behind bars, then Eliza shouldn't be in danger anymore and no more craziness should happen out at the Meyer ranch. Mr. Friedman was pretty convincing.

He seemed to think that Lucas was behind everything at the quarry as well. As a diversion."

It was great to think that she wouldn't receive any more threatening notes, but that would only be true if Lucas Meyer was truly guilty.

The sheriff slapped his hat against his leg, dust flying off it. He settled it atop his head and nodded at the pair. "I need to get back to the ranch. My deputies said that two more hired hands wanted to give testimonies."

"Thank you for letting us know, Sheriff." Devin shook hands with the man and watched him walk away. Once he was out of earshot, he turned to Eliza. "If it were just the word of the brother-in-law who we heard was a gold-digger anyway, I wouldn't believe it. But if several people have the same testimony . . ." With a shake of his head, he grimaced. "I guess then maybe it's true."

The sound of horse's hooves pounding the ground made her turn. It was the young boy from the telegraph office.

His horse skidded to a stop, and he hopped down. "Miss Mills, this is for you."

She reached into her pocket and handed him the only coin she had with her. "Thank you." And took the envelope. "I hope it's not from Grandmama. Prayerfully all is well at home." Lifting the flap, she opened it and pulled out the small piece of paper.

Miss Mills,

Apologize for delay. Train hit a herd of cattle. Waited on repair, but my wife has gone into labor, and I must cut trip short. I shall travel to DNM at a later date.

Dr. Masterson

"Wait a minute." She read it again and then shoved the paper at Devin. "Is that saying what I think it's saying?"

Devin took the missive and read it. Then he looked at her, his blue eyes wide. "So, if Dr. Masterson never made it out here . . ."

Eliza swallowed hard, pressing a hand to her racing heart. "Then who on earth was that man we spoke with?"

thirteen

"I can't seem to quench my thirst to solve the greatest problems."

~Earl Douglass

"When you asked me to come out here, I had no idea what I was getting into." Devin sat in the Adamses's parlor with Eliza and twisted his hat in his hands.

"Believe me, had I known myself, *I* might not have come." She sniffed and pulled out a hankie. "Forgive me. I'm tired and overwhelmed and thoughts of home bring thoughts of Grandfather." After she wiped at a few tears and blew her nose, she lifted her chin. "I'm fine. Don't worry."

"I'm just thankful you've decided to go home with me in a couple days. I know there's a big mess here, but they can get it all figured out." He patted her hand.

She huffed. "What I don't understand is the man who said he was Dr. Masterson. Why? Why come here? And his charade was very good. He knew things about paleontology, about my

191

paper, about the *real* Dr. Masterson. I'm of a mind to send a telegram to the real man about what has happened here."

"That's probably a good idea, but the real Dr. Masterson's wife was having a baby. Do you think they will stay in New York for a while?"

Eliza shrugged. "I need to alert Mr. Carnegie as well. He's the one who told me Dr. Masterson was coming in the first place." She pinched the bridge of her nose. "What a mess. I'll have to tell him the whole story."

"I think that would be best. Perhaps you should wait until we get home so that you can speak to him in person. Surely he'll understand."

She nodded. "I will alert him to the imposter and then tell him the whole sordid tale once I'm there. It's a good thing we're going home so I can see him."

"You're leaving?" Adelaide entered the room with a tray of refreshments, the cups rattling on the tray.

Eliza stood and wrapped her arms around the young girl, whose shoulders were trembling. "I'm sorry. I should have told all of you as soon as we arrived. But I think I was in a bit of shock."

Mrs. Adams and the rest of her daughters entered the parlor as well. "What's this?" The mother went to her crying daughter.

Before the rest of the room erupted in tears, he better do something. If anyone wanted to be upset about Eliza's departure, they could blame him. "My apologies, Mrs. Adams. Eliza and I were just discussing that we will be leaving to head back to Pittsburgh the day after tomorrow."

"So soon?" Louise almost fell into a chair, her face pale.

"My train tickets were already in place, and I'm about to take Eliza to the station to see about her arrangements as well." Devin kept his voice calm, but it was best for him to get away from his young admirer anyway.

Eleanor stepped toward Eliza and grabbed her hand. "But Mama told us that the sheriff caught the bad guy. Why are you leaving early?"

Eliza crouched in front of her. Devin watched as she tenderly smoothed blond hair away from the girl's wet face. "I'm so sorry. But I'm not able to do my work here for a while, and since my grandfather passed away, I think it's best for me to go spend time with my grandmother."

Louise stood and fled the room, tears streaming down her cheeks.

Mrs. Adams sent Devin an apologetic look while Mabel buried her face in her mother's skirts and joined the chorus of crying. "Girls, why don't we give them some time to discuss everything. We'll get to spend time with Eliza this evening, right?" She pointed the question toward Eliza.

"Yes, ma'am." Eliza looked on the verge of tears herself. "I'll take care of everything this afternoon and be back for dinner."

Mrs. Adams escorted her girls out of the room just as someone knocked on the front door.

"I'll get it, Mrs. Adams." Eliza rushed to the door.

"Thank you." The older woman tossed the words over her shoulder as the girls' crying escalated.

One of the workers from the quarry stood there, hat in hand. "Come on in, Charlie." Eliza waved a hand toward the parlor. "What brings you here?"

"Oh, I can't stay, miss. I was sent to let you know that while they're keeping the quarry closed to visitors for a good while yet, we're going to get back to excavating. Mr. Douglass would like your help. He said to tell ya that he got your note about the Meyer ranch, and once we hear from the authorities about whether we can excavate there or not, he wanted you to be in charge if you'd like." Charlie nodded at Eliza and then waved at Devin. "Good to see you, Mr. Schmitt."

"You too, Charlie."

Well. So much for Eliza going home with him. Surely this news would sway her into staying. He held his breath.

She darted a glance to him, chewing on her lip. But he didn't miss the light in her eyes. "I'll have to let you know what I plan to do. I was just discussing heading back to Pittsburgh."

"Oh." Charlie deflated. "Well, you'll be sorely missed if you choose to go. I'll let Mr. Douglass know that you're thinking about it."

"Thank you." She watched the man for a few seconds before she closed the door and then turned to Devin. "What do you think I should do?"

He studied her face for a moment. If he had his way, he'd get her on the first train back home. But this was a decision she needed to make for herself. "I can't tell you that, Eliza. As much as I was looking forward to you being back in Pittsburgh this summer, I know this is your dream. But I only want you staying as long as it's safe. What if there's more vandalism, or those women come back to confront you? Will you be able to handle another onslaught?" He'd tried not to give his opinion, but it seemed to come out anyway.

It wasn't as if he blamed her for wanting to stay. The thrill of a new discovery would be difficult for anyone to ignore, let alone someone as passionate as Eliza. Still, this place was just a bit too dangerous for his taste.

Eliza sighed and pushed away from the door, making her way across the room. "Looks like I have a decision to make."

"I'm guessing you want to delay a trip to the train station."

"That's probably best." She stepped over to the settee and sat next to him, giving him a half-grin. "I want to be excited about my work again."

"I understand that." Boy, did he ever. More than a decade of friendship and memories had drilled the importance of her work into him. The intensity of the thought surprised him. Did he resent her love of science? He let the thought simmer for a moment. No. He couldn't keep her from what she loved . . . what God had created her to do.

"But I'm also weary from everything that has happened." Eliza leaned against him. He let himself relish the feeling of her shoulder against his. The comfort they found in one another was truly a gift. One he wouldn't spoil by voicing his concern for her safety and his desire for her to return home. He needed to trust the Lord with her, as he had done in the past. *Father, help me to support her and not be selfish in my desire to keep her close to me. Especially when I have no claim on her heart.*

So he kept his mouth shut and nodded, afraid that if he spoke, his heart would spill out.

***

TUESDAY, JULY 18, 1916 • JENSEN

Now why would Lucas Meyer take the blame?

Having him behind bars complicated things. Why did the sheriff believe that Horris was right about his brother-in-law and that everything Lucas had done all these years was to search for the family gold? Were they also blaming Lucas for his family's disappearance . . . ?

She pressed her lips together. Well, while this wasn't exactly as planned, she could make it work. Although it meant she couldn't do any more sabotage out at the quarry or keep them from digging. And she couldn't make a hullabaloo at the ranch anymore, which would have had the hired hands running for the hills and continuing the rumor that the place was haunted.

Bother! It all worked against her objectives.

Well, if she couldn't buy herself more time, she'd have to take the risk and grab the gold in the middle of the night. The bones would have to stay. By the time they dug them up, figured out who they were, and put two and two together, she would be long gone.

There was nothing keeping her here anyway.

~

WEDNESDAY, JULY 19, 1916 • JENSEN

It was time to go home. The melancholy and silence that had followed Devin around like a cloud after Eliza made her decision was even greater today. But he'd have to shove it aside and say good-bye.

It was best this way—that's what he told himself over and over. He could tell her good-bye as he'd originally planned. Then he could go back home to his routine and work to carve her out of his heart.

It was almost time to head to the train station. Devin shoved his hands into his pockets and wandered around the quarry in search of her.

When he found her, she was sitting on a rock. Staring off toward the horizon.

"Eliza?"

Her head slowly turned toward him. Her green eyes were puffy and red. Her smile forced. She stood. "Hi."

"Hi." He took off his hat and held it in his hands. How was he supposed to do this?

"You're dressed in your traveling suit. I guess it's time?" Her face was pinched, but she was clearly trying to make this good-bye a bit easier.

Bless her. "Yeah. I don't want to miss my train."

Her shoulders hunched and her face fell. "I had a feeling you'd say that, but I still hoped you'd change your mind and stay a . . ." She didn't finish her statement.

Even so, the words gave his heart a tiny boost. She would miss him. But it was time for her to walk on her own two feet.

196

For good. She was amazing. Maybe his friendship had held her back. And he couldn't live with that. "I've got a little bit of time, will you take a walk with me?"

"I'd like that."

He led her away from the tents, away from the sounds of hammers and chisels, away from anyone who might be able to hear them.

"Did you hear back from Mr. Carnegie and Dr. Masterson?"

"I did." She pulled telegrams out of her pocket. "Dr. Masterson was appalled that someone would impersonate him and wanted to speak with me about the details when I return home. And Mr. Carnegie was upset about it because he thinks it was someone who wanted to attack him and give his work a bad name. I spent a great deal sending them both long, detailed responses because I couldn't wait for them to know the whole story." She curled her fingers around the slips of paper and kept her eyes on the packed dirt path. "Once it was out there, I felt a lot better. Mr. Carnegie was disappointed about the situation, but he said he would take care of it. Dr. Masterson said that his imposter knew far too much about him and was concerned he might do it again."

Devin scratched the side of his face. "I don't know what I would do if I found out someone was impersonating me. On the other hand, being an English professor isn't as glamorous as paleontology."

Eliza let out a little chuckle. "Oh, I don't know. The steady job of an English professor looks pretty enticing right now." She bumped his shoulder with her own, then continued. "Dr. Masterson even said that yes, he was a new believer and was doing exactly what our fake Dr. Masterson said he was going to do. He's concerned about his research and his wife and new baby. Which is completely understandable."

"Was he upset with you?"

"No." She glanced his way, giving him a small genuine smile.

"And that was a great relief, as you can imagine. But the situation is still a mess for him."

Devin could only imagine the headache Dr. Masterson had on his hands with an imposter on the loose. "Once things calm down, you'll have him in your corner and will be able to correspond with the man you've looked up to for a long time." He nudged her with his elbow. "You can tell him the truth from the very beginning."

Another smile lifted her lips. This time, it filled her face. "You're right, I just hate that I was a part of this fiasco."

They walked several more paces in silence.

Each step made Devin's pulse pound harder. He had so much to say to her it felt impossible to formulate a coherent thought. It was time.

Lord, help me.

Once they were out of sight of everyone and everything, he stopped and turned to her. "Eliza. I need to say something."

She waved her hands in front of her and shook her head. "No. I'm the one who needs to say it. I'm sorry. Sorry for the mess I caused. Sorry for dragging you into all of it. Sorry for asking you to lie for me. I'm sorry for all of it."

Did they really need to go into this again? Still, it wouldn't do to snap at her right before he shared his heart. "I told you already that it was forgiven. We've been friends far too long to let something like that come between us."

Eliza nodded. "I know that. I just feel so horrible about it." She paused, then caught his gaze with her own. "I've decided to help here and with the dig out at the Meyer ranch for a few more weeks. Train Deborah a bit more. Then I'm coming home. As much as I love all this, I think I've caused enough trouble out here. It's time I rethink things. You know?"

What? What had happened to her? "No. I *don't* know. And frankly, I think you've lost your mind. What happened to Eliza Mills who would drag her best friend all over God's creation just so she could dig up a few bones?" He stepped closer to her, grabbing her hand. Why couldn't she see the truth? "What happened to that girl who was so excited about what she learned reading a boring research paper that she couldn't wait to tell her tutor and friend? And what happened to that young woman who went to college to study paleontology and couldn't wait to tell her best friend about her studies? Every. Single. Day."

"She failed. That's what happened to her." She handed a piece of paper to him.

He took it and unfolded it.

You are a disgrace to women everywhere. Just look at all the trouble that has arisen since you've been here! You are a sad example to our young people, touting your science, wearing men's trousers, and carousing with men. We will not stand for it. Go home.

He wadded up the paper and threw it. "How exactly have you failed?"

Eliza threw her arms wide, her voice thick with frustration. "Did you not read the letter? I've let people down. I haven't been a good example of my faith. I even heard Mrs. Adams tell her daughters that just because I wore pants to dig in didn't mean that it was appropriate for women to dress in such a way."

Devin inhaled a sharp breath. She was pouting like she had when she was a child. "I can't believe what I'm hearing. You are being utterly ridiculous, you know that? What are you so afraid of?"

Her eyes snapped to his, eyebrows drawn tight together.

That got her ire up. Good. Her needed her to pay attention. "Ridiculous?"

"Yes."

She huffed and lifted her chin. "Who says I'm afraid of anything?"

He shook his head. "You. You were afraid of telling the truth. You're afraid because some people have attacked you. You're afraid of continuing on with what you love now. So I'll ask it again. What are you so afraid of?"

She bit her lip and tears pooled in her eyes.

The Eliza he'd known all his life was strong but had never had to take this many blows. She seemed to be so knotted up in her own feelings she couldn't see that those silly notes were just lies designed to discourage her. And because she couldn't see that, they'd worked.

But the hurtful words had also exposed a deeper issue than believing some silly lies penned by silly women. How could he help her?

Tell her the truth.

The thought hit him again, more insistent than the last time.

He didn't want to hurt her.

The truth will set her free.

The truth from Scripture came to him, bringing with it a peace he hadn't felt this whole trip. He loved Eliza. He'd done everything he could to encourage her in her grief and confusion. But maybe it was time for some honest talk about what was really going on. *God, please give me the right words.*

Devin stepped forward and took her hands. "You refuse to trust other people, Eliza. You rely on yourself too much. I hate to say it, but I don't think you're trusting God either. For your future. For your work. For anything."

She blinked rapidly but didn't say a word.

Well, it was time to lay it out on the table. "You know how much I care for you. How much your friendship means to me. And I'm not trying to wound you . . ." His words tumbled out. For an English professor, the difficulty he had putting a coherent sentence together made his cheeks flush red. But he refused to give into the frustration tightening his chest. "Eliza . . . you need to know something before I go back to Pittsburgh. I don't want you to say anything, just . . . hear me out." How should he say this . . . ? He shook his head and just plowed on from his heart.

"We've shared everything—well, almost everything—with each other for twenty years. What you don't know . . . is that I love you, Eliza." Just speaking it out loud, his shoulders loosened. Perhaps the truth was setting him free too. While his insides tumbled, he also relaxed. Relief? Probably. After all these years, it spurred him on. "And not just the love of family or friendship. I've loved you with my whole heart since I was still a kid. At sixteen years old, I knew my heart was yours. No other woman has ever interested me. Not even when all my pals tried to set me up on dates. It's always been you."

The band around his heart was all but gone. Not that he wanted his love to be a burden, but he wanted . . . no *needed* her to know why he had always championed her with such vigor. The difficult part was she also needed to know why he'd never acted on it.

He licked his lips and squeezed her hands in his. "But we come from two different worlds. Thankfully, those worlds collided when my father became your tutor. And I will be forever grateful. I wouldn't trade our relationship for anything. I wouldn't trade all the years I've loved you for anything."

Taking a deep breath, he looked her in the eye and fought the tears clogging his throat. "But I've got to let you go now."

The questions in her eyes were almost too much for him. He couldn't tell her that he'd made a promise to her grandfather. That might make her think less of the man who raised her, and he couldn't do that to her.

A sob escaped her lips. "Devin—"

"You've got to let me finish." He held up a finger. "I'm releasing you. I have to. Before my heart shatters and can't be repaired. Perhaps I'll go back to Pittsburgh and find a nice, boring librarian to court. Or someone from church." An awkward chuckle escaped him. Perhaps his stupidity would break the tension. "You need to continue with your work and let that passion guide you. God gave it to you for a reason. Use it."

She studied him, tears streaming down her face, but didn't say anything. Her green eyes were full of . . . what?

He wasn't sure.

"Stop being afraid, Eliza. Trust God." He dared to step even closer. Releasing her hands, he cupped her cheeks, her skin soft against his hands. Never would he forget this moment. It was seared in his memory.

With a brief kiss to her forehead, he closed his eyes and released her. Finally. "I'll always be your friend. I promised. Remember?"

She nodded and a couple of tears slipped down her cheeks. "I remember. But Devin"—she blinked several times, her mouth snapped shut, then opened again—"I—"

"Good-bye, Eliza." He couldn't let her say something that would make him feel better. He'd shared his heart. Released the burden.

It was over.

Something inside him wrenched apart. He turned and walked back to the wagon that would take him to the train.

"Good-bye." Her soft word didn't soothe.

It cut and sliced and stabbed at him.

fourteen

"Sometimes I think I am a fool."
~Earl Douglass

Sunday morning dawned bright and warm. As Eliza watched the sun rise, she reread the article from yesterday's paper—an article that had originated in New York, which meant the whole world had seen it by now.

Paleontologist Lies about Authorship of Paper!

The author compared her to Cope and Marsh, and her deceit to their underhanded dealings. Then the writer of the article dared to throw her faith in there. What a shame the good little Christian girl couldn't tell the truth. What else was she hiding?

The paper even mentioned that her dearly departed grandfather was close friends with Andrew Carnegie and she worked for the Carnegie Institute—implying she'd gotten the job on that merit alone.

No matter how many times she read it, she couldn't deny

203

what was there. Yes, it painted her in a very bad light and twisted the story to give support to the author's opinion, but nevertheless, it was true.

It. Was. True.

She'd lied. Plain and simple.

The man impersonating Dr. Masterson was behind this. But she couldn't help wondering . . . who was behind *him*? He was obviously a talented actor. So who was pulling the marionette's strings?

Eliza folded the paper back up and tossed it aside.

Another sleepless night. She needed to be in church today. No matter what she looked like. No matter how she felt. Devin had been correct about her fear and trust. His words had been all she could think about until that wretched article appeared.

Devin.

The crux of their conversation before he left came back to her with such force that she had to close her eyes. He loved her, but they couldn't be together. Why? Because of money? Because he didn't think she loved him? It didn't make sense.

After all these years, all the time they'd spent with one another . . . he'd loved her like that for more than a decade? Why hadn't he ever said anything before now?

Images of him flowed through her mind and heart. How he listened and shared life with her . . . how he was willing to challenge her and say hard things . . . the look in his eyes when he saw her . . .

Eliza shook her head. *That's* how she should have known. He'd shown her every day how much she meant to him. The more she examined her own heart, the more the truth sank in.

The only man she'd ever wanted was Devin.

Had she ruined everything in spectacular fashion like always, or could she do something about this?

As she dressed for church, she allowed the tears to fall. She'd been afraid, so she hadn't been honest. But could she have been? All those years ago? Would her papers have been published if the powers that be had known she was a woman?

At this point, she'd never know.

Then there was Devin. Her confidante. Her best friend. Her "partner in crime," as Devin's father used to always say.

She washed her face and squeezed her eyes tight against all the memories.

Every major point in her life, every big accomplishment, every low point . . . Devin had been there.

The Adamses had been awfully quiet after the paper arrived. She'd been too exhausted to talk to them about it. And yet, the small buggy was ready for her as usual. Their kindness and hospitality warmed her heart. Perhaps they weren't judging her like she'd assumed everyone would.

She drove the small conveyance to her new church and allowed all the beautiful reminders of Devin to keep her occupied. She refused to focus on the fact that he'd told her good-bye. Her heart couldn't take it. Had he really meant *good-bye* good-bye?

Once she arrived and had her horse and buggy secure, Eliza slipped into a chair at the back of the room at the ranch house. Because the congregation was so small, it was difficult to sneak in unnoticed. Still, she was thankful they were singing a hymn. Less attention would be directed at her tardiness. Or her presence in general.

The liar.

The pariah.

Taking a deep breath, Eliza focused on the words being sung.

> So I'll cherish the old rugged cross,
> Till my trophies at last I lay down;
> I will cling to the old rugged cross,
> And exchange it some day for a crown.

The words stung. She had no more trophies. And she hadn't really had the opportunity to lay them down before the Lord. No, she'd clutched at them and held on to them until they'd been ripped from her. Eliza bit the corner of her lip. How was she ever going to face anyone again?

All the events of the past week scrolled through her mind. All the times she should have done something different, said something different. All the mistakes.

"What are you so afraid of?"

Devin's question was like a pebble in her shoe. Irritating and rubbing her the wrong way.

Yet it was the question at the heart of the whole mess.

Foolish. She was foolish and silly and look where it had gotten her. Alone.

Her eyes burned. Exactly what she'd been afraid of.

And her own actions had driven her there.

"The LORD bless thee, and keep thee: the LORD make His face shine upon thee, and be gracious unto thee." The recitation of the service benediction drew Eliza from her thoughts.

Her face burned. She'd missed the whole message! She dropped her head in her hands with a groan. Was she so self-absorbed that her problems were more important than studying the Word?

Ugh. What a wretch she was.

Eliza felt the seat next to her shift and she looked up. Mrs. Winters sat beside Eliza, her brow furrowed. "My dear Miss Mills, I couldn't help but notice how pale you are this morning. Are you all right?"

"I am." Eliza gave the kind woman a thin smile even as her heart clenched. Yet another lie? What was wrong with her?

Mrs. Winters's brown eyes seemed to bore into Eliza's soul, as if the woman knew all her secrets. "Hmm . . . It looks as though you have the weight of the world on your shoulders, Eliza. You don't mind if I call you by your given name, do you?"

Eliza shook her head, unable to speak past the lump in her throat.

"Good." She patted Eliza's hand. "You can call me Mary. Now, why don't you tell me what's bothering you."

The lump broke into a sob. Eliza buried her face in her hands. How she still had tears left after the last week was beyond her. But here they came again, cascading down her face.

"Oh, my dear." Mary slipped a soft arm around Eliza's shoulders and pulled her close. "Whatever it is, it can't be as bad as all this, now, can it?"

"I've m-made an a-absolute mess o-of my life." Each word was a stab to her heart.

The woman's arm tightened around her. "Well, who hasn't from time to time? Here's a hankie. Dry your face and tell me all about it."

Eliza took the small cloth and mopped away the tears. The scent of jasmine lingered, soothing her frayed nerves. She took a deep breath and explained the events of the last few days to Mary, sparing no detail. Every bad decision and wrong move was laid out. After explaining how Devin's declaration and probing question left her stunned, hurt, and confused, Eliza sat back in her chair with a sigh.

"I've let everyone down. Devin is gone. That horrid article is out in the paper. I'm sure Mr. Carnegie will be rather upset. I've brought dishonor to his museum. Who will want me representing them in any scientific field after this? And through all of it, I was afraid of being alone. But that's exactly where my actions brought me."

To Eliza's surprise, Mary smiled and even chuckled. Eliza's jaw dropped, then snapped shut. Well. She hadn't just bared her soul to have this woman mock her!

Mary reached out and patted her arm. "I'm not laughing *at* you, Eliza. I will say, I appreciate your flair for the dramatic. No, no. Don't be offended. I can hear your pain and your worry and embarrassment. And indeed, it is quite the situation you find yourself in. But"—the older woman took Eliza's hand in hers—"it is not insurmountable. You are a beautiful young woman. Full of life and joy. You're clearly brilliant and success-ful. But you have put entirely too much pressure on yourself. We all do it. We put ourselves in a place where we think *we* have to orchestrate our own lives. As if we are the masters of our destiny and not in the hand of the living God who loves us and knows what is best for us." Mary squeezed Eliza's hand, a gentle smile on her weathered face.

"Perhaps before you make all sorts of plans about what you should do, take some time and get alone with Jesus. Pour your heart out to Him like you just did to me. And wait on Him. He is faithful, Eliza. He loves you. And I think He wants to remind you that your life belongs to Him. Maybe He needed to get you alone so you would *listen* to Him. Wholly and completely."

Eliza swallowed. Her heart constricted as Mary's gentle words settled in her. It was true. She was *still* trying to man-age her life and fix the wrongs she'd done, all on her own. She twisted the hankie through her fingers. "You're right." She sighed. "But what if He's disappointed in me too? If He's decided I'm too much of a problem to redeem?"

Mary shook her head. "Impossible, dear girl. He longs for us to run to Him, even when we sin. There is no condemnation for those who are in Christ Jesus." She tapped Eliza's forearm with her finger, emphasizing her words. "Confess, repent. Be honest with Jesus. He will forgive you, Eliza. Give Him control of your life. Pray about what you need to do next. Give the Lord time to work. And stop worrying so much about what everyone else thinks."

Eliza offered the woman a wobbly smile as the room emp-tied. "I'm sorry for keeping you, but thank you. For checking up on me, for your words of wisdom . . . you've given me a lot to think about."

"I'm glad you're a part of our church, Eliza." Mary stood and patted Eliza's shoulder. "I will be praying for you. Don't hesitate to find me if you need a friend."

Eliza watched the slender woman make her way outside through the thinning crowd, greeting several people. Clearly Mary was well known and liked, judging by the smiles gracing the faces of fellow believers as they conversed with her. She'd been kind yet firm, speaking truth and wisdom into Eliza's hurting soul.

Maybe Mr. Adams would let her borrow the carriage for the afternoon so she could get away and get alone.

An hour later, Eliza was stocked with a lunch basket, her Bible, a blanket, and permission from Mr. Adams to use the carriage as long as she needed. So she set out toward Green River, just half a mile from the Adams's homestead.

The wind rippled through the mane of the horse as she maneuvered the carriage toward the river. The sun was bright in a cloudless blue sky. A gentle summer breeze ruffled the grass of the prairie on one side, and the branches of trees on the other. It was the perfect summer day. A day that she usually would have spent telling tourists about the wonders of dinosaurs, and having lunch with Devin, maybe even enjoying dinner with her host family.

But that wasn't where God had her right now.

Spotting a small grove of trees several feet from the riverbank, Eliza directed the carriage to a spot with enough grass for the horse to graze for a while. After pulling the brake, she grabbed the small basket containing her lunch and Bible, the blanket Mrs. Adams had lent her, and hopped to the ground. She walked a few yards, then settled under the shade of a tree, her back pressing against the bark. The water rushed by her, its rapids like a mirror of her swirling thoughts. But her mind kept coming back to one fact . . .

Devin was right about everything.

Under all her ambition, enthusiasm, and drive, Eliza was insecure.

Afraid.

Her bravado was a bluff, daring anyone to call her out and prove she didn't belong in the scientific community.

Her reputation and drive to prove her scientific acumen blinded her to the impact of her actions on her family, friends, and colleagues. The minute she had the chance to own her work, to walk in true confidence in who God made her to be, she chickened out.

Tears slipped down her cheeks. Devin told her she didn't trust the Lord.

He was right.

Her carefully constructed life was in tatters. All because she tried to do everything on her own.

But through all of it, Devin had declared his heart. He loved her. No. It was deeper than that. He was *in* love with her.

Eliza shook her head. She'd been blind for so many years. Buried so many feelings. Worn a façade for so long she didn't even know who she really was anymore. Devin's revelation of his feelings and his thoughts about her behavior made that abundantly clear.

She pulled her Bible out of the basket and held it for a moment. It had been a gift from her grandparents on her sixteenth birthday. The black leather and gold gilt pages were faded with time and use. It was her most prized possession, outside of the first fossil she'd found when she was seven. However, it hadn't been opened much lately.

That had to change.

Mary's words from earlier that morning came rushing back. Eliza had run long enough. It was time to seek the Lord and live her life according to His Word, not her own blind aspirations and dreams. This time she wouldn't let shame keep her from the Lord. She would run to Him.

Eliza opened the Bible and thumbed through it, not sure what she was looking for. She skimmed through several chapters in John when a verse from chapter fifteen caught her eye. "'I am the vine, ye are the branches: He that abideth in me, and I in him, the same bringeth forth much fruit: for without me ye can do nothing.'"

The words plunged into her heart, awakening her to the depths of the Truth.

Without Jesus, she could do nothing.

Finding fossils with Devin when she was fifteen. The accolades awarded her in college. The chance to study God's creation alongside some of the finest minds in the country. Getting a job with Mr. Carnegie in his magnificent museum. Every opportunity had been a blessing, not because of herself, but a gift from God. She could proclaim with confidence that God created the heavens and the earth. The very sky above them and soil beneath them declared the glory of God!

Yet even as she'd declared that with her lips, more and more, she'd depended on her own abilities and intelligence. When had her focus shifted from seeing her aptitude for science and learning as a gift from God to thinking them the results of her own efforts?

Eliza wiped her face, but the tears kept falling. It was pride, plain and simple. No wonder confusion and uncertainty dogged her every step. Attempting to walk in the way of Jesus without actually walking *with* Him, without letting Him work through her, was a sure recipe for disaster. The fruit of her actions proved that.

She lifted her face to heaven. "Lord! I am so sorry. I have been careless and prideful and full of fear! Please forgive and cleanse me."

Her tears slowed from great gulping sobs to soft sniffles. Her shoulders relaxed and her breath evened out as peace settled over her—a peace far warmer than the light of the sun above her. The weight . . . the heavy burden that had been a part of her for so long was now gone! In its place was the knowledge she was forgiven and loved by her Savior.

Mary was right, there was no condemnation for her as a child of God. *Thank You, Lord.*

Eliza watched the light flicker through the leaves of the trees above her. The rumble of her stomach cut through the air and she looked at the watch pinned to her shirtwaist. Definitely past lunchtime. Her stomach rumbled again. *Hours* past.

She opened the basket and pulled out her sandwich. The hearty scent of beef made her mouth water. She unwrapped the handheld deliciousness and laid back on the blanket with a sigh. Munching on the homemade bread, fresh roasted beef, and cheese, she stared up into the sky and listed off everything in her life she could think of that she'd held on to and gave it over to the Father. Everything she'd tried to control. Everything she'd hoped and dreamed.

The more she lifted her burdens up to Him, the cleaner and lighter she felt and the more her words tumbled out one after another.

A couple hours later, the basket was empty and her heart was full. Eliza gathered her things and headed back home. Tomorrow, she would send a telegram to Mr. Carnegie about the article. She couldn't control what people thought or said about her, but she could be honest with him. Then she would request to dig out on the Meyer ranch again. Maybe Deborah would still help her. It would be nice to get to know her better. Become even better friends than they were now. The thought warmed her.

As she drove toward the house, she noticed another carriage in the yard. Perhaps the Adamses had a visitor staying for supper.

Deborah Hawkins stood up on the porch, a deep frown on her face. She walked down the steps and toward Eliza.

"Is this true?" She held up the newspaper, fire in her eyes.

"Please." Eliza sent a quick prayer toward heaven. "Allow me to explain." She climbed down from the buggy and took a deep breath. "I wrote many papers under a male name years ago because I was afraid they wouldn't publish a woman paleontologist."

Deborah's face softened a bit. "So what did you lie about?"

Eliza winced. "I asked Devin to say that he wrote them. But he wasn't comfortable with lying for me so we told the truth to Dr. Masterson. Well, the man we thought was Dr. Masterson. But he was an imposter, and he must've gone to the papers with it."

"Oh." Deborah blinked several times. "My husband said there must be an explanation, and Earl agreed. Mr. Carnegie had sent out a lot of telegrams about the impersonator to all his people around the country."

Eliza nodded. Mr. Carnegie had told her he would inform his connections to keep a watch out for the man posing as Dr. Masterson. "I'm sorry about all this, Deborah."

She shook her head and rolled the newspaper up in her hands. "After working with you, I couldn't believe it would be true. Then a group of women protestors turned up on the road by the quarry and they've been saying some pretty hateful things. Couple that with the article and . . ." She shrugged. "It doesn't matter, I shouldn't have doubted you."

Eliza put a hand to her chest. What a gift this woman and her friendship were. "Thank you. I'm sorry that I've caused such a mess."

Deborah grabbed Eliza's free hand and squeezed it tight. "Earlier today, I was excited because the sheriff came to see us and granted permission for you and me to continue excavating on the Meyer ranch. Then I read this and listened to the protestors and—" She shook her head. "I'm so sorry!"

They were allowed back on the ranch! "You have nothing

to apologize for. And that's wonderful news from the sheriff." She gripped her friend's hand tighter.

"Isn't it? I can't wait to get back there and figure out what we've discovered. But you're the expert. I can't do this without you." Deborah smiled, and Eliza's heart warmed. *Thank You, Lord, for friends who are so quick to forgive my stupidity.*

"Does that mean you'll help me tomorrow?" Eliza held her breath.

"I'd love to."

fifteen

"What a wonder, the bursting forth of unnumbered myriads of leaves and flowers. The plum and apple trees are in their bridal robes and the air is laden with sweet odors."

~Earl Douglass

Nelson's time in Utah couldn't have gone better. His friend had played his part perfectly, and the newspapers ran with the story.

Miss Mills's reputation would soon be in tatters. But just to make sure, he had another card up his sleeve. His ace in the hole.

Once the obstacle was out of his way, he would win. Everything.

He'd barely lifted a finger to destroy Eliza Mills and her career. No, she managed that on her own, lying about her authorship on her paper. Making her friend, that inane English professor from the university, say he'd written it? He rolled his

215

eyes. Did the man have no self-respect? To let a female wind him around her little finger showed a lack of spine.

Never mind. The professor was none of his concern. And with Miss Mills just a few steps from career destruction, she wouldn't be for long either. His path to power had one last brick to be laid: removing her from the museum staff.

Mr. Carnegie's note to all the employees about being aboveboard and honest in all things had made Nelson smile. The great man's encouragement only reinforced Nelson's plan. No matter how long Carnegie and Mr. Mills had been friends, the philanthropist and wealthy mogul wouldn't dare to keep Eliza Mills employed. Not once Nelson was through with her.

Carnegie would be free of her. And he'd be grateful.

To Nelson.

A knock at his door interrupted his thoughts. "Come!"

Two men shuffled into the room, eyes glued to the floor. A grin lifted his lips. It was good to have junior scientists who actually knew their place on the food chain. Both young men shifted, waiting for him to speak.

"Turner. Lincoln. I appreciate you making time to meet me here. I have a proposition for you. Please, sit." He gestured to the two chairs in front of his desk.

They did as told and finally looked up at him. "Thank you for inviting us to meet with you, sir." Turner's eyes darted from side to side.

"Yes, it's an honor, sir," Lincoln echoed, locking eyes with him. Good. At least one of them needed a bit of backbone for what he had planned.

He steepled his fingers together and took a deep breath. "What I am about to say to you does not leave this room. You are to tell no one of my involvement. You will not speak of my part with anyone. Not your family, friends, and certainly not with each other. Trust me, I will know if you violate this agreement, and it will not go well for you. Is that understood?"

At their vigorous nods, he continued. "It has come to my attention that someone has been stealing donor money. Money allocated to erect the many beautiful dinosaur skeletons currently sitting in the preparator's warehouse."

Turner's brow furrowed. "I've not heard of this, sir. To our knowledge, donor funds are flush and—"

"You will speak only when I allow you to. *Understood?*"

The junior scientist shrank back with a nod.

"Good. Now, as I was saying. This discrepancy has just now come to my attention. And I need to know if there is truth to the rumors. So"—he opened the top right-hand drawer of his desk and pulled out two thick envelopes—"I am offering you each two hundred dollars to find out who is behind this nefarious act. If you catch the culprit, there is another hundred dollars in it for each of you."

The two men exchanged wide-eyed glances, then looked back to him.

"Turner, I'm sure this money will be most helpful for your mother, especially with her poor health of late."

Turner went pale but nodded.

He swung his gaze to the fair-haired Lincoln. "And I know you have a young wife with a baby on the way, correct?"

Lincoln nodded. "I'm sure the extra funds will go a long way toward their comfort this coming winter."

They both grabbed the envelopes. Lincoln shoved his in his coat pocket. Turner clutched his in a white-knuckled fist. "Where do you want us to start?"

He smiled. Truly, it was almost too easy. "Well, I would look first at Miss Eliza Mills. Her department's budget seems to be larger this year than last year. Make sure you are thorough in questioning every expense, deposit, and withdrawal of hers."

Lincoln shifted in his seat. "But we're only juniors here, sir. How can we get this information?"

Since he had already changed the books, they played perfectly into his hands. "Oh"—he waved them off—"don't worry about that. The museum has an open-door policy. I've had her books collected for you. Mr. Carnegie is fastidious when it comes to our generous patrons' donations. And if Miss Mills is abusing those funds, he has every right to know. Make sure you ask all your colleagues if they've heard anything about Miss Mills stealing this money. And take it to the head of finance as well. Leave no stone unturned."

The two men nodded and stood to leave.

"One more thing." He folded his hands on his desk. "If anyone is able to trace this request back to me, I will not only take the money back, but I will ensure you are fired from this museum and never hired again in the field of paleontology."

Turner nodded and practically ran out the door.

Lincoln hesitated. "Why can't they know you are the one instigating this investigation?"

Nelson stood and released what he hoped sounded like a gracious sigh. "My dear young man. You haven't been here long enough to understand the politics involved. I wouldn't want the head of finance getting his nose bent out of shape—or worse, losing his job—because he missed something important." He affected a humble shrug. "I'm simply trying to do what's best for the museum. I had someone come to me in confidence with information about Miss Mills. But because of her family's connection to Mr. Carnegie and their vast wealth, they were afraid of repercussions."

"Oh. I see." Lincoln dipped his chin. "You have my word, sir, I'll do my best." Then he left the office, the door shutting behind him with a sharp click.

There. That was done. No doubt those two would have the rumor mill churning by lunchtime.

What would Miss Mills do when she returned home and found her precious reputation demolished? How would she respond when Mr. Carnegie, furious over the misappropria-tion of funds, fired her and made sure she would never work in any museum again?

He sighed and leaned back, the leather of his chair creak-ing with the movement. Oh, watching everything unfold was going to be a joy.

WEDNESDAY, JULY 26, 1916 • PITTSBURGH

The evening sun was about to dip below the horizon. Devin watched from his seat on the porch as the last edges of it disappeared and the sky darkened.

The clouds put on a display of color until the remnants of light vanished. The sky became a dusky midnight blue and then deepened to its black cloak speckled with the stars of the universe.

Leaving Eliza had hurt more than he'd ever thought pos-sible. Even worse was the fact that he'd laid his heart on the table.

Why had he *ever* thought that would be a good idea? While it had given him a brief moment of relief to unburden himself, it had made the good-bye even more wrenching.

When she first said she was coming home with him, he'd gotten his hopes up. Something he never should have done. But he couldn't blame her for changing her mind.

Now that he'd been home a few days, he'd poured all his time and energy into his work at the University. Even added two more classes—literature this time—to teach. That should keep him busy. He might exhaust himself into oblivion, but that would only help keep his thoughts away from Eliza.

He glanced at the stack of papers on the small table to his right.

His latest project. It gave him something to pour himself

into when he came home and the long evening hours tempted him to thoughts of her.

Dad had been great. He'd listened. Encouraged. Prayed. Then this morning, he'd promised to not bring Eliza up again. He'd only speak of her if Devin brought it up.

That had been the biggest gift.

If only his heart would get the same message. And his mind. How would he ever get over her if he couldn't stop thinking about her? Devin let out a growl and shoved his hands in his hair.

Maybe he was going insane.

He had to be. He was still writing Eliza. Still expecting a reply. Still lulling himself with the thought that he'd promised he would always be her friend. And friends wrote each other letters. There was no harm.

Ha.

Maybe he should do as he'd said to her and go find a nice, quiet girl to court. Someone who could—over time—help him to love again.

A tap from inside the front door brought him out of his thoughts. He chuckled. "You don't have to knock to come out on the front porch."

The door creaked a bit as Dad poked his head around it. "I brought you some tea. Thought it might help you relax and sleep. You've been burning the candle at both ends."

"Thanks, Dad." He reached for the steaming cup. "Would you like to sit and chat for a while? I could use the company."

"Sure. You know how much I love to look at the stars."

He sipped the hot liquid. Time was so precious. He might not have a lot of years left with his father and he wanted to treasure every one.

Once they were settled in a couple of rocking chairs, Dad took a sip from his mug and put the chair into motion. "What's on your mind?" He didn't look at Devin. Just stared out at the night sky.

"How did you . . . ?" He cleared his throat. Why was it so hard to ask this? "How did you do it, Dad? How did you go on with life . . . heal, and mend your broken heart after Mom died?" He began to rock as well. "I mean . . . I remember snippets of you crying. I know you were grieving for a long while. But most of my memories are of you strong, smiling, and taking care of me."

Dad rocked for several moments. "Healing only took place after I gave my intense grief over to the Lord. Oh, it was still there. Losing your mother made me want to crawl into the grave and join her. Heaven is a place with no more tears, no more pain." He sighed, his head bobbing with the rocking of his chair. "I desperately wanted to rid myself of the pain and tears. But then, I'd see you. Our incredible son. And I could hear your mother's voice in my mind, telling me to keep going and to take care of you. She always challenged me to find the joy in everything. Whether it was a good situation or a difficult one." He took another sip and fell silent.

Devin studied him for a long time. The man had sacrificed so much to raise him. Never once complaining. Then it hit him.

"So *that's* why you made me memorize James, chapter one."

"Your mother loved the book of James." Dad didn't smile. He seemed lost in thought. "When you lose someone, son, you are plagued with all the regrets of what you could have done better. All the things left unsaid. I loved your mother with my whole heart, but there were times I was so focused on my work that I neglected her and you. I vowed not to do that with you after she was gone."

Devin reached over and gripped his dad's forearm. "You were always there for me. And I know it was tough, trying to fill the hole she left. Wrangling a young boy who missed his mother."

"I don't know what I would have done if Mr. Mills hadn't

hired me to tutor Eliza." Dad's voice was rough and choked. "God truly paved the way with that job." He cleared his throat and paused for several seconds. "I wouldn't have been able to keep up my teaching and taking care of your needs. But God provided. I was able to teach my own son along with their granddaughter, and I wouldn't trade that time with you for all the riches in the world." His father finally looked over at him. Tears pooled in his eyes.

It shook Devin. That Dad would share his heart in this way . . . "I'm thankful for all you did for me." He whispered the words, fighting his own tears.

Dad stopped the motion of the chair and turned toward him. "I know you said you needed to let Eliza go. And if you truly need to do that, I'm behind you. I promise. But please . . ." His voice cracked, and he ducked his head for a moment and then lifted it again. "Please pray about it a bit more. Don't give up on a love that may only come once in a lifetime. You still have a chance, son. Eliza is alive. I don't want you to live with regrets." Dad choked up again and stood. "What I wouldn't give for one more day with your mother. I see that same love in your eyes for Eliza. Don't throw it away."

Dad walked into the house and left Devin sitting on the porch.

He'd questioned God a lot about Eliza over the years. About his promise to her grandfather and honoring his word. But no clear answers had come. So he'd taken matters into his own hands. Thinking that it must be the right thing to do . . .

Lord, did I jump ahead of You?

His gut clenched. Was it selfish to try to guard his own heart because it simply hurt too much to love Eliza knowing it would never be reciprocated? He started. Oh . . . wasn't that exactly what he'd accused Eliza of doing? Being afraid?

What a hypocrite he'd been! He buried his face in his hands, heat burning its way up his neck and cheeks. *Lord, I told her the truth about her fears and lack of trust. But I couldn't see the same things in me. Forgive me!*

He sat back in the chair, his confession bringing no immediate relief. His chest was so tight it was difficult to draw a breath. But a bigger question hit him, the weight of it almost crushing. What if he'd made the wrong decision?

FRIDAY, JULY 28, 1916 • MEYER RANCH

The weight of the chisel in her palm was warm and familiar. She rolled the smooth wooden handle back and forth for a moment, joy welling within her. A smile broke out across her face. She had several hours of tedious, backbreaking work ahead of her.

But she didn't care.

She was digging for bones again!

Eliza and Deborah had met out at the ranch every day for the last four days, working on the fossils closest to the surface of the rock. No one had bothered the two of them. Only a few hired hands remained on the ranch—those who believed in Mr. Meyer and didn't believe in any haunting rubbish—and they kept the cattle far away from the dig location.

Deborah told her yesterday that the protestors had finally stopped at the quarry when the sheriff got onto them. Nobody was out there to hear them anyway. Several of the ladies fumed, but they left and hadn't been back. And talk in town finally died down about the newspaper article.

Funny thing about it, Eliza never had to defend herself. Her new pastor, his wife, and Mary had come to visit her at her request. She told them the truth about all that happened and found understanding, forgiveness, and open arms waiting for her. It was a beautiful thing.

Mary even wrote a short and succinct article for their local paper clearing it all up.

The Lord's lovingkindness was overwhelming after the mess Eliza had created. She tapped a chunk of rock and watched it break apart. Just like the burden she'd been carrying for so long. But when she relinquished control and sought Him? The results were amazing. Most important was the peace she felt.

She continued to work her chisel around a rounded bone. It seemed to be a vertebra, but it was so buried in the rock, it might take her weeks to get it out. That was fine. The exacting work kept her occupied and focused. And gave her plenty of time to think.

Devin's confession sat on the edge of her memory, his words rushing through her mind every time she had a quiet moment.

It was becoming ridiculous. Still, his candor was refreshing. It always had been.

How she'd wanted to talk it out with him before he left, but there'd been no time. And now . . . now she saw the wisdom in the time and distance between them.

If only that would stop the ache squeezing her heart.

She wiped her hands on her pants and sat back on her heels, glancing around. Where was her canteen? She spotted it next to the small picnic basket Louise had packed for them.

The gesture had been a surprise. Poor Louise was still mourning Devin's departure and would barely speak to Eliza.

In some ways, she admired the young woman. There was a youthful freedom in wearing her heart on her sleeve. Eliza had never possessed that. And she'd started examining why she couldn't or shouldn't be so bold and unafraid in her own emotions.

Much of it had to do with Grandmama's society training. A lady never let on what she was thinking or feeling. One never knew who might be offended.

Eliza leaned forward and grabbed the small aluminum

bottle and unscrewed the cap. A bit of water softened the dirt around the bone. Using her fingers, she dug away the mud and rocks, a bit more bone emerging from the ground.

But why must she always have her guard up? How was she to ever truly know anyone if she was always fiercely protecting herself against what they might think? Even with Devin, who knew her better than anyone else in the world . . . she was still afraid to let him in completely. It was ridiculous. She'd always been able to share anything and everything with him.

Why had she never allowed herself to think of him as a suitor? He was her favorite person on earth!

"Eliza, what do you think of this one over here?"

Eliza shook her head free of her thoughts and looked over at Deborah. Her friend had chiseled a good deal of rock around what appeared to be a large fossil. When they'd started digging, it had been impossible to decipher what type of bone they were looking at.

But now, with Deborah's detailed and careful work . . .

Eliza laid down her chisel and hammer and jumped up and down. "Deborah!" she squealed. "That's a giant rib!"

"I was hoping you'd say that." Her friend joined her in a celebration. "So we have a dinosaur?"

Eliza twirled around, lifting her face to the sky. "Yes! I think we do!"

sixteen

"What is the use of anything only to make others and myself as happy as I can while I live. My greatest ambition is to earn enough money to make my folks comfortable and do the work I love. Although I have not reached that time yet the prospect seems better than ever before."

~Earl Douglass

"I wish that girl would come home." Dad set the biscuits on the table with a bit more force than usual.

Devin felt the same but had been working to tame his anger. He'd been so focused on his work when he got back that he hadn't bothered to read the papers. Dad struggled with his eyes, and the doctor told him not to read for a while until a new pair of spectacles came in for him.

So yesterday, when a colleague at work teased him about the newspaper article on Eliza, Devin took the ribbing good-naturedly, pretending he knew what the man was talking

226

about. As soon as he was able, he rushed home to find the article.

He read each horrible word, fingers turning white, he gripped the paper so hard. He tossed the paper aside. Was *that* what passed for journalism these days? Salacious gossip? Poor Eliza. What had this done to her? Why hadn't she written him about it?

He took a sip of coffee before responding to Dad. "I'd like to take the next train west and get her, but I have no idea what's happening out there. That article has been out for a while. Have they even seen it out West?"

"Hard to tell. But with the wireless telegraph and such these days, it would be hard to escape it." Dad squinted at him. "Exactly why didn't she come home with you again?"

"They started to dig again—and not just any dig. Eliza was put in charge. Earl Douglass is a phenomenal mentor, and she's learned so much from him." Devin ate a few more bites, then reached for a biscuit. "You'd enjoy seeing the quarry. Especially once you see the museum and how they've put together some of the large skeletons."

Dad barely kept his grin hidden. "You sound like a supportive and encouraging *friend*."

"And what is so wrong with that?" Devin rolled his eyes. "Here we go again. You said you wouldn't bring it up."

"Well, after you asked me about your mother, it's only fair. I'm not going to walk on eggshells about Eliza." His dad laughed. "You seriously believe that the two of you—as close as you've always been—can stay apart? Especially now that you told her how you felt?"

Devin groaned and shook his head. He should have never told his father about his feelings. Ever since that night on the porch when they'd talked about Mom, Dad had been on the constant prowl to play matchmaker.

The telephone rang, and Devin got up and laid his napkin on the table. "I'll get that."

He went to the phone on the wall and answered. "Hello?"

"Is this Devin Schmitt?" A female voice he didn't recognize.

"Yes."

"Hi. I'm sorry to bother you at home, but I needed to talk to you right away. I'm Sarah Limon. I'm a friend of Eliza's at the Carnegie Institute."

Something in the tone of her voice set him on edge. "Is everything all right?"

"No. There are some terrible rumors going around at the museum about Eliza. They're accusing her of stealing fossils and donor money. It's awful. But once the rumors started, they just got bigger and more outlandish. And then that newspaper article fueled it all, even though Mr. Carnegie issued a statement to all the employees here about that. I'm worried about her, and she's not here to defend herself."

His blood began to boil. These shenanigans had gone far enough! "Who started the rumors?"

"I don't know." Crackling sounded through the phone. Then her voice was even softer. "But you know, there are plenty of men here who don't like a woman working in the paleontology part of the museum." Another crackling sound. "Eliza talked about you all the time, and I knew I could trust you. I'm just a secretary, so I don't have any power to do anything to help. But I knew you could." Some more crackling. "I'm sorry. I have to go."

The line disconnected.

Devin hung up the phone.

"What was that all about? Rumors?" Dad had come out of his seat.

Devin filled him in as he paced the small area around the table.

"What are you going to do?"

Devin laid his hands on the back of the chair and leaned down. His mind swirled. Oh, he'd like to punch whoever started those rumors. And he'd like to make sure that anyone who said anything negative about Eliza was fired. And never able to come near her again. Unfortunately, that wasn't in his power.

He straightened. But *one* thing was. "I'm going to have a meeting with Mr. Carnegie, that's what I'm going to do."

Dad's eyes widened. "Have you ever met the man?"

"Once. With Eliza at the museum." The wealthy philanthropist probably wouldn't remember him, but he didn't care. He would wait as long as it took to see him. No, he would *demand* to see him.

"It's a noble thing you want to do, son, but I'm not sure you'll be successful. Especially since we really don't have any idea what's happening."

Devin narrowed his eyes. "I'll tell you what's happening. Someone is trying to ruin Eliza's reputation by lying about her. Whoever it is was bold enough to send an imposter out West and now this. And I'm not about to allow that to happen." He straightened and slapped his napkin on the table.

Just let anyone *try* to stand in his way.

~

MONDAY, JULY 31, 1916 · DINOSAUR NATIONAL MONUMENT

She could've sworn this was where she'd buried the gold. But no matter how many holes she dug, she hadn't found it.

It was dark though, with only the light of the moon. She couldn't risk a lantern out here. Especially since the man running the quarry had started having men patrol at night.

But she had to find the box of gold. It contained the only map with detailed instructions as to where the rest of the gold was hidden all over the ranch.

She sat back on her heels and took a deep breath. That's what all this was for. That bullion was her ticket to a new life. She deserved it after all she'd endured. It. Was. Hers.

With it, she would disappear to Europe forever and live like a princess. She would shed the shell of the woman she'd been and become anything she wanted to be. She was young. She could be vibrant once more.

Never . . . *never* again would she allow a man to control her, beat her down, and crush her spirit.

With fresh vigor, she went back to the boulder by her marker and counted her steps. Perhaps she'd been off by a step or angled in the wrong direction. But she came to the same spot. Then she gasped and went back to the crevice in the large rock wall. Her marker was gone.

She growled out her frustration. No wonder she hadn't been able to find it. Now she'd have to dig up this entire area.

She would find it. She would.

And woe to anyone who tried to stop her.

~~~

WEDNESDAY, AUGUST 2, 1916 • ADAMS FARM

Two weeks had passed since Devin left. She'd shed more tears in the past few weeks than in her entire life.

But it had been worth it. Because now she knew the truth.

Devin Schmitt was the best thing that had ever happened to her. Not only his friendship, and not only his speaking truth into her last month . . . but his unconditional love for her.

His honesty.

His fierce loyalty.

His knack for pushing back with her and making her think.

She asked herself over and over why she hadn't paid more attention to that all these years. But now, after several prayer sessions with Mary and a good deal of time in the Word, she was ready.

Ready to cast aside all her fears and fully trust in the Lord.

Even though every day was a struggle.

Even though, every day, she wished she could talk to Devin. Tell him what was in her heart.

And even though, most of the time, she struggled for words to express what she felt.

Despite all that, she would no longer deny she loved him. And was, as a matter of fact, *in* love with him.

Just the thought brought a smile to her heart.

It was time to send him a long letter. If she could only get the words right. She preferred to tell him in person . . . but that would be weeks away.

When her commitment here to Carnegie for the summer came to an end, she would tell her wonderful boss that she preferred returning to the museum. But in the time she had left here, she would grow and trust the Lord to help her conquer her fears and insecurities.

Stepping back onto the porch, she stared out at the sunset. Tomorrow promised to be hot and full of visitors since the men at the quarry directed the ones who weren't satisfied to wait for her direction. She didn't mind. That was, after all, why she was out here. Perhaps she should go to bed early and catch up from all the sleepless nights.

She turned and walked in the door. The house was quiet, so she slipped up the stairs to her room.

Under the door, an envelope was tucked there.

She picked it up and smiled when she saw Devin's handwriting. He'd followed through with his promise to write her. Even with her lack of correspondence to him. Goodness, she wasn't good enough for him.

She went into her room and closed the door as she ripped into the envelope.

Dear Eliza,

I hope you are doing well. Dad sends his love to you.

I returned back to work to find a mountain of paperwork waiting for me. I should have known. But it has kept me busy.

Leaving Utah was difficult, but I'm thankful you have people there to pray with you and guide you. Scripture is clear that older women and older men should help to guide the younger women and younger men, but rarely do we see that in action anymore. I think that church family will be a great one for you for a long time. I'm so happy for you.

Since I challenged you to follow your passions and abandon your fears, I decided it was only fair that I do the same thing. I can't give you all the details yet, but you can be praying for me.

Dad and I are doing well, we've gotten back into our usual rhythm of life.

He went on about the new classes he would be teaching and the new organization of the department. Funny, in the past, she hadn't paid as much attention to the details of his work, but now she found them fascinating.

She finished his letter and placed it on her small desk. She sat in the chair and stared out the window, wanting to write him back. But something Mary had said earlier kept coming back to mind.

"What are you striving for?"

Eliza hadn't understood at first, but Mary continued to push until she did.

For so long, Eliza had thought she'd taken the apostle Paul's approach and had been content in whatever circumstances she was in. But Mary confronted her on that.

Eliza *hadn't* been content. She'd been passionate about her work, yes, but she'd been searching and longing and striving for something else. Thinking she hadn't achieved what she was supposed to.

As she and Mary talked, she told her that she'd written dozens of papers. She'd studied for years. She had a degree in paleontology, for goodness' sake. Plus she'd earned the position at the Carnegie Museum and now was out here at Dinosaur National Monument . . .

And even as she talked, she finally understood.

It was all striving.

Because she was so afraid of failing. And because she was striving over and over . . .

She wasn't content.

If she had been content, she would have continued on no matter what naysayers said. She would've plopped her own name on those papers and been content with whatever God wanted to do with them.

She would have trusted Him. And His love for her—

Oh.

His love. For her.

She leaned back in the chair, closing her eyes. *Is that it, Lord?* She waited, and the confirmation rang through her heart and soul.

This was what Mary had been trying to get through her thick skull. Eliza was afraid, yes. But not just of failure. Or being alone.

She was afraid of love.

No . . . she was afraid of not *deserving* love. God's love. And then . . . Devin's.

She stood and tried to catch her breath.

She'd thought all these years that the *something missing* was something she hadn't found yet. Something she needed to search for, or research, or study.

But it was right in front of her the entire time.

Taking deep breaths, she worked to calm her heart. She'd

love nothing more than to run to Mary and tell her the epiphany she'd just had. But it was getting late.

Eliza plopped back in the chair and picked up her pen.

No. These words shouldn't be written in a letter to Devin. She needed to tell him face-to-face.

But she wrote them down anyway, just for herself.

I am loved by God.

Wholly. Completely. Unconditionally.

She couldn't help but laugh with the joy bubbling out of her. And in that moment . . .

Her heart cracked open wide.

God. *Loved.* Her.

And He gave her Devin. Her best friend. Her constant support.

Her beloved.

She *loved* him. And now she knew God had given him to her to share life and faith with.

Laughter bubbled out of her again. No wonder she extracted that promise from him all those years ago! She must have known in her soul that without Devin, she wasn't who God intended her to be. He completed her. She completed him. God made them to love each other.

Thank You, Lord. Thank You for helping me finally see.

She. Loved. Devin.

FRIDAY, AUGUST 4, 1916 • PITTSBURGH

The loud banging at the front door had Devin rubbing at his eyes as he threw on his bathrobe and rushed to answer it. He peered out the small window in the top of the door.

There stood the same man who'd summoned him to Mills Manor when Mr. Mills had passed.

He opened the door. "Good morning." His voice croaked, and he ran a hand through his hair.

"Good morning, Mr. Schmitt. Mrs. Mills requests that you take breakfast with her this morning, if that is amenable to you."

Wait. What? Had he heard the man correctly? "She wants me to eat breakfast . . . with her?" Was he dreaming?

The man smiled and nodded. "Mrs. Mills also apologizes for the early summons. But it is most important."

The words finally penetrated his sleep-addled brain. "Oh! Yes. What time is she expecting me?"

"Twenty minutes?" The man pointed behind him to a motor car. "I'll be glad to drive you as soon as you are ready."

Devin blinked. Mrs. Mills ate breakfast at six a.m.? Didn't the wealthy sleep in and have breakfast at their leisure? "I'll be right out." He closed the door and rushed back down the hall. No time to waste. He tapped on Dad's door—the man could sleep through a tornado. When he didn't answer, Devin went back to the kitchen and wrote a note in large letters so his father would be able to read it.

In record time, he showered, shaved, dressed, and was out the door with just a few minutes to spare.

On the short drive, he worked to rid his brain of the cobwebs that had taken up residence while he slept. What would Mrs. Mills request of him this time? It didn't matter. For Eliza's sake, as long as it was in his power, he would help her grandmother.

The driver parked the car and opened the door for Devin.

He took the front steps two at a time and the butler opened the door before he could knock. "This way, sir." The man bowed.

Devin followed him into the morning room. A gorgeous and airy room painted yellow on two walls and full of windows on the other two.

Eliza's grandmother sat at the table.

"Good morning, Mrs. Mills." He bowed. Was his suit wrinkled? He hadn't even thought to check.

"Good morning, Devin." Her smile was bright. "Please have a seat."

The butler pulled out a chair for him, and he sat. A huge plate was taken from the warmer and placed in front of him.

"Would you bless the meal, please?" Mrs. Mills raised an eyebrow at him.

He cleared his throat and bowed his head. "Father God, we thank You for this bounty before us. Bless this time together. In Jesus's name, amen."

"Thank you, dear." She began to fill her plate as the servants came around the table with different dishes.

He did the same, but it was difficult to think about food knowing that there was something important coming. Devin placed his napkin in his lap and picked up one of the three forks in front of him, praying it was the correct one.

"You're probably wondering why I asked you to come today." Mrs. Mills glanced at him.

He chuckled when he saw the sparkle in her eyes. "The thought crossed my mind, yes, ma'am."

She took a bite of her quiche and then took a sip of juice. "I've been doing a great deal of thinking since my husband passed. God rest his soul."

"Oh?" His stomach rumbled. Might as well enjoy the incredible food in front of him. The first bite of quiche practically melted on his tongue. What was in this glorious concoction?

"You see, I'm the one who insisted that my husband ask you to make that promise to him all those years ago."

He swallowed, and it plummeted to his stomach like a brick. He set his fork down and picked up his juice glass. Nerves prickled his skin. Was he about to be told to stay away from her again? For good?

"I could tell that you adored Eliza, and I was concerned."

The warmth in the woman's eyes made him bold. "Concerned I wouldn't treat her well?"

"Heavens, no. I knew you'd loved our girl from a young age. You've always been a man of integrity. But . . . my father and my husband's father were both men of the old regime. Money ruled all. There was no mixing of the classes. Old money trumped new money, and new money trumped no money."

"Funny, your husband said something like that to me that day." No matter how good the food was, he wasn't about to eat anything else. He couldn't. He waited for whatever Mrs. Mills had to say.

Mrs. Mills placed her fork on her plate and waved for the servants to leave them. She focused her gaze on Devin. "Over the years, I've watched my granddaughter flourish in her pursuit of paleontology. But she has never *once* shown any interest in any man we tried to introduce her to. She never truly enjoyed all the balls and galas—even though we made her go. You were the only one she shared her life with other than us. You were her best friend, and we respected that.

"But last year, my husband began to try and convince me that perhaps we had been wrong and a bit judgmental. Your father is one of the finest men we know. As are you. You hold my Eliza's heart, even if she doesn't realize it."

What? He leaned back in his chair.

"A bit shocked, are you?" She seemed amused. "Eat your food, son, I promise I won't bite."

What on earth was happening here? Devin sat up straight and picked up his fork out of respect but wasn't sure he could swallow anything until he knew for sure what Mrs. Mills was saying.

"I don't care about money. Eliza will inherit enough money to care for generation upon generation beyond her. If you two don't wish to live here, that's fine. If you want to continue as the English department head, that's fine too." She paused and raised a hand to her chest, mindlessly toying with the string of pearls around her neck. "If Eliza wants to work in the museum for the rest of her life, or if she chooses to wear pants and dig in the dirt, I won't stand in her way."

He took another sip of juice and prayed it would go down. "Ma'am, I'm a bit confused." But hope sprang alive like a well within him.

"Let me be quite blunt."

Devin straightened and looked Eliza's grandmother in the eye. "Yes, ma'am."

She smiled at him, and Devin was struck at the strong resemblance between the woman and Eliza. His heart ached. How he missed her. "You are released from your vow."

What did she just say? His heart seemed to stop for a moment.

Mrs. Mills continued. "Eliza's grandfather and I both knew that you are the man for our girl. The way you have loved her and stood by her all these years is a credit to the man that you are."

His lungs released as if they'd been bound up for years. "Thank you, ma'am." He stared at his plate and was all of a sudden ravenous. Picking up his fork for the third time, he hesitated, his thoughts in a jumble. Even with Mrs. Mills's blessing, there was no guarantee Eliza felt the same way about him. Sure, there had been glimpses of something more in Utah. Yet some of her last words were about what a good friend he was. He said as much to Mrs. Mills.

"I do love Eliza, Mrs. Mills. But I don't think she cares for me the same way. She's never said—"

"Let me stop you right there." She held up a hand and her smile became . . . mischievous. "She loves you, Devin. I know my granddaughter. She may not even admit it to herself because her grandfather instilled in her from a very young age to keep a fierce guard on her heart. She always took whatever

238

he said to be written in stone." Her wistful expression was beautiful. "But rest assured. She loves you. That's why there has never been anyone else."

Mrs. Mills took a sip of water and licked her lips. "Now that we've solved that . . . what are we going to do about this mess with the museum?"

seventeen

"Am anxious for the evening to come, so I can continue working out the puzzle."

~Earl Douglass

SATURDAY, AUGUST 5, 1916 • MEYER RANCH

The sun beat down on Eliza's back through her long work shirt. What she wouldn't give for a good, strong breeze. Unfortunately, the air was stagnant and just plain hot.

As much as she loved retrieving a fossilized bone from its resting place, when the heat made it hard to breathe—and sent sweat trickling down her face, neck, and back—she'd rather be back inside the museum.

Back home she'd loved educating people at the museum and putting together activities and plans to get families fascinated with the great beasts. She also loved talking to those visiting the quarry about the incredible work they were doing. If she had to choose between the actual excavation and teaching others about it . . . well, she couldn't decide.

At least out here in the quiet of the ranch, she had time to think. How was she to talk with Devin about her feelings for him? Women of society weren't usually encouraged to share their love with a suitor.

But . . . he *had* shared with her first. That made a difference, didn't it? Oh! How she longed to tell him.

And ever since her heart began to blossom toward Devin, her longing for love and family blossomed as well. She grinned. What would Devin's response be to *that*?

She sat back on her heels. Whew! Was it possible the air was even hotter now?

She giggled. No, but it was possible her thoughts made it seem so.

She wiped her hands on her dungarees, leaned down, and blew on the fossil she'd been meticulously chiseling at for the past hour. Then she brushed away all the loose pieces of rock and dirt and studied it. This one was proving difficult to get out.

Taking a sip of water, she leaned back on her heels again and looked up at the cloudless sky.

Mary had encouraged her to take her time determining how to share her feelings. To pray. And only then to share her feelings in a letter to Devin.

Eliza had started a letter at least ten times. Pouring out her heart and soul in flowery sentences and hoping that he would appreciate her effort.

But he knew her better than anyone else.

Devin would expect honesty, *not* flowery words.

She lifted her broad straw hat and ran a hand over her hair. Perhaps it would be better to tell him in person. What if, by the time she returned to Pittsburgh, he had followed through with his idea of courting someone else?

That thought was enough to make her want to hop on a train home today. But she'd made a commitment to Deborah and Mr. Douglass. She couldn't leave now.

The work here was rewarding. But the longer she stayed, the more she knew she was supposed to return to Pittsburgh. Prayerfully, after everything that had happened, Mr. Carnegie still had her position at the museum available. She really couldn't wait to get back to it.

Perhaps she had finally found what she was supposed to do.

Oh, and wouldn't it be nice to be back in the city! To visit Rufaloe's. And perhaps purchase a new hat or two. Of the smaller variety.

She giggled and peace flowed through her heart. Yes. It was the right decision. As much as she loved the quarry and this new discovery here, she couldn't wait to get back to shops and activities. And most of all, Devin.

She missed him. It seemed like every moment of every day.

Maybe after she was done here today, she should simply go back to her room and write him a short letter. And why not? Why shouldn't they correspond over the last weeks she was here? Or, if she bared her heart, then they could both look forward to their reunion.

Footsteps sounded to her right and she lifted her face to her visitor.

"Miss Mills. I'm sorry to intrude, but I was told I could find you here." Gregory, one of the workers at the quarry, tipped his hat to her and then removed it. Another man stood behind him.

"Good morning, Gregory." She brushed some more loose fragments away from the fossil. "It's a scorcher today, isn't it?"

"Indeed it is, miss." He chuckled and pointed to her denim-covered legs. "I told my wife that you often liked to dig in a pair of men's pants, and she said she couldn't blame you. The heat must be intolerable in all the layers you women wear."

She glanced up at him with a laugh. "And skirts can make it difficult and sometimes even life threatening to dig, depending on the location." She shrugged. "I guess we all have to evolve to get the job done."

"Very true, miss." His hat was in his hands.

She studied him for a moment. "Is there something else you needed?"

He twisted his hat. "I was wondering . . ." He looked down at his feet.

"Yes?"

"I was wondering if you would talk to our daughter one day? She's nine and loves what we're doing out here." He scuffed the dirt with his boot for a moment, then looked back at Eliza. "My wife was a bit concerned at first about her being so fixated on paleontology, but the more we talked about it, the more we realized that you could be a good example to her." He raised his eyebrows.

She recognized the pleading in the man's eyes. Most of these workers didn't have a lot when it came to monetary wealth. "I imagine you're wanting your daughter to have the best opportunities for her future. I would love to speak with her about paleontology."

His face relaxed into a big smile. "Oh, thank you, Miss Mills. We are grateful to give her this chance to pursue her dreams."

"You're welcome."

"I'll have my wife speak with you about when is a good time."

"I look forward to it. But I will only be here for a few more weeks."

He plopped his hat back on his head, nodded, and walked away.

Eliza took up her chisel again and smiled at the fossil. God had given her another reminder that she was using her gifts for Him.

No more striving. No more discontent. She could step forward in the joy of knowing that she had a purpose. And no matter what she did, she would do it to the best of her ability for the glory of God.

"What are you doing here?"

The quiet voice made Eliza jerk and she fell on her backside as she turned toward the sound. With a hand to her heart, she found Mrs. Friedman standing there. "Gracious, you gave me a fright."

The slight woman smiled. "I'm so sorry. I wasn't expecting to find anyone here."

"Your brother gave us permission to dig up these fossils. The sheriff did as well, after your brother was arrested." Eliza swallowed. "I'm so sorry about that, by the way. Your brother always seemed like such a nice man to me."

She put a hand over her mouth and several seconds passed before she spoke. "Thank you. This has been extremely difficult. But it's been good to hear there are people who believe in him."

The poor woman! "Is there anything I can help you with? Did you need something while you were out here? I know it's pretty abandoned."

She shook her head. "No. I simply promised Lucas that I would check on things as often as I could."

"That's understandable." She stared down at the tools in her hands. What else should she say? Should she give her condolences for the loss of her husband?

"It was good to see you, Miss Mills. Thank you for your great kindness to my brother. I hope the fossils are all you imagined and more." The smile didn't reach her eyes, but the woman had lived through so much hardship and grief, Eliza wasn't surprised.

"Thank you. You are most welcome."

The woman walked through the long grass back toward the ranch house.

An hour later, Eliza couldn't take the heat anymore. Time

to ride back to the Adams's home for a reprieve until Deborah came. Swinging up into the saddle, she patted the horse's neck for a moment, then urged it into a gallop.

When she walked in the door, Mrs. Adams was kneading bread dough on the butcher block in the middle of her kitchen.

Red-faced and smiling, her hostess greeted her. "It shouldn't take long for the bread to rise in this heat, should it?"

Eliza went to the washbasin and washed her hands. "Here, let me give you a bit of a break." She stepped up beside the woman and watched her movements. It didn't look that difficult.

One of Mrs. Adams's eyebrows rose while her lips twitched. "Have you ever kneaded bread before?"

Eliza laughed. "No. But at least allow me to give it a try." The next quarter of an hour was filled with her chatting with her hostess and learning the special techniques of kneading dough.

When Mr. Carnegie had offered her this position at the monument, she'd made sure that he knew she didn't want any special treatment. And while this lovely home was much better than living in a tent, it was much different from anything she'd ever experienced. It had been good to see the way this family cared for one another and pitched in to make a home and life together.

"Not bad, Eliza. I'm impressed. Most women who've never done such a chore don't have the arm strength."

Eliza curtseyed in her pants and long work shirt. "Thank you very much. It must be all the time I've spent digging in the dirt for bones."

"Thank you for your help. I'm sure you're anxious to get back to your fossils." The woman glided around her kitchen, preparing other dishes for dinner and humming as she worked.

Eliza left the room. What did the Adams family really think of her? The daughters had been wide-eyed several times when

Eliza came down the stairs dressed in her regular clothing and one of her big hats. She'd tried to bring the plainest and sturdiest of her clothes, but apparently, they were still a bit fancy for this area of the West.

But every time she went to work in her pants, Mrs. Adams seemed a bit . . . uncomfortable.

Still, they'd never spoken a cross word to her. Even with all the danger and drama she'd brought into their lives. Perhaps a nice gift would be a good way to end her time here. She would think of a way to thank them for their hospitality.

She made her way up the stairs to her room and fanned herself. Even though her window was open, there still wasn't any breeze and it was stifling.

Opting for a washcloth and hoping there was some cooler water in the basin, she wiped away as much of the dirt from her face and neck as she could. The clock on the dresser showed that she still had an hour before Deborah would be back out at the ranch to help dig.

She went to her desk and looked at her correspondence and her Bible. Mary had been meeting with her twice a week for prayer and had become a friend. Eliza hadn't had many female friends until she'd gone to university and then to work for the museum. But Mary made it easy and shared many Scriptures with her about how women were to be there for one another. Especially the older guiding the younger, just as Devin had mentioned in his letter.

They'd been making a list together of all the different ways Eliza could use the gifts God had given her.

What a wonder that God could use her simple gifts in so many ways. That He used each and every believer in unique and wonderful ways.

The hair on the back of her neck bristled all of a sudden, and she whirled around.

Louise stood in the doorway, a scowl on her face.

"What's wrong?"

The girl didn't answer, just spun on her heel and stomped down the hall.

~

TUESDAY, AUGUST 8, 1916 • CARNEGIE INSTITUTE

Devin paced outside Andrew Carnegie's office. He'd left a message with the secretary *days* ago only to find out that the philanthropist was out of town. So much had happened since then, he wanted to meet with the man and then rearrange his schedule so he could get back out to see Eliza as soon as possible.

When he'd gotten word this morning to come in for an appointment, he'd canceled everything.

Eliza's reputation was on the line, and he was going to do everything in his power to help her. Whoever was behind this was doing an elaborate job.

The ornate wood door opened and Mr. Carnegie himself stood there. "Mr. Schmitt, please come in."

Devin wasted no time and headed straight for the man. He shook his hand. "Thank you for seeing me, Mr. Carnegie."

The door closed behind him and then Carnegie walked around his desk. "Please. Have a seat."

"Thank you, sir." He sat, but it was hard to stay still.

Carnegie folded his hands on the desk in front of him. "You left a message that this was urgent about your friend Miss Mills."

"Yes, sir." Devin immediately went into the details of the phone call he'd received from a secretary at the museum. "I knew I had to come see you as soon as possible. Sir, I've known Eliza—Miss Mills—almost my entire life. She would never steal anything from the museum or from donors. I am aware that you were close friends with her grandfather, so you know

247

her integrity as well. I don't know who is out to destroy her reputation, but it must be stopped."

He hadn't meant to get so worked up in his speech, but he lowered his voice and kept eye contact with the man who held Eliza's fate in his hands. "I promise you, sir, I will help you do whatever it takes to get to the bottom of this and clear Eliza's name."

Mr. Carnegie leaned back in his chair, his eyes narrowed, and then he drummed the desk with his fingers. "I heard that there were missing fossils and donor money unaccounted for, but I hadn't heard any of these rumors." He narrowed his eyes. "Eliza's grandfather was a friend of mine for years, God rest his soul. And I've known Eliza from childhood. I don't think for a second that she could be responsible."

"You don't?"

"No." A thin smile showed through his facial hair. "But since I just returned to Pittsburgh to check on things, I do believe that I need to handle this situation myself."

"You do?" His shoulders relaxed. He'd expected to have to fight for Eliza.

The man nodded and he drummed his fingers on the desk again. "I don't like having dishonest people in my employ. Whoever started the rumors is probably behind the thefts as well. Someone eager to have the blame and focus on another person." His lips pinched together. "After the fiasco with someone impersonating Dr. Masterson, I must say that I am concerned. In my gut, I believe it to be the same person."

That made sense. "That would take a fair bit of planning on their part, sir. Do you think they had help?"

"I would imagine. Smearing Eliza every which way he or she can, both here *and* in Utah, would mean several people are involved. But why? To come after me? Or simply to ruin her?" His voice had taken on a darker tone the longer he spoke.

Devin wouldn't want to be the recipient of the fury building in this man.

He met Devin's gaze again. "Thank you for coming to me. Rest assured, I will handle it."

"Thank you, sir." Well . . . now what? Nervous energy had built up inside him every time he thought about Sarah's phone call, and here he didn't even have to convince Mr. Carnegie of Eliza's innocence. He stood. "Will you let me know, sir, when things are corrected?"

"Yes, I will make sure to do that." Mr. Carnegie stood as well. "Eliza is fortunate to have a friend like you, Mr. Schmitt."

They shook hands once again, and Devin found his way out of the office. On the way home, he wound through the streets of the city he loved so much. But he would give all this up if it meant that he could be with Eliza.

By the time he returned home, Devin had come to a solid conclusion.

He was going out to Dinosaur National Monument and declaring his love for her. Again. As soon as possible. Too much time had been wasted as it was.

When he walked in the door, he stopped abruptly, as his dad stood there. "It's a telegram for you."

A telegram? He couldn't recall the last time he'd received one. Devin ripped into the envelope and pulled out the paper.

Need your assistance in the investigation. Please call as soon as possible.

Sheriff Jensen

"Is it Eliza? Is she all right?" Dad's eyes were filled with concern.

Devin shook his head. "I don't know. I hope so. But it's not from her. It's from the sheriff."

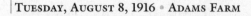

Eliza bounded down the stairs. She was *so* close to retrieving the first fossil out of the rock bed on the ranch! It was always an exhilarating feeling, and she couldn't wait for Deborah to experience it.

"This came for you." Louise stiffly handed her an envelope. The girl hadn't smiled at her since Devin left.

Eliza put on her biggest smile, determined not to let the young woman get to her. "Thank you."

Once she was outside and loaded up her horse, she took the moment to open the envelope and read.

> *Everyone has to evolve? Is that what kind of "Scriptural truth" you are spreading with your work? Haven't you caused enough trouble in this town? Go home, Miss Mills. Before something worse happens.*

Eliza wadded up the paper and shoved it into the saddle bag with a grunt. Obviously, the judgmental church ladies weren't going to give up until she left.

Well, it wouldn't be too long before she was gone. Let them spew their hate. She wasn't hurting anyone by digging up fossils. She was helping to educate people. Bringing history to life.

She shook off the nasty way the letter made her feel and mounted her horse.

Today was going to be a wonderful day.

But as she rode, her mood kept turning foul.

Everyone has to evolve . . .

When had she said that? And to whom?

Lord, why can't I get that letter out of my thoughts? Why do people hate me so much?

It made her want to lash out and call them all ugly names—

Oh dear. This would not do.

"God, sometimes I wonder why You put up with me. But I'm grateful You do. I'm angry and upset about that letter. Goodness, I know You probably are too since this has to do with You. But You're God and I'm not. I'm facing a mighty big giant. I know You're on my side. I know that. But I need You—I'm asking You—to banish this fear. Help me to have clear answers for whoever might venture out and have questions today. Help me to be gracious and to show Your love—especially when I don't want to. I need Your words. Your peace. Your strength. And the power to shut my mouth if I need to. Lord . . . help."

She reined the horse to a stop and just waited. Listening.

Not much stirred the silence. But within her, peace stirred and grew. She drew in the Lord's presence.

"Okay then. Let's face whatever happens. Even if they call me an evolutionist and a God hater. I can do this. Through Him Who gives me strength." She rode to the path leading to the top of the bluff where she had her tent set up.

Today could either be a huge victory or massive disaster. Either way . . .

She wasn't alone.

eighteen

"The country is beautiful now as everything except the
exposed rocks is covered with verdue. There are many
flowers in bloom. I wish I knew the names of them, but
I know but few."

~Earl Douglass

He had often wondered what utter victory tasted like. Today,
it tasted like the rare whiskey at his club, rich and smooth on
his tongue. The amber liquid warmed him from the inside out.

Had he ever felt so happy? Not that he could recall.

Turner and Lincoln had done their jobs exceptionally well.
Better than he anticipated. Eliza Mills was the laughingstock
of the scientific world. The moment was ripe for him to step
into the spotlight and let his peers and leaders see just how
vast his knowledge and expertise were. And just how indebted
they were to him for his brilliant, forward-thinking mind.

He would now become Carnegie's most valuable asset. And he
could hardly wait to let the world know exactly that. Finishing
his whiskey, he stood and strode out of the club. Scanning the
street, he spotted a five-cent jitney car sitting down the street.

Placing his fingers between his lips, he let loose a whistle, high and sharp.

The driver looked up and gave him a nod, driving his black automobile up to the edge of the sidewalk. The balding man poked his head out the window. "Where to, sir?"

"The *Pittsburgh Post-Gazette*." He opened the back door.

The man whistled. "That's clear on the northwest side of town."

He settled in the back seat and glared at the older gentleman. "I'll pay you double if you can get me there in twenty minutes."

Bushy white eyebrows shot up on the driver's wrinkled forehead. "Yes, sir!"

Eighteen minutes later, he was walking up the front steps of the newspaper building. Pushing through the large doors, he entered a room of chaos. Typewriters clacked loudly, cigar smoke hanging in the air.

A young man with slicked-back hair and wire-rimmed glasses nodded from the desk at the front of the room. "What do you want, sir?"

He adjusted his tie and approached the large oak desk. "I need to speak with someone about a scoop of a story with the Carnegie Museum and Mr. Carnegie himself."

The young man gazed at him, dark brown eyes large and unblinking behind his thick glasses. "And who are you?"

"I am a leading scientist at the Carnegie Museum. Here is my card." He slid the rectangular paper across the smooth surface of the desk. "Trust me when I say one of your writers will want the scoop of the year regarding the Dinosaur National Monument, the Carnegie Institute, and skeletons. In the closet and otherwise."

He smirked. Such a clever turn of phrase. He was in rare form today.

"Hmm . . ." The clerk took his card and studied it for a moment.

Oh yes, the interest was there. His pulse thrummed. His rightful recognition was almost in his grasp.

Finally, the wiry young man pushed back from his desk and entered the frenzy of reporters behind him. He walked to a desk in the far-right corner and whispered something in the ear of a man who looked to be about forty, with sandy brown hair and a serious expression.

The two men walked back toward him. The clerk pushed the swinging gate open for the writer with him.

"This is Bradley Hopper. He is our national news writer and has covered many events out at the museum."

"A pleasure to meet you, Mr. Hopper. Might I take you out for a cup of coffee? I promise an afternoon with me will not be wasted. The story I have for you is a scoop to capitalize on the dinosaur mania sweeping our fair country."

"There's a small deli about four blocks from here." Mr. Hopper motioned toward the door. "A good spot to discuss your . . . scoop."

So. The writer was skeptical. Not to worry. By the end of the afternoon, and on the heels of a generous tip for running his story, the article would be queued up for the paper's run the next day.

The next morning, he stepped out of his boardinghouse, a bounce in his step and humming a jaunty tune. The stories couldn't have been better. He pulled the newspaper from under his arm and snapped it to its full length.

Carnegie Museum Scientist Is Real Genius
behind Dinosaur National Monument
Female Paleontologist Steals from Museum

They were beautiful. Mr. Hopper had outdone himself. The articles were perfect. In fact, he had almost memorized them both in their entirety. But his favorite paragraph was the one outlining his spectacular accomplishments in discovering Carnegie's beloved Dippy, his direction to Earl Douglass to dig just a bit farther to the northwest of the quarry, and his prestigious post as the Carnegie Museum's curator.

As curator, Mr. Nelson has brought several popular displays to the Carnegie Institute. Responsible for the discovery of Diplodocus carnegii, fondly known as Dippy, Mr. Nelson launched Andrew Carnegie's dream of paleontological science into the stratosphere. Not only is his Diplodocus carnegii beloved by kings and world rulers alike, it is the cornerstone for the magnificent Hall of Dinosaurs. Conceived by Mr. Nelson's keen oversight and care, the Hall of Dinosaurs is the number-one attraction at the museum. And he only plans to make it bigger and better.

"I am determined to make Carnegie Institute the crown jewel of paleontology," he told this reporter. "And with the discoveries from the Dinosaur National Monument, we will have species of dinosaurs to display for decades to come. I am sure Earl Douglass thanks his lucky stars every day when he remembers it was I who encouraged him to dig just a few hundred yards farther to the northwest in what is now Dinosaur National Monument."

Mr. Hopper had eaten every detail right out of his hand. Nelson almost crowed. It was *he* who had single-handedly changed the face of paleontological science in America. That little Miss Mills was painted as a thief. She'd never work in the field again.

Job offers would start pouring in, giving him leverage with Carnegie to force the man to pay him what he was actually worth.

He would bring more fame and honor to Carnegie than Douglass could ever have dreamed of doing. First, he would drain Carnegie Quarry of every last bone and fossil, ensuring the museum's displays would not only be the largest in the world, but would have his name on each one.

Then they would move all dig operations to Montana and capitalize on several quarries producing various fossils in the Badlands. And from there, who knew what heights he could reach?

Finally, everything was going his way.

~~~~~

FRIDAY, AUGUST 11, 1916 • CARNEGIE INSTITUTE

Mr. Andrew Carnegie sat behind his massive desk and looked up at Devin over the rim of his spectacles. "Thank you, young man."

"You're welcome, sir."

"Had you not come to me about the rumors that were going around, I would have learned about this debacle far too late." He lifted the morning's paper and shook his head. "Mr. Nelson would have covered his tracks, I'm sure. And I would have lost the best preparator and authenticator I've ever had." The older man leaned back in his chair.

"All thanks to one of the secretaries at the museum, sir. Sarah called me because she knew Eliza wasn't guilty. You should thank her as well." Devin stood as straight as he could. This was the second time he'd been in Mr. Carnegie's office, and he still couldn't believe he was here.

Never had he been in the presence of anyone who had so much wealth, nor anyone who'd given so much wealth away. Other than Eliza's family. It was truly impressive.

Carnegie removed his spectacles and smiled at him. "I will make sure to thank Sarah as well as soon as I've dealt"—he poked the paper with his index finger—"with this."

"Thank you, sir."

"Are you sure you won't sit and have lunch with me? I'd love to hear about your work in the English department and your many years of friendship with Eliza."

"As wonderful of an offer as that is, sir, I'd like to get to the train station as soon as possible." Devin glanced at the massive grandfather clock in the corner of the room. If he could finish with Mr. Carnegie in twenty minutes, he'd make the afternoon train with a few minutes to spare.

Carnegie quirked one eyebrow. "Headed west?"

"Yes, sir."

"To a quarry in Utah, might I presume?"

"Yes, sir." Devin tried not to chuckle, but it came out anyway. "Might I ask a favor before I go?"

"Fire away."

"Might I use your telephone? The sheriff in Jensen sent me a telegram asking me to call, and I haven't been able to get through."

"Go right ahead." Mr. Carnegie turned the phone toward him. "And if you or Eliza need my assistance in any way, I'm ready to help."

"Thank you, sir." Devin didn't waste any time putting in the call with the operator. This was the part that took a while, if the call could make all the connections. When the sheriff answered, Devin breathed a sigh. "Sheriff, this is Devin Schmitt. I received your telegram."

As the man gave him the rundown, Devin nodded and lifted his shoulders. "I'll be on the next train, sir."

<hr />

Saturday, August 12, 1916 • Jensen

That female paleontologist was ruining everything again.

She'd probably found the painted rock, her special marker, and took it. Made it part of her silly fossil collection.

All it did was make finding her box of gold much more difficult.

To make things worse, that woman was back at the ranch digging for fossils again. Why hadn't all that stopped when Lucas Meyer was arrested? Most of the workers had left—it had been perfect.

She should have been able to get out there and follow the map in peace. As it was, it would probably take her a good week to find it all, dig it up, and cart it off.

Now Miss Mills's presence was delaying that even more.

But what could she do?

She paced the hallway and chewed on her thumbnail.

After several passes, the only solution stared her straight in the face.

She'd have to do it.

It was the only way she could leave with the gold. She wasn't about to give up now.

What was one more death to achieve her dream?

Monday, August 14, 1916 • Dinosaur National Monument

Finally. The quarry was open to visitors again, one day a week.

Eliza was excited to get back out there and speak to people. Much easier out there at the monument, which people really wanted to see. And if anyone asked her about the newspaper article and the papers she wrote, God would help her handle it. As He'd helped her when a man in town stopped her at the hardware store to point out that scientists were always arguing with one another so why should anyone believe them?

His logic pained her.

She'd worked with other paleontologists for years. Yes, she disagreed with several of them on different issues. But they'd all agreed to disagree and focus on the work.

However . . . now that she thought about it, her family's wealth was well known. As was the fact that their money often funded whatever dig she'd been on.

Could that have kept people from saying anything negative in front of her until the chaos this summer? Had someone been jealous of her and over the years formed a plan against her?

She hated to even think it, but that was the way of the world, wasn't it?

It was a wonder Mr. Carnegie had believed in her like he did.

With a deep breath and a prayer for wisdom and strength, she went to the visitor tent.

Time to put on her best smile and welcome them.

"Good morning." She prayed no one would be divisive or argumentative. But as the group moved toward her, she noticed there were two young girls present. Dressed in their finest, even in the hot landscape of the quarry. Their eyes sparkled.

Now *there* was a look she knew well. Eagerness to learn.

A fresh wave of energy rushed through her.

It didn't matter what mean-minded people said, there were so many others passionate to discover the truth. And if she could point some to the Creator, that's what it was all about, right?

She motioned the two young girls forward and gave them each a fossil to hold.

Mesmerized, the girls stared, eyes glowing.

Smiles lit the adults' faces.

"Thank you for coming out to Carnegie's quarry at Dinosaur National Monument. Who's ready to talk about dinosaurs?"

———— ⁓ ————

WEDNESDAY, AUGUST 16, 1916 • MEYER RANCH

"Miss Mills?"

Eliza started. The young kid from the telegraph office was beside her.

Wow, she must have really been focused on the fossil she'd been attempting to pull from the rock for the last hour. She hadn't even heard him approach. "Good morning." She smiled and got to her feet.

"I've got another telegram for you. Mr. Clarence wanted me to apologize. It should have been delivered a while back. Somehow it fell behind the counter."

"Oh, thank you for bringing it to me." She took it and smiled at him, handing him a coin. Hopefully it wasn't anything of great consequence.

He rushed off without another word.

Eliza slid her finger under the flap of the envelope and pulled out the sheet of paper. Dated more than ten days ago.

Someone spreading rumors. Accused you of stealing fossils and donor money. Called Mr. Schmitt for help. Sarah

What!? Who would do such a thing? Sweat broke out across her back, making her shirt stick to her. Where was a cool breeze when she needed one? Fanning herself with the envelope and paper, she tried to calm her breathing. What did Mr. Carnegie think? Would he believe it? She hadn't heard anything from him in a while. Her stomach plummeted. Oh, this was terrible. And she wasn't even there to defend herself? What was she supposed to do?

Taking a deep breath, she paced. She had to think this through.

What were her options?

If she rushed back, would they believe her? Or would trying to defend herself simply make them think she was more guilty? Especially in light of the horrible article by the imposter. Would that previous article make people assume she *was* guilty?

A woman in this day and age didn't exactly have the same clout as a man. No matter what her last name was.

At least Sarah had called Devin. She hated dragging him into something else, but he would defend her. In her heart, she knew he would. But he hadn't said a word about it either. Why?

She tapped the envelope against her hand as she continued to stomp her frustrations out into the desert-like terrain.

Deborah had gone off in search of the outhouse near the cattle shed, which meant Eliza could growl out her frustrations to the sky without being heard.

She marched through the grass, mumbling under her breath. There had to be something—*any*thing—she could do.

But Pittsburgh was a world away.

She had no idea who her accuser was.

And she had no control. No idea what was happening. No solution whatsoever.

Wadding up the telegram, she released a scream to the sky. When that didn't help, she stomped around some more. *Why, God? Why?*

Eliza buried her face in her hands, trying to stem the tears. Again. But an ominous click made her freeze in her tracks.

Was that . . . a gun?

"Turn around slowly, Miss Mills, and your friend won't get hurt."

nineteen

"Bitterness and despair rolled away and left me happy again."

~Earl Douglass

WEDNESDAY, AUGUST 16, 1916 • CARNEGIE INSTITUTE

Was it normal for giddiness to last this long? He didn't know and he didn't care. The article had accomplished everything he intended it to do.

People were looking at him differently now. Asking his opinion. Seeking him out for direction with various displays at the museum. It was only a matter of time before Mr. Carnegie visited him and they could sit down and renegotiate his contract. Even the great steel magnate should be able to see he'd be a fool to let him go now. Not without destroying the reputation of his beloved museum.

He picked up the newspaper outside his office and tucked it under his arm. With a few clicks, he unlocked the massive wooden door and strolled to his desk. In short order, the rough draft of his new paper on the profitability and sustainability of natural history museums and their contributions to the well-being of American culture was spread on his desk.

If he was to truly make his mark in paleontology, he had to show that their science had to be a money-making enterprise. Now that they knew the plains and mountains out West were rife with fossils, it was time to start capitalizing on their vast monetary value.

Pulling up his chair, he frowned. Where was his fountain pen? Shuffling papers and peeking under folders, he searched and searched. Picking up the newspaper, he spotted it beneath . . .

He froze.

What did that headline say?

Dread prickled along his skin. With slow movements, he unfolded the paper and read.

Carnegie Denounces Fraud Curator—"Earl Douglass Is the Real Genius"

Blood roared in his ears. What on earth was this? He scanned the article, all feeling draining from his body.

No. It couldn't be possible. How could Andrew Carnegie do this to *him* of all people? After he'd sacrificed his life to make sure that stupid Hall of Dinosaurs was the ultimate shrine to the massive beasts. Slaving away to make sure the museum was a success.

A sharp rap at his door made him jump. But he didn't have time to give permission to enter before two police officers pushed their way into his office, their faces grim.

"Mr. Nelson?"

"What do you want? I didn't do anything wrong!"

One police officer moved toward his desk. "We have signed witness statements from two scientists and a journalist that say you bribed them to smear the reputation of one Miss Eliza Mills. And to print a profile on you that is factually untrue."

He pushed his chair back. This wasn't happening. It couldn't be! "You have no proof! You've got nothing on me! I was acting on the orders of Mr. Carnegie himself!"

The other policeman let out a dry chuckle and slipped around the left-hand side of his desk. "Sure you were. No use in fighting us. We have plenty of proof. You are under arrest for unlawful bribery and criminal menacing." The officer leaned closer, his low voice rumbling in Nelson's ear. "They're also investigating you in the fraud and impersonation of a Dr. Masterson."

No! He wrested one arm from the officer's grip. "I have proof. *Proof!* Look, look . . ." He fumbled through the papers on his desk. Where were those notes? Aha! He scooped up the small slips of paper and shoved them at the policeman. "Here! Direct orders from Mr. Carnegie. I acted in his stead."

The officer took the papers, an eyebrow raised high on his forehead. He shuffled through the messages, then looked at Nelson, his gaze hard. "Is this a joke?" He glanced back down. "'Please order more brass name plates for displays.'"

"See? He wanted me to order new brass name plates so that we could correct the information on them. They should have *my* name on them. *I'm* the genius behind their discovery."

The officer blinked at him, then flipped to the next note. "'I will be out of the office on Tuesday and Wednesday. —C'"

"Exactly!" What was wrong with these imbeciles? "Clearly, he wanted me to take action while he was gone. To show initiative. That's what Mr. Carnegie expects of a good leader."

"But that's not what it says." The officer looked down on him—as if he were a child—and held up the note.

Fool! Cretin! "You don't know Mr. Carnegie like I do."

The officer shook his head. "There is nothing here that shows Mr. Carnegie had anything to do with the crimes of which you are accused. He didn't instruct you to do it. You did that all in your own wild mind."

Nelson snatched the papers back. "Just you wait until Mr. Carnegie hears about your treatment of me. I will—"

"Mr. Nelson!"

Andrew Carnegie's voice cut across the room. The small Scotsman stood in the doorway as the other officer grabbed Nelson's arm.

Nelson straightened, fighting against the officer's painful grip. He waved his fistful of papers toward his employer. "See? Mr. Carnegie is here to defend me. Yes, he left the note letting me know of his absence." He glanced at Mr. Carnegie with a grin. "That's when I knew, sir. I *knew* you wanted me to take charge. Show my initiative. Prove I am worthy to run your glorious institute. And I have!"

Mr. Carnegie strode across the thick Persian rug and stood before the desk. He leaned forward and pressed his fingertips onto the shiny oak surface. But his voice, when he spoke, was calm.

And ice cold.

"Are you ill, Mr. Nelson?"

The same strange look that had been on the officer's face now filled Carnegie's.

Nelson straightened his jacket and lifted his shoulders. "I am perfectly fine, *sir*." Why was he kowtowing to this man? They had no idea who they were dealing with.

Carnegie straightened. "It will take a professional to diagnose if there is something wrong with your mind." He glanced at the officers, who nodded. What were they nodding about? Was this a conspiracy? They were *all* out to get him!

Carnegie's gaze came back to him. "But regardless, you, sir, will cease making a scene in my institute. As of this moment, you are fired and barred from ever walking these hallowed premises again. And if, indeed, you are fine, as you say, not only will you be prosecuted for your crimes, but I will ask the judge to ensure any sentence you receive includes a written apology to Dr. Masterson, Earl Douglass, and Eliza Mills for the damage you've done to each of them with your lies."

Nelson clenched his jaw. So. This explained it all.

The great man was mad!

"That woman will *never* get an apology from m—"

The officers grabbed his hands, wrenching them behind his back and snapping handcuffs on him.

"Don't you touch me! This is all a gross misunderstanding. You can't *do* this to me." He writhed against the cold metal digging into his wrists.

Ignoring his protests, the two officers gripped his biceps and shoved him forward, cutting him off from any further response.

No matter. He would have his day in court. That would be the day Andrew Carnegie would regret thinking he could ever defeat him.

⁓

WEDNESDAY, AUGUST 16, 1916 ∙ JENSEN

This was not what Devin had planned.

He thought he'd get off the train, go see the sheriff, and then spend the evening with Eliza and ask her if she loved him. If she said yes, he'd propose.

Simple.

But no one knew where she was.

Mr. Hawkins went straight to the sheriff after he'd gone to tell his wife that her mother was ill. But Deborah hadn't been at the dig site. Neither had Eliza. Tools were scattered about, and neither one of them ever left their tools unattended.

Devin paced the sheriff's station as they gathered the deputies and men from town to help in the search.

One of the deputies raced up. "Sheriff! Herb said that he'd delivered a telegram to Eliza."

"How long ago? And *where*?" The sheriff's thunderous voice revealed his aggravation that they'd been a few hours too late to catch whoever kidnapped those women.

"Almost six, sir. He delivered it at the Meyer ranch."

"All right, men." The sheriff climbed on a chair and looked at each man in the room. "We'll start by combing every inch of that ranch. Lucas Meyer will be with me. He knows it better than any of us. Let's divide into ten groups. Fire three shots in succession into the air if you find them. Doc will be waiting at the ranch house in case anyone is injured." He hopped down. "Let's get out there. Only a few more hours until we lose daylight."

As the men left the sheriff's office and mounted up, what looked like a sea of horses headed out toward the Meyer ranch.

Lucas Meyer rode next to Devin.

Devin glanced at the ranch owner. He'd gotten awfully thin sitting in a jail cell all this time. "You holding up?"

"Yeah. Just wish we'd been able to go through with the sheriff's plan."

"Me too. Before anything happened to Eliza." He gulped back the worries his statement conjured up.

Thank heaven the sheriff had taken Devin into his confidence when he arrived, explaining that he and Lucas came up with the idea to arrest Lucas as a ruse, to trap the real killer. It was a brilliant plan and should have worked.

The sheriff told Devin that Lucas had seen hints of the truth of what happened over the years, but it wasn't until his animals were killed that his suspicions were confirmed. Then, when seven of his own workers died, he'd gone to the sheriff with everything he knew.

They'd been so close to snatching up the killer. If only Devin had gotten there earlier. They could have stopped the kidnapping from happening.

"I'm so sorry about everything you've had to go through, Lucas. It must have been horrific to endure all the loss and tragedy you've experienced."

Lucas rode in silence for several moments, then shook his

head. "I can't say it's been easy, but the good Lord has been with me. Even when I've felt completely alone, He's been there." He shifted in the saddle. "For a long time, I thought all the loss was my punishment for leaving the ranch and my family. That the only way to make it up to them was by keeping the ranch going. But now . . ." His hands tightened on his reins. "I think it's best if I just sell the ranch and start over somewhere else. There's too many bad memories there. Too much grief."

They reached the edge of town and the men all pushed their horses to run at full-speed.

As the hooves pounded the ground, Devin pleaded with God to keep Eliza and Deborah safe.

Too many people had lost their lives.

He couldn't lose Eliza. Not when he was so close to finally making her his own.

WEDNESDAY, AUGUST 16, 1916 • JENSEN

"They're sure to search the whole ranch tonight." Melissa stared at her captives. "And then tomorrow, they'll widen the search and go elsewhere. That's when you three will help me dig up my gold."

The young Adams girl sobbed.

Melissa rolled her eyes. The girl had no idea what suffering was.

"I'm so sorry, Eliza." The girl spoke between whining and gulping for air. "I wanted something bad to happen to you. Mrs. Friedman said you'd done bad things at the ranch— damage to the property. Even stolen things! She was so mad and wanted to know where you were."

Melissa had to give it to the Mills woman. She was calm, as though she were sitting in a drawing room and not restrained by ropes in a shack. "It's not your fault, Louise. You're forgiven. She already knew where we were. We saw her the other day."

Aha. The paleontologist's soothing tone had grown angry with the last statement. So maybe she had some backbone after all. That would make this more interesting.

And fun.

The woman pointed her icy stare at Melissa. "Since we're going to be here all night, why don't you tell us what this is all about? Did you kill all those animals? And your brother's workers too?"

Melissa allowed a small laugh. She sat on the last chair in the little shack, resting her Colt on her knee. Aimed right at her guests. "Little miss paleontologist princess thinks she has it all figured out?" She looked at the other woman. Deborah? Was that her name? "What about you? Do you think I'm a murderer?"

While this woman showed more fear than Miss Mills, she clamped her lips together and didn't answer.

As for the blasted paleontologist, she didn't give up. "You did it. You killed them. And you were behind the stolen tools and the vandalism, weren't you? And all the events on the ranch that made people think it was haunted. For how many years?" Her eyes filled with disdain. "All for what . . . gold?"

How *dare* she mock her! "You *would* belittle it. From what I heard, you grew up in a mansion and your family has scads of money. You wouldn't understand what gold could do for me. I have nothing! Nothing beyond what I've taken. And yes, I killed for it. But you missed one. I also killed my good-for-nothin' husband. Now what do you think? You with your fancy clothes and hats."

Melissa stood, knocking her chair over. In two paces she was in front of that little rich girl, her gun pointed straight at the interloper's heart. "You have no idea what it is to suffer at the hands of controlling men. To be the daughter of a wealthy man and never see a *penny* of it. To be sent out every night on rat duty because that's all a girl was good for." She gulped. "To long to be loved and taken care of, and when you meet someone you adore, your father tells you it's forbidden to marry a bum like him."

She didn't owe this woman any explanation! But having started, she couldn't stop.

"And when you do get married, the man turns into a hateful, greedy monster, and your family disowns you. They all *deserved* to die. This ranch should be mine. That gold *will* be mine. Don't judge me until you understand what it's like to be m—"

Crash!

The door behind her fell off its hinges, and men flooded into the shack.

"No!" She turned toward Eliza and pulled the trigger.

twenty

"There are many things I wish to remember and keep some thing like the sequence of events. Sometimes one event a day will serve as a string to hold many remembrances. I have made a mistake in not realizing this in the past."

~Earl Douglass

WEDNESDAY, AUGUST 16, 1916 • JENSEN

Devin pushed past the sheriff and his men, shoving shoulders and bodies as hard as he could. He had to get to Eliza. Was she shot? Was she even . . . still alive? His heart threatened to beat out of his chest.

When the door had crashed in, he'd felt as if time stopped—then started again, but slow, moment by moment. He watched it all unfold.

The woman turning and pulling the trigger.

The bullet heading straight for Eliza.

Some kind of guttural noise escaped his mouth as he surged forward.

271

Eliza screaming. A sickening thud.

Someone called to him from far away. "Mr. Schmitt—"

"I need to be by her side." He didn't know or care who spoke and tugged at his arm. No one would stop him.

Two deputies had hold of the guilty woman's arms, and they pulled her back. She was ranting and raving about something, but Devin didn't listen.

Eliza was on the floor. Eyes closed. A pool of red expanding around her left leg.

Noise from the room rushed in and filled his senses. He blinked and then went into action. Devin stripped off his jacket and pressed it against the bullet wound in Eliza's leg. Stop the bleeding. That's what he had to do. But it soaked through so fast . . .

He pulled the jacket away, folded it, and then used the sleeves to tie it around her leg as tight as he could. "Where's the doctor?"

"He's riding up as we speak, son." The sheriff crouched beside him and gripped Devin's shoulder. "She's still breathing . . ."

"Why isn't she conscious?" Was that his voice? That hoarse, desperate sound?

The sheriff studied her. "She must have hit her head when she fell."

He nodded. Everything he wanted to say to Eliza bubbled to the surface. If she'd only move. Open her eyes—

He couldn't take it anymore. He lifted her into one arm, untying the ropes from her wrists with his free hand. Then he cradled her, pressing his face against her hair. "I love you." His whisper was choked by the emotion clogging his throat. "Don't you dare leave me now. You made a promise, remember?"

She moaned, and he pulled back a few inches. Her eyelids fluttered!

"That's my girl. Stay with me, Eliza. Forever." He kept his words soft as he pressed a kiss against her temple.

Another moan and her hand came up and gripped his shirt. Even as her face relaxed, her grip on him held tight.

He whispered to her, lips against her ear. "Doc is coming. You're going to be right as rain." *Lord God in heaven—please. Please!* "You've shared your hopes and dreams with me since we were barely as tall as the shrubs at Mills Manor." Strength surged into him. He willed it to seep out of his hands and into her body. "Well . . . my hopes have been long buried. So I'm going to tell you a secret. I'm writing a book, Eliza. You have to be here to read it . . . to tell me where I can make it better."

A commotion at the door pulled his gaze away. The doctor.

He whispered against her hair. "You're all I've ever wanted, Eliza. A life with you. I love you . . ."

The doctor reached her side and examined the wound in her leg. "I need to get her back to my place as soon as possible. Let's get a tourniquet even tighter and keep the wound from being jostled too much." The man's piercing gaze snagged Devin's. "You up for holding her steady in the back of a wagon?"

"Yes, sir." He clenched his jaw.

"Good. It's going to be a long, hard ride." The doc went back to her leg. "I'll pack the wound, but time is of the essence."

Devin held Eliza's shoulders as the doctor made quick work of bandaging the wound.

"Why?"

Devin glanced into the corner where Lucas Meyer hovered over his sister. "I don't understand why you would do such a thing . . ." The man's upper body began to quake. *"You* killed our family?" Great sobs erupted out of him.

The woman turned her face away. Her expression was hard. Angry.

Disgusted.

What could make someone so cold? And evil? What could be so terrible it drove people to do horrific things?

Lucas collapsed onto his knees, and several of the sheriff's men stepped to put a hand on his shoulders.

"All these years, I've carried the guilt and shame . . . thinking it was my fault . . ."

Such pain in the man's words, it almost took Devin's breath away. *God, help him . . .* He glanced at Eliza's pale face.

Help us all.

⁓

THURSDAY, AUGUST 31, 1916 · MAGEE-WOMENS HOSPITAL, PITTSBURGH

A whooshing sound continued next to her in a steady rhythm. What *was* that?

Where was she?

Eliza listened a little more intently. But there wasn't another sound. Wait. What was *that*? Was someone snoring?

Where *was* she?

She took a few deep breaths. Ooh . . . everything hurt. But the more long, deep breaths she took, the clearer her mind became.

She worked to open her eyes. Only her right one cooperated at first. But with persistence, her left opened a little as well.

The room around her was bright.

But it wasn't home.

It wasn't anywhere she knew in Utah.

Her memory was fuzzy.

Oh! The shack. Tied up. Melissa Friedman. A . . .

A gun aimed at her!

She jolted in the bed and gasped for air. Why couldn't she sit up?

"Eliza?"

Oh, that voice. Calm washed over her. "Devin?"

274

"I'm here."

"Where is here?" She licked her lips. "And can you get me some water?"

"Of course." He lifted a cup to her lips.

Never had anything tasted so delicious. She wanted to gulp the entire thing down.

"Let's take it a little at a time."

Who was that strong voice?

Eliza managed to look at the doorway. A man entered the room and stood at the foot of her bed. "Good to see you awake and alert, Miss Mills. I'm Dr. Dover."

Even in her dazed state, her eyes widened. "You're Mr. Carnegie's physician."

"That I am." He stepped closer. "I went out to Utah to fetch you in Mr. Carnegie's personal train car. I've had to give you a lot of pain medication because you kept writhing, and we didn't want you to be uncomfortable and open up the wound. But you're here now." He touched the sheet covering her legs. "May I take a look?"

"Yes, Doctor." But even as she answered, she frowned. *Wound? What woun—?*

Oh. That's right. She'd been shot in the leg.

She closed her eyes against the memory. The sound of the shot. The pain that hit her. Blood gushing from the wound . . .

Then nothing. She must have passed out.

The doctor covered her leg again and looked down at her. "It's healing. Finally. But it will probably take months for it to *completely* heal." The doctor gave her an encouraging smile. "It was providential that I made it when I did. They hadn't been able to get the whole bullet out before I arrived in Jensen. You'd lost a great deal of blood, and they didn't want to sacrifice your leg. I did surgery immediately, and once you were stable, we brought you back here." He patted her shoulder.

She sent him a smile. "Thank you, Doctor."

"I'll leave you to catch up with your boyfriend here. Mr. Carnegie said he would be by to visit you soon. Won't he be ecstatic to see you are awake." And with that, he strode out of the room.

She turned her attention back to Devin. "My boyfriend." She grinned as wide as her chapped lips would allow.

"That is, if you'll have me." Devin lifted her hand so gently and rubbed his thumb over the top. "I know we have a lot to discuss. Especially after—"

"Hush." She croaked the word. "I can't take any more of that. After facing this, believe me, I don't want to dwell anymore in the past. My grandfather told me when I was just a little girl that I must guard my heart against falling in love so that God could show me the man He had for me. Grandfather instilled such a fear in me, that I never realized how much I had guarded my own heart. Until you came out this summer and my stomach flipped over itself and my heart pounded out of my chest. That was when I knew that I not only loved you, but I was in love with you."

His head jerked back a bit as his eyebrows shot up. "Your grandfather made me promise him over a decade ago that I would never pursue you. Out of respect for him, I agreed. It was like being stabbed in the heart. When I left you in Utah after telling you how I felt, my intentions were to let you go. My heart couldn't take being in love with you and never being with you." He swallowed. "But when I returned, your grandmother summoned me to the manor."

Eliza swallowed. Grandmama *summoned* him? Had she been kind? Rude? Cold? "Oh? What did she say?"

"She released me from that promise and told me she and your grandfather both knew the last couple years that I was the man for you." His grin stretched almost from ear to ear.

For a moment, Eliza forgot to breathe. Then the full meaning of his words flooded her. They had Grandmama's blessing!

And Grandfather's—God rest his soul. Tears filled her eyes. How good the Lord had been to them! Eliza gave Devin a wide grin. "Well, if that's the case, I don't want to take another moment for granted. Devin, I love you. With all my heart."

His face lit up and his eyes softened. "I love you too. I can't stand the thought of living without you by my side. I've wanted—longed—for more than friendship with you all these years. Never thinking it was possible." He laughed. "But look at what God has done."

Heat rushed to her cheeks.

He chuckled. "Look at that. You've finally got color in your face." He dropped a light kiss on her forehead.

Eliza closed her eyes for a moment, Devin's nearness washing over her, warming her. Was it possible to live in a moment like this forever?

Devin pulled away and sat back in his chair, but he picked up her hand, lacing his fingers through hers.

She could twirl for days with the happiness flowing through her. That is, once she got out of this hospital bed. For now, she would rest and heal. And catch up on all the latest news.

She tugged on Devin's hand. "Now that we have the important things out of the way"—she grinned—"what's been happening while I've been in here? Am I the culprit behind all the thefts at the museum?"

SUNDAY, SEPTEMBER 3, 1916 • MAGEE-WOMENS HOSPITAL

Eliza held her breath as Devin leaned in close.

A throat cleared at the door. "Excuse me for interrupting."

It took her a moment to realize who was there, she'd been so caught up in Devin's eyes. "Mr. Carnegie!"

"Eliza, my dear. I'm so thankful you are awake now." He approached the bed, carrying a bouquet of flowers in a lovely crystal vase. He set it on the table and stood at the foot of the bed, hands clasped in front of him. "Devin has told me he already filled you in on what happened here several weeks ago?"

She nodded. "I still can't believe I was here for weeks before I woke up. And I'm so sorry about Mr. Nelson and the trouble he made for you."

Mr. Carnegie inclined his head. "None of us realized the poor man was so ill in his mind. Driven, power-hungry . . . yes, I knew that. But he was excellent at what he did. I guess, eventually, it became an obsession? At least he's getting the help he needs now."

"And I want to tell you how sorry I am for my part—"

"Don't worry, my dear. All of that is in the past."

Just like that, she was forgiven. Had anyone ever been so blessed as she by a loving God?

Mr. Carnegie went on. "I came to reassure you that all is well. Thanks to Mr. Schmitt here, who came to me in a flurry demanding an audience and insisting you were innocent." Mr. Carnegie chuckled and shook Devin's hand. "I approve, by the way." He sent her a wink.

Oh good heavens! From the heat in her face, her cheeks must be getting redder and redder. But she couldn't stop the grin tugging at her lips. "Thank you, sir." He had interrupted an *almost* kiss.

"Now, I'm not one to stay. Hospitals are not among my favorite places to be, but I had to come make the offer in person."

"Offer?" What could he be talking about?

"I'd like to offer you the job of curator at my Hall of Dinosaurs." The grin that covered his face stretched his white mustache and beard wider than she'd ever seen them.

"Curator? Truly?" She put a hand to her chest. *Lord, You are so good! "Curator?"*

"Yes, Miss Mills. Does your reaction mean that you accept?"

The word *yes* sat on her lips, but she paused and looked

at Devin, lifting her eyebrows. Without a doubt, he would support whatever decision she made. But she was done with leaving him out of this or any decision. They were facing a new future *together*. This wasn't about just her hopes and dreams anymore . . . nor his. It was about *their* hopes and dreams.

He squeezed her hand, giving her a grin. "Well, my love? It's a dream come true, wouldn't you say?"

Eliza tightened her grip on his fingers and let out a laugh. "Mr. Carnegie, I would be delighted!"

EPILOGUE

"I am more and more convinced that we have a prize."

~Earl Douglass

Devin helped Eliza out of the motor car and then carried her up the steps to her home. Eliza bit her lip. She would not cry. But she longed to be able to race up the steps and throw herself into Grandmama's arms.

However, the doctors had told her it would take a great deal of time before she could walk again.

The bullet had damaged not only her muscle and tissue, but it had fractured the bone as well. It would be months before she could stroll in a park on Devin's arm. Or even walk through the house with Grandmama.

But she wouldn't complain. After all, Devin insisted on carrying her anywhere he could. What on earth was there to complain about in that?

She studied his profile, a small smile lifting her lips. He'd been so patient with her. Waiting for her to realize how much she loved him. His care of her this last week had been a balm in the midst of her frustration and pain. And he wasn't afraid to call her out on her grumpy attitude.

Instead, he pointed her to God. Together they sought the Lord to heal Eliza in His time. To give her the strength to face the coming months. To help them grow in love for one another.

So she would just take advantage of this time to rest and be with her grandmother. And with Devin.

She smiled again and nestled closer to his chest. What would it be like to be properly courted by her best friend? She didn't know, but she couldn't wait to find out—

Heat filled her cheeks. Oh! She *had* become bold.

And frankly, she didn't care.

Devin set her down at the top step, where one of the staff waited with a wheeled chair for her. Devin helped her to get situated with her leg propped up and then knelt down in front of her.

"Eliza."

"Yes?" She wiggled in the seat. Something was poking her in the rear end.

"I've already spoken to your grandmother about what I'm going to say. Just so you know."

"Okay." She winced and tried to maneuver away from whatever jabbed her. But it only made it worse. She scrunched up her nose and lurched in the seat, making her leg ache. "Ow!"

Devin laughed and shook his head. "Are you even paying attention?"

"Yes, I'm paying attention." She wiggled one more time. "But something in this chair—" She huffed and her massive hat tumbled down over her face. The weight of it made her feel like she'd been punched in the nose. "Ouch!" Maybe they were monstrosities after all. Her maid rushed forward and took the hat.

Done with ladylike behavior, she grunted and pushed and

heaved until she moved the cushion to cover the horrid piece of wood that had tried to impale her. "There. Whew. That's better. What were you saying?"

Devin rubbed his fingers along his jaw, his lips twitching. "I was attempting to ask you a question."

"Well then, all right. I'm ready whenever you are." She folded her hands in her lap and looked up.

"I don't know . . . what to do." He blinked at her and pointed to her head.

She reached up and felt the mess her flopping hat had made of her hair. Removing the pins, she worked her fingers through her hair and let it fall around her shoulders.

His eyes widened. "I've always loved it when your hair is down."

The butler cleared his throat behind them.

"Sorry." Devin quirked a smile at her and straightened. "Eliza . . ."

"Yes?" At the look in his eyes, her stomach fluttered. He wasn't about to . . . was he?

"Will you marry me?"

He was! He *did!* "Yes! Yes, I'll marry you!" She flung her arms wide and leaned forward to hug him. At this point, she didn't even care that they had an audience. She pulled him close.

Devin came to his feet, leaned over her, and placed his hands on either side of her face. "I've loved you forever and will continue to love you forever." He lifted her completely out of the chair and into his arms.

Then he kissed her.

Not a little peck. And not even a chaste and sweet kiss because they were in front of the staff.

No. Devin *kissed* her.

She wrapped her arms around his neck and kissed him back. Every nerve ending in her body screamed to life, her skin tingled, and her head swam.

"Let's get married soon." She spoke the words against his lips.

"I'm in agreement."

"Good." She kissed him again. "I'm sure Grandmama can throw something together."

He laughed, deep and long. As he set her back down in the chair, she glanced around at the staff. Hmm . . . they'd multiplied in numbers since she'd last looked up.

Then the applause started.

Devin took her hand and looked at the appreciative crowd. "I've loved Eliza since we were young. One day, she made me promise to be her best friend forever and to never let anything come between us." He shrugged. "What can I say? A promise is a promise."

NOTE FROM
THE AUTHOR

I'm so thankful that you joined me once again for this final book in my TREASURES OF THE EARTH series.

Earl Douglass was a huge inspiration for these stories. The work that he did not only will help to educate and amaze people for generations to come, but I was fascinated with the man himself.

"He was who he was because of what he wrote." (His grand-daughter, Diane, told me that once, and I wrote it down.) Earl journaled for forty-seven years of his life—incredible.

And fun fact, if he was ever stranded? He wanted all the works of Shakespeare and the Bible with him.

If you read his journal entries and wander through his work in the book *Speak to the Earth and It Will Teach You*, you'll see the great struggle he had himself with his faith during this time of scientific discovery.

I can only imagine being a believer during this time and hearing the shift in the field of science from believing in a Creator to negating Him. Today, we have many more resources and studies and technology to help us to understand, but the debate is stronger than ever.

In these books, I wanted to share with you what it might

have been like historically to be in this position. Earl is a great example of that. And what a thrill that he was the one who found the bones that led to Dinosaur National Monument and what it is today.

His dream was fulfilled when they indeed left bones in the quarry wall and put them on display.

At the end of this note are two of Earl's poems. Within his journals, he wrote a lot of poetry. I've loved reading his quotes, haven't you?

When I was doing research out in Vernal and at Dinosaur National Monument, I met a wonderful woman named Marilyn Wallis, who was the office manager at the Vernal Chamber of Commerce. She shared the coolest story with us. One that was passed down in her family over the decades.

Her great-great-grandparents were William and Eliza Neil. There is an old log house right before you enter the monument that was theirs. They lived there, and Earl pitched a tent there while he was looking for a great find. Their son, Frank—Marilyn's great-uncle—went with Earl so he wouldn't be alone. Earl was about to give up digging in their area when they encouraged him to go out one more day.

He did, and that was the day he found the bones.

Earl sacrificed a lot in his lifetime because of his love for paleontology. While rich men like Cope and Marsh did some pretty awful things to gain fame, Earl remained honest and a man of integrity.

His dream wasn't vast amounts of wealth—he often sold what he found just so he could get more schooling or go on the next expedition—but to see the great beasts and their history come to life for generations to come.

He was a true scientist.

It has been an honor and a privilege to present a little of his legacy to you.

Dinosaur National Monument wouldn't be what it is today

without Earl Douglass. The title of this book takes on even greater meaning for me because Earl's hope for the monument was finally brought to fruition decades after his death. The visitor center encases an enormous wall of fossils that guests can walk up to and see. It is magnificent and well worth the visit.

I'm looking forward to hearing what you think of this special series, and I hope you'll join me for my next historical with Bethany House, which takes place during World War II—tentatively titled *The Pianist*—coming in September of 2025.

Until next time,

Kimberley

Hymn of the Wilderness

Speak to the Earth and It Will Teach You: The Life and Times of Earl Douglass 1862–1931. (BookSurge Publishing, 2009), pp. 342–343

> I wander in the midst of the olden hills,
> Mid rude rocks carved by tempest's rage
> In days unknown. A mystery fills
> The primal scene, sublime with age—
> Sublime, for Nature reigns alone
> Upon her everlasting throne.
>
> Here altars rise on every hand
> That mystic reverence inspires,
> And ancient, silent temples stand;
> And though I hear no chanting choirs
> From near and far there seems to roll
> A mystic music to my soul.
>
> Here, freed from man's contending thought,
> That makes a din of hate and strife,
> I find what long in vain I sought,
> A nearness to the source of life;
> Where scenes are fresh and thoughts are free
> My deeper self returns to me.

Here are no books, no written words
That man ignores or blindly heeds.
No sound of human voice is heard,
No narrative of human deeds.
Yet to the one whos list's are told
Strange stories of the days of old.

In this wild land of sagey plains
And sculptured, rocky-templed heights,
Where bigotry has left no stains
And tyranny no scourging blights,
Should not the poet love to roam
And freedom's lovers find a home?

With songs and hymns these rocks ne'er rang;
These hills the prophets never trod,
Nor sages e'er these wonders sang
Nor seers have heard the "voice of God"
Yet here the Spirit dwells, divine,
That spake with men in Palestine.

If prophet, genius, sage, and seer
Would flash deep truths in human speech,
Would read the revelations here,
The Spirit's inspiration teach,
Their words would live through tempest shocks,
Their thoughts survive these crumbling rocks.

A Picture of Gethsemane
Speak to the Earth and It Will Teach You, pp. 408–413

It was a picture on a wall—
A painted picture—"that was all".

It was a picture of despair;
Forlorn the one in anguish there.

No light was in the darkened sky;
No flower or blade of grass was nigh.

With head on arm and tangled locks,
One lone form knelt on barren rocks.

No face was seen, but attitude
And raiment were with woe imbued.

Arms, hands, and all were telling there
The awful language of despair.

O, what a type I thought in tears,
Of all the fruitage of the years!

Because of these I scarce could see—
Had I not known Gethsemane?

Did e'er a brush with truer power
Portray a darker, sadder hour?

Loe one whose hopes had been so bright
Until that last and fateful night!

Faithful you labored 'till that hour
To break the tyrant's fearful power;

Boldly pursued your daring plan—
The freedom of your fellow man.

Then came the last, despairing night
With scarce a single ray of light.
Had you believed "The Father's" power
Would save you in that trying hour?

Or trust that sympathy for man
Lay deep and sure in Nature's plan?

But no one came to set you free
From that dread hour at Calvary.

How often had the words you spake
Pierced the sad heart that swelled to break!

"My God, My God, I trusted thee!
Why hast thou now forsaken me?"

Sad were the words that Caesar said
When from his Brutus' sword he bled;

But that a man's or empire's loss;
Not a world's fate upon the cross

Did you believe man e'er would be
Worthy and able to be free?

Did you not know that deaf and blind,
The living truth we seldom find?

Even the few at our right hand
Could not your message understand.

So long as men are willing slaves,
Worship and serve designing knaves,

So long those who would set men free
Shall end in dark Gethsemane—
So long in vain seems Calvary.

I've often wondered if you knew,
After your time, what men would do?

How they would take your name and plan
The bondage of their fellow man;

Would fill the world with shame and crime
Through all the centuries since that time;

And tyrant systems named for you
Would cancel all you tried to do—

Systems that all your precepts wrecked,
And made your words of none effect.

Your precepts given to make us free
Were turned to tools of slavery.

In that dread hour was there a gleam
That made the future darker seem?

In murky skies did red light break
From martyrs burning at the stake?

And on the earth a redder flood,
Where Christians shed their brother's blood?

The banners, with your name unfurled,
Long waved above a blood-stained world.

They used your name to trap mankind,
Self-blinded leaders of the blind;

Who nothing did you bade them do,
These were the ones condemned by you.

"Great is Diana," shouts the mob
And in her name the people rob.

"Great is the Christ," and many sell
In his great name the fears of hell.

The noble man that should have stood
For all that's manly brave and good.

How oft' the "House of God",
since then, Has been a murderous, thievish den!

And yours, the greatest of all names,
Yet used for greater lies and shame.

If these things you could then foresee,
How black, indeed, Gethsemane!

O, hero of the true and good,
Two thousand years misunderstood!

Has your cause met unending shame!
By counterfeiting your name?

Is all so dark? Are there a few
To your high aims and purpose true?

Many there are—a quiet throng
That help the world and men along

To aim for higher earthly goal
And for the freedom of the soul;

Who, in a wilderness of fears,
With love and hope have gilded tears.

These are the followers of thee;
And many know Gethsemane.

Though near the end of mortal life
Did you see far beyond the strife,

Down through the ages yet to be,
Past many a sad Gethsemane,

Glad Freedom's flag at last unfurled
Above a long-enduring world?

Will men thy potent message see—
Or the world's last Gethsemane?

Still for some future good we grope,
Inspired by sympathy and hope.

Many will die in brutal fight
But few, like thee, will die for right.

Truth on a cross is sanctified
And men, not truths, are crucified.

Not silenced at Gethsemane
That first clear voice to set men free.

I know not what the truth may be,
But this, that picture said to me.

ACKNOWLEDGMENTS

This series would not be here without Jessica Sharpe (my editor at Bethany House) saying, "Dinosaurs! Who doesn't love dinosaurs?" And without the incredible editing prowess of Karen Ball who, somehow, sees the beauty in my stories amid the mess. Then helps me to turn it into something incredible.

Then there's Carrie—my project manager—and dear friend. She's so great. Navigating this year since my dad went on to his home in heaven has been a challenge. *Catching up* after needing to take time off after he passed has been like a thousand-car train barreling toward Hurricane Gulch in Alaska and the bridge is out.

Yeah, it has been a year. But God is good. He is sustaining. And somehow, some way, we've made it through. And in a couple weeks, I will be completely caught up. (I probably won't know what to do with myself, so there's that . . .)

I'd like to shout out one more time to the incredible man who found the first bones and worked and dreamed at Dinosaur National Monument for more than a dozen years: Earl Douglass. I wish I could have known you, but I feel like I do through all your writings.

Diane Douglass Iverson, thank you for giving me permission to use your grandfather's quotes and poems from his personal journals and writings. And thank you for sharing from your heart with me about the man behind this incredible discovery. It is a blessing to know you.

I owe a huge debt of gratitude to Dr. Sue Ann Bilbey, who agreed so graciously to meet with me and answer questions. Her expertise in the field is incredible, and her experience is inspiring. In explaining how difficult it is for women in the field of paleontology even to this day, she said, "Keep track of everything. Women in the field are rare—I was the only female in class. And it's imperative to always get everything in writing." Her passion for the field also helped lead to the book about Earl getting out there. I am so grateful to Diane for connecting us.

Thanks are also due to Marilyn Wallis for sharing her family stories with us. How incredible to add that other little piece of Earl's legacy to us.

Ken Carpenter's research on the Douglasses was also a huge help to me as I worked on this series.

And then there's Devin Cetnar—who I named the hero in *A Hope Unburied* after—thank you for all your encouragement, your constant smile, and your love of books. Please give your family hugs from me. When are you coming to visit?

I couldn't do what I do without the readers. Thank YOU for being such a huge part of my life.

To my family—I love you all so much. Jeremy, for almost thirty-three years of marriage that just keeps getting better and better. Our kids—Josh and Ruth, Kayla and Steven—thank you for loving your mom even though she has so many flaws. And to my grandkids, Nana loves you so much! What a joy to get to live this beautiful life with you all.

Finally, to my Lord and Savior, who makes all this possible. The Author of all. The Creator. I stand in awe of You.

For more from Kimberley Woodhouse,
read on for an excerpt from

A
DEEP
DIVIDE

When her father's greedy corruption goes too far, heiress
Emma Grace McMurray sneaks away to be a Harvey Girl at
the El Tovar Grand Canyon Hotel, planning to stay hidden
forever. There she uncovers mysteries, secrets, and a love beyond anything she could imagine—leaving her to question all
she thought to be true.

Available now wherever books are sold.

one

Something touched Emma Grace's shoulder. But she was so tired, her eyelids too heavy.

"Next stop, Grand Canyon and El Tovar!" The shout jolted her fully awake. Clutching her bag to her chest, she blinked away the last vestiges of dreams in her mind. The three-hour ride from Williams, Arizona, had passed in the blink of an eye. At least it seemed that way . . . probably because she fell asleep. Not something she was prone to do, but not sleeping for three days straight as she traveled across the country had obviously taken its toll.

With a deep breath, she sat up straighter and swallowed down every emotion that tried to climb up her throat. Working for the Fred Harvey Company the past five years had brought her to the top ranks. When she heard the El Tovar would be opening, she put in her request that very day. It was Harvey's crown jewel, after all. But why was she doubting? She was good. All her managers even wrote *the best* on her recommendation letters. She deserved this, didn't she?

The job would be great—this was something she could do

almost with her eyes closed now. But the jitters in her stomach persisted. It was starting all over again that intimidated her. Five years she'd done it, at seven different Harvey Houses along the rail line. Each time it seemed to get more difficult. But her circumstances demanded it. She needed to increase the distance between her and Boston. A new place was necessary.

This was the farthest west she'd ever been. And it was remote.

But was she far enough away that *he* couldn't find—

"Miss Edwards?" The conductor held out a slip for her. "This is for your luggage. But not to worry about it, they will take it directly to your room."

She pasted on a smile. "Thank you."

"I know Miss Anniston is looking forward to your arrival." The man gave a small nod.

Emma Grace put a hand to her throat. "I'm looking forward to it as well." The fact that the conductor on the train, in addition to some of the railroad personnel in Williams, had spoken of Miss Anniston and her anticipation of Emma Grace's arrival made her throat a bit dry. How lovely that the woman had spoken so highly of her, but would she be gracious and kind? Or would she be a tyrant?

That remained to be seen.

A couple of the head waitresses Emma Grace had worked under were hard—almost to the point of being callous and mean. No two ways about it. But it had made her a better waitress, and if she were honest with herself . . . a better person as well. The training had been difficult, but she had the upper hand of knowing what customers expected in fine dining establishments. She'd lived that life. Been that customer. It gave her a bit of an edge, but she realized quickly how much she truly had to learn about humanity.

Even though she loved being a part of the working class, there were times she had to remind herself about her position in society. She couldn't speak to people the same way she could as Emma Grace McMurray. Not that she had ever been a snob—oh, she prayed she hadn't been—but speaking her mind had been her norm. As a socialite, she could do that. As Emma Grace Edwards, she could not.

Was she doing the right thing? The same question haunted her everywhere she went. She lifted her reticule to her lap and opened it. The aged newspaper article's edges peeked out of the side. But she shoved it deeper inside the bag. Now was not the time. She practically had it memorized, anyway.

This was what new situations did to her. They brought up the past and everything that went with it. All she wanted to do was move forward. Live a simple life. But after all this time, she doubted it was possible.

Still, it didn't keep her from hoping.

The whistle blew, and the train slowed. As it chugged its way into the depot, she took a moment to straighten her hair and pin her hat back into place. It was nice to not have to deal with the wigs anymore, nor push glasses up her nose. It had been five years since she'd let her blond hair be seen. Five years of disguises, different at each place she'd lived.

But it was time to let her natural look be her new disguise. No one had recognized her in all this time. And it wasn't like she hadn't matured over the years. For too long she'd been thin and scrawny—too thin. But she found out the hard way that not eating wasn't a good way to be able to withstand the rigors of her job and its twelve-hour shifts. After a bath one evening, she'd even passed out. When she finally allowed herself to eat and fill out, she found she liked her sturdy frame and curves. She didn't look at all like the young girl who'd run away from . . . everything.

She shook her head of the thoughts and gripped her reticule. That was the past. And it needed to stay there. No man would control her. No one would ever fool her again. No chance that money would dictate her choices. She loved her job and her life. And she had the opportunity for a completely fresh start here, one that hopefully would include new friends and a warm atmosphere. Like family. Something she'd craved for far too long.

As long as it wasn't anything like what *her* family had become.

The brakes hissed, and the train stopped moving. Out the window, the snow-covered, rocky landscape appeared dry and dusty and was dotted with scrubby-looking trees—some tall, some short. It certainly didn't look like much. Could one of the most glorious wonders of the world really be here? She'd seen photographs of the Grand Canyon. It was hard to imagine that such a place even existed.

Passengers scooted out into the aisles of the train. It was time.

Time to face this new world and tackle her job.

The past didn't matter. All that mattered was here and now.

With rhythmic steps, they all shuffled down the aisle toward the door. Emma Grace took a peek around the man's shoulder in front of her. Only a few more steps and she'd have some fresh air and room to breathe.

She closed her eyes for a moment and then stepped forward again. It was almost her turn to disembark. What she wouldn't give to be able to stretch all of her muscles—touch her toes and reach for the sky—but that wouldn't be very proper. She'd have to wait until she was in the privacy of her room. Whenever that would be.

Another step.

Oh, it made her antsy. Only one more person, then she could get off this train.

The conductor nodded at her as he tipped his cap. "Enjoy the most amazing wonder you'll ever see." His smile was genuine as his eyes twinkled. "I look forward to seeing you in the dining room."

"Thank you. I look forward to it as well." Emma Grace turned toward the steps and ventured down.

As she exited the train, the chill of the air took her breath away for a moment, and the wind threatened to take her hat with it.

A lovely dark-haired woman approached. Probably a good ten years her senior, she was still young and beautiful and seemed nothing like the harsh spinster barking out orders that Emma Grace had dramatically conjured up in her mind.

Several inches shorter than Emma Grace, the woman had a soft, warm appearance and moved with confidence and grace. Her hands tucked into the pockets of her long black coat. One eyebrow quirked upward. "Miss Edwards?"

"Yes." She stepped forward as butterflies filled her stomach. Why was she so nervous? She'd done this many times and had years of experience to rely upon. "I'm Emma Grace Edwards."

"Welcome to El Tovar. I'm Ruth Anniston, head waitress." She tilted her head toward what appeared to be the hotel. "Let's get you out of the cold and settled. The rest of the girls don't arrive for another two days." While the greeting wasn't at all unamiable, there was only so much to ascertain in the brisk breeze and bitter temperature.

"Oh? How many are you expecting?"

"Twenty-five in all. We've hired the best of the best. And while they've all been Harvey Girls for at least a few months, there will be training for the El Tovar in particular, as it is expected to attract the most elite of clientele. You—along with the other senior waitresses—will be assigned a trainee."

That made Emma Grace's nerves jitter even more. Would Miss Anniston approve of her? It was so important for her to make a good impression. She wanted this job to last for a long time. Hopefully for the rest of her life.

Following the woman from the rail tracks to a set of stone steps that would take them up the hill, she gazed at the massive structure. As she made her way up the steep incline, the large building loomed in front of her. This side of it was a half-hexagon shape. From where she stepped, she could see that it stretched in length for a substantial distance before her. The large stones at the foundation were topped with giant logs and then more dark wood siding as the building rose for several stories above her. Basement . . . one, two, three stories. Was there even a fourth up there? As they walked around and up the hill, she noticed a turret at the top that seemed to almost touch the sky from this angle. Was that in the center of the hotel? She got dizzy with her neck craned back.

While its height was not much compared to the tall buildings in the cities back east, this one stretched out in breadth even more than its height. The closer she got, the larger it loomed. Its unique design drew her in. "It's a lovely hotel."

"Mr. Whittlesey—the architect of El Tovar—envisions it as a mix of Swiss chalet and Norwegian villa. Would you agree?" Miss Anniston stopped and gazed up with her.

Emma Grace did indeed agree, but she didn't dare say that out loud. The real Emma Grace had seen Swiss chalets and Norwegian villas, but Emma Grace the waitress most certainly wouldn't have had the privilege of vacationing in Europe. So, she shrugged. "I can't say that I have an opinion one way or the other." She let out a light laugh, hoping to convey the innocence of a poor young waitress. "It's a beautiful building though to be sure."

Miss Anniston started walking again before her abrupt stop outside a basement door almost made Emma Grace collide with her. "You'll find your way around quick enough. Are you terribly cold?"

What did her question imply? Was this some sort of test for her ability to work here? She shook her head slightly to rid herself of her anxious thoughts. Everything put her on edge when she was in a new place. "It's chilly, but I'm all right."

A secretive smile spread across the woman's face. "Good. Because I think there's something you need to see before we go inside." With her hands still stuffed into her coat pockets, she tilted her head again—this time away from the hotel—beckoning Emma Grace toward the west side of the building. "Follow me. Just be prepared—it will get even colder at the rim."

Chicago, Illinois

A centimeter to the left should do. Ray Watkins straightened the pencil jar on his desk. There. Perfect.

Before he could get to the stack of reports waiting for him, he'd have to deal with the chaos that was his workspace. While blowing at a piece of lint on the blotter, he caught something out of the corner of his eye. One of the files on top of the cabinet was askew. He'd have to ask his secretary one more time to make sure he stacked the files appropriately. He walked over to the mahogany cabinet and straightened them. Might as well put them in alphabetical order while he was at it. The satisfaction of the simple task steadied his breathing. As he shuffled them back into a neat position, his mind cleared.

Much better.

With a tug on his pinstripe vest, he went back to his chair.

The tedious reports where he checked the work of the accounting department weren't his favorite task, but alas, it fell to him. His father had poured his whole life into Watkins Enterprises, and one day Ray hoped to be able to add to it. He'd have to earn his way, that's for sure. Dad hadn't created it overnight—a fact Ray was reminded of often. It was a privilege to be able to follow in his father's footsteps.

A few years ago, that hadn't been his opinion, but God had changed him. Each day was a gift now. A chance to live out his favorite verse in Colossians. The words tumbled through his mind, *"And whatsoever ye do in word or deed, do all in the name of the Lord Jesus, giving thanks to God and the Father by him."*

So, even the mundane reports needed to be done well and with a good attitude—something else he needed to be reminded of on a daily basis. His hope was that one day all of the empire his father had built and hoarded could be used to help the poor or used for missions . . . however God directed him.

Two hours into the afternoon, he stretched his arms and back as a sense of accomplishment filled him. He dipped his pen and signed the last page, conveying that he'd checked and double-checked the work. Another task complete.

Shifting his gaze to the window, he took in the sunshine and perfect white clouds dotting a blue sky. It would make for a great picture. Made him imagine what it would look like through the lens of his new camera. The clock chimed the hour. Perhaps he'd be able to get away in time to drive by Lake Michigan. His favorite view.

"Ray!" Dad's booming voice pulled his attention away from the window. Looming in the doorway, with a catlike smile on his features, his dad stroked his beard. "I've got exciting news." Even if it wasn't exciting for anyone but him, Dad would expect anyone and everyone to listen and nod their agreement. His father's presence dominated no matter where he went. "I'm sending you out to the new Harvey House at the Grand Canyon. I've been in discussions with the Harvey boys about the investment opportunities in the West. They've agreed to advertise for us, and we will do the same for them here."

Ray leaned back in his chair. Dad was always looking for new ways to expand and get his name out there. "What exactly will they advertise for us? It's not like we have the same attraction as the Grand Canyon."

"I asked them to start with our art galleries and jewelry stores. Since the wealthy will most likely be the ones to make that trip, it will give them something to look forward to when they come home. Or perhaps those who aren't from Chicago or New York will want to take a trip so they can visit one of our fine establishments. I'm even thinking of building out west myself. Oh, make sure you pack that box-camera-photograph thing of yours." He waved a hand, as if that would make the right word appear.

Ray's eyebrows shot up. "Oh?" He couldn't trust himself to say much more. All he could do was attempt to mask his shock. When had Dad ever expressed *any* interest in his photography?

Dad sat in the chair across from him and leaned back with his hands folded across his chest. "It's supposed to be a grand affair—the El Tovar I believe is what it's called. My investors are eager to hear how we can capitalize on the Atchison, To-peka, and Santa Fe rail line. Everyone is fascinated with the West and wants their piece of it. Harvey has a good corner of it now, so we need to find our own niche."

Ray's heart sank a bit. It was just another errand for the investors. What would he have to do this time? Make a list of all the Harvey Houses along the way? Journal the food that people could purchase along the line? His initial shock about being asked to bring his camera faded fast. Another waste of money for Dad and a waste of time for him. He let out a sigh. Not exactly the good attitude he'd been aiming for.

"The brand-new hotel is a charming, Swiss-chalet-looking lodge. Supposedly it has every amenity the social elite will enjoy." He leaned forward and lifted his chin, that telltale sparkle in his eye. "But next door—or across the court-yard—is the Hopi House, designed by a Miss Mary Colter. She's been a decorator for Harvey and a designer. But she knows the Indians. It's a lovely Pueblo structure that repre-sents the magnificent people of the West and houses their art. Apparently, they've got real Indians from nearby villages who create the art right there in front of people. This is Harvey's new plan, to have Indian art and souvenir shops next to their hotels. But at this location, they've put an exhibit of rare and costly specimens. It's the priceless Harvey collection that won the grand prize at the Louisiana Purchase Exposition."

That actually *was* interesting to Ray. "So, you'd like me to visit and detail what El Tovar offers its visitors?"

"Yes, but I also need you to think bigger. Our class is fascinated with the West, didn't you hear me? *Fascinated.* Primitive as it may be."

Next would come the lecture on how to charm the rich into spending money. Again. Investing in something new and interesting. Building the company into something bigger than Rockefeller or Vanderbilt dared to dream. Ray had heard the spiel before, but he nodded at all the appropriate places and listened.

His father had been criticized often for his unfocused way of doing business. Rather than investing in oil, steel, coal, the railroads, or even creating or making something, Ray Watkins Senior was all about trying his hand at everything: investing in real estate, jewelry, art, restaurants, hotels . . . it was all over the map. And he'd made quite a fortune, but their investors were always looking for more. Lots more.

"What I'm saying is that I'm giving you an incredible opportunity. You need to ponder the tough questions. What could we—our investors—capitalize upon? What else could we build there that could attract our social crowd? What would people want to spend money on? I've heard that more and more people are willing to venture down into the canyon. The stories good ol' Ralph Cameron has sent state that he's getting a hefty profit from his toll on the Bright Angel Trail. You need to find out if we can get in on something like that too." Dad stood and began pacing. A sure indicator that he was winding up for even more ideas.

Not one to usually interrupt his father when he was on a roll, Ray couldn't let one thing pass. "Why did you want me to bring my camera?"

Dad's face turned very serious. "To send me pictures, of course. I need to see what's there: the canyon, the hotel, the opportunities, the art." Dad pointed a finger at him. "Don't forget the art. Perhaps we could even acquire some of it for the galleries here." He went back to stroking his beard. "I know this is a larger task than I've given you before, and it will be quite time consuming, but I need you to be my eyes and ears. It may be some time before I can get away myself. So be thorough."

He clasped his hands behind his back and lifted his chin. "I'm counting on you. This could be huge for us. Expansion into the West is our future." With a dramatic flair, Dad sat back down in the chair and leaned forward. "I'll send at least two or three men with you to help. Put them to work for whatever you need, but keep in mind I've got several other errands for each of them to run."

Of course he did. Dad always had an agenda other than just the errands he'd send Ray to pursue. But one day, through hard work and perseverance, he was determined to have his father trust him with the entirety of the business. But Dad wasn't one to let things go easily. He liked being in complete control. "How long do you want me to stay?"

"It will probably take several weeks. Or even perhaps a couple months, I would imagine. I'll let you know when you've accomplished all that needs to be done. Once I've had time to look over everything you send, I'll need to meet with the investors here and possibly bring some of them out to see it for themselves. That's why it's crucial for you to send me detailed reports—something I know you are outstanding at producing."

"Thank you, Dad." He'd take the compliment, seeing as his father didn't hand them out very often. "When would you like me to leave?"

"Within the week, if possible."

Ray stood, straightened the papers he'd been working on, and placed his pen back in the holder. He offered Dad a smile. "I guess I better start packing then. I wonder what the weather is like in the Arizona Territory this time of year?" He shrugged. "I guess I need to prepare for multiple seasons if I'm to be away for a couple months."

His father stood as well, gripped Ray's upper arm with his left hand, and shook his right hand vigorously. "I'm excited for this next stage for you, son. One day, I know you'll make a fine head for this company—my legacy—and bring even more pride to the Watkins name."

Still shaking Dad's hand, Ray smiled. "I hope to make you proud."

"You have." With a brief nod, he turned on his heel and left.

Ray sat back behind his desk and pulled a small notebook out of a drawer. Best to start a list of all he needed to bring with him, especially if he was to be away for months. Which really wasn't a problem. It wasn't like there was anyone or anything that truly tied him to Chicago. The senior Watkins had sent him on many trips since he'd come home as a college graduate hoping to take on the business. At least this one didn't seem to be as tedious or even as frivolous as so many of the others had been. Perhaps Dad was ready to start handing him some more responsibility. It was an encouraging thought.

The patience he'd learned the past few years after he'd turned his life around had begun to feel like it would never bear fruit. Today was proof that Reverend James had been correct. The pages of the notebook in front of him blurred as his thoughts rushed back to their last conversation.

"You've been given a second chance. Don't waste it by complain-

ing about what you wish you could do. Instead focus on what you can do. Be grateful to Almighty God. It's time to show your family that you've changed. You've given your life over to the Lord and are allowing Him to work in you. Perhaps you will have an impact on them as well. The wild Ray Watkins of your youth is gone."

"But there's still so much guilt inside," Ray had replied. *"How do I get past the horrible things I've done? Is it even fair for me to have a fresh start?"*

"Thankfully, the good Lord doesn't give us what we deserve. Your sins were covered on the cross. They're paid for in full. Now, go and live for Him." Reverend James squeezed his shoulder and then headed for the door. Hat in his hands, he turned back toward him. *"You didn't kill that young boy, Ray. Remember that."*

Kimberley Woodhouse (KimberleyWoodhouse.com) is an award-winning, bestselling author of more than forty fiction and nonfiction books. Kim and her incredible husband of thirty-plus years live in Colorado, where they play golf together, spend time with their kids and grandkids, and research all the history around them.

Sign Up for Kimberley's Newsletter

Keep up to date with Kimberley's latest news on book releases and events by signing up for her email list at the link below.

KimberleyWoodhouse.com

FOLLOW KIMBERLEY ON SOCIAL MEDIA

Kimberley Woodhouse   @KimberleyWoodhouse   @KimWoodhouse

More from Kimberley Woodhouse

Anna Lakeman has spent her life working alongside her paleontologist father. When they find dinosaur bones, a rich investor tries to take over their dig. As Anna fights for recognition of her work and reconnects with an old beau, tensions mount and secrets are unburied. How can they keep the perils of the past from threatening their renewed affection?

The Secrets Beneath
TREASURES OF THE EARTH #1

When paleontologist Martha Jankowski discovers an intact dinosaur skeleton, she has the opportunity to make a name for herself, but only if she can uncover the full skeleton before another competing dig. As she races against the clock, she meets a man who shares her passion for science and faith—but is he friend or foe?

Set in Stone
TREASURES OF THE EARTH #2

Eleanor Briggs travels to Kalispell, Montana, with her conservationist father to discuss the formation of Glacier National Park, and sparks fly when she meets Carter Brunswick, despite their differences. As the town fights to keep the railroad, the dangers Eleanor and Carter face will change the course of their lives.

With Each Tomorrow
THE JEWELS OF KALISPELL #2

BETHANYHOUSE

 Bethany House Fiction

 @BethanyHouseFiction

 @Bethany_House

 @BethanyHouseFiction

 Free exclusive resources for your book group at BethanyHouseOpenBook.com

 Sign up for our fiction newsletter today at BethanyHouse.com